Behind the Yellow Filter

A Former Enemy Becomes the Camera Capital of the World

Lynn !
Enjoy the book with
as much fun as I had
writing it. Thank you for
your support,
Stuart

Stuart Held   3/27/06

Outskirts Press, Inc.
Denver, Colorado

This is a work of fiction. The events and characters described here are imaginary and are not intended to refer to specific places or living persons. The opinions expressed in this manuscript are solely the opinions of the author and do not represent the opinions or thoughts of the publisher. The author represents and warrants that s/he either owns or has the legal right to publish all material in this book. If you believe this to be incorrect, contact the publisher through its website at www.outskirtspress.com.

Behind the Yellow Filter
A Former Enemy Becomes the Camera Capital of the World
All Rights Reserved
Copyright © 2006 Stuart Held

This book may not be reproduced, transmitted, or stored in whole or in part by any means, including graphic, electronic, or mechanical without the express written consent of the publisher except in the case of brief quotations embodied in critical articles and reviews.

Outskirts Press
http://www.outskirtspress.com

ISBN-10: 1-59800-290-2
ISBN-13: 978-1-59800-290-4

Library of Congress Control Number: 2005938904

Outskirts Press and the "OP" logo are trademarks belonging to Outskirts Press, Inc.

Printed in the United States of America

Dedication

This book is dedicated to my family without whom there would be no reason to continue in this world. My partner and soul mate – my wife, Nina – is my best friend and the facilitator who literally keeps our family going. This has been a labor of love and fun to do. Many of my friends have encouraged me to continue with this project. It has awakened many memories of my past years of international travel that I wanted to share with everyone – in particular my family.

Thank you to my pre-publishing readers for their help and advice;

Anthony Capetola, George Feinsod, Debra Leder,
Sheila & Myron Polkes, June & Melvin Rabin, Linda Sardone, Rebecca Speziale, Christine & Michael Swirnoff

A special thank you to Jack Klein, my pre-publishing reader and copy editor.

I can't thank you enough. You made it a readable book and made sure it was still my book.

Introduction

The world's reliance on a former enemy that develops into the camera capital of the world

Giving the reader a taste of how business is done in Japan.

Competition between the 'Super Powers' to obtain a strategic part used in a computer.

Preface

In the 1950's the news of the day was the War in Korea and the McCarthy hearings in the Senate. It was only a few years after World War II. In retrospect the times seemed to be simpler and easier.

This book talks about the fledgling photographic industry in the United States. Manufacturers in Japan could not afford to sell to the US customers directly – they required a distributor to be able to reach their customers.

The distributors sold their wares to camera stores. Many of the stores in the 1950's were owned by individuals and were referred to as "Mom and Pop shops". There were a few chain operations but the heart of the business was in the hands of individuals.

Many of these individuals became storeowners because they were photographic hobbyists. Or, they were European immigrants with some technical background who eased into a business that didn't cost a large initial investment. Many of them didn't have a formal education beyond high school.

The largest customers for photo equipment were department stores - discount pricing was not the watchword of the industry. Some smaller camera shops would actually say "We don't normally carry that kind of camera but, if you look in at Macy's or Abraham and Strauss and take down the model number, I will get it for you. Then I can teach you how to use it." Price was not the object at that time, service was.

This book, will discuss a young, newly wed marketing engineer working for a camera distributor, who becomes an unwitting CIA agent. He gets involved in an international espionage scheme and is forced to mature overnight.

Many of the experiences discussed actually happened to the writer and were worked into the story. The book, a postcard from the past, tells how business was done in Japan.

The dark side of the book is the Yakuza, the Japanese Mafia. The origin of the Yakuza goes back to 1612. They then were known as the "Crazy Ones". They became particularly strong during World War II and the US occupation. They created the black market for foodstuffs and provided 'protection' for the local business.

Between 1958 and 1963 the number of Yakuza members was 184,000, more then the entire Japanese Army. The Yakuza were influenced by the American gangster movies and began to dress in black suits with white shirts, black sunglasses and cropped hair. Tattoos are the clan's badge of honor. The origin of the tattoo comes from the Bukato. A black ring is tattooed on a Yakuza's arm for each crime he committed. The tattoos over the entire body illustrated that you were unwilling to accommodate yourself to society's rules and norms.

I was engaged in the photographic industry for many years. This book is written from my experience and memories over a period of fifty years in the business world. Nevertheless it is a story, a fictional story. Many of my friends have helped me edit the book so that it would read using English properly. My one and most important editor is my wife who is the only person I tried some of my ideas on to see if they should be incorporated into the book.

This is a work of fiction. All names, characters, and incidents, except for certain incidental references, are products of the author's imagination and do not refer to or portray any actual person.

Table of Contents

Chapter	Page
1. How it all started	1
2. On to Virginia	8
3. The training	12
4. A short trip and stay at home	20
5. Japan – For the first time	27
6. My first meal in Japan	32
7. The Domestic Crime Agency	35
8. The head office of Nippon Kogaku, K.K.	45
9. The Ohi-Machi factory – Sinagawa-ku District	52
10. Dinner with Dr. Masao Nagaoka and directors of Nikon	60
11. Thursday – Another day has start	67
12. Fuji Photo Film, K.K. – Aasaksa District – Tokyo	70
13. An air controlled room for a demonstration	75
14. Another air controlled room and demonstration	79

Table of Contents

15. Dinner with friends in a sushi restaurant — 84

16. The evening was just getting started — 88

17. Secure telephone call with Luke Albert — 97

18. Another breakfast meeting in the Orchid Room of the Palace Hotel — 104

19. A short meeting with Chief of Police Hiro — 108

20. Michico Iishida the president of Mamiya — 111

21. The Japanese Defense Agency — 116

22. A fifty million dollar offer — 122

23. A night spent in darkness — 129

24. Another breakfast and more Information in the Orchid Room — 135

25. Planning the Nikon 'F' introduction — 139

26. The set up before the bidding gets more interesting — 146

27. Face-to-face negotiations — 151

28. Awake and an update — 159

Table of Contents

29. The debriefing	163
30. In memoriam	167
31. Lunch with the Changs	172
32. A meeting with Hiro and a call to the office	178
33. The 'Incident'	182
34. The Jewish Community Center of Tokyo	186
35. The arrival of Luke Albert	193
36. A morning of surprises	201
37. The Tamron visit proved to be a little more then optics.	208
38. Breakfast with Luke Albert	223
39. Tying up loose ends at the Nikon factory	230
40. A special lunch with the Changs	237
41. Odds & Ends	245
Epilogue	249

CHAPTER One
How It All Started.

On a hot smoldering summer day in New York City aboard the BMT subway I stood with my arm wrapped around the porcelain pole reading the Daily News. It was unbearably hot in my wool purple splashed tweed suit – pink high collar shirt - Billy Eckstein style- and wide flower tie. I was in style for the early fifties but, I was uncomfortable this very hot day in July.

The train arrived at Dekalb Avenue, went into the East River Tunnel – Brooklyn to Manhattan – and at about 8:30 AM I got to my 14th Street - Union Square - station stop. I climbed the stairs and was finally able to emerge from underground only to be greeted by a wall of city heat. With the sun blazing on my back I was walked past Union Square Park – across the street from S. Klein department store on the way to my office.

At 21st Street and Fifth Avenue I walked into a relatively new office building (it was only twenty years old) that had 'air cooling'. It was refreshing to feel the 'cold' air as we waited in the lobby for the elevator. When I arrived on the fifth floor, I found my company's door and walked into the office where that cool feeling quickly dissolved. "There is some kind of problem with the cooling system," Doreen shouted. All of the electric fans were ablaze with the underlying buzz that would stay with you throughout the day. "Just try to talk above the noise," I said to myself trying to keep calm and cool looking in my new suit.

Doreen Parks was the office manager. She was round and motherly looking but seemed to act like a prison guard when she had to issue instructions. She was loyal to the company and whenever you called no matter the time of day she was there. She had dark hair pulled back in a bun, wore black-rimmed eyeglasses and a matronly styled dress, and spoke in voice that sounded like a throaty whisper. When she told you to do something – you did it. She could be very demanding and even though, from afar, she looked like a pushover, I am sure everyone in the office was scared to death of her.

Doreen stopped by my desk and whispered "Mr. Albert wants to see you at 11:00 – and be on time." Mr. Albert was my boss. We didn't know too much about Luke Albert other then he had a very successful record in the 'Company'. He was a good-looking man with short-cropped black hair - a college type who was in his late forties and had an athletic way of moving around.

Luke Albert was a retired field operative who was put out to pasture, as we were told, because of an incident that happened on his watch. Naturally, no one told us what the incident was and being in a company built around secrecy that was not an uncommon reality. For now, Luke Albert was the President of TAG Photographic, Inc.

The Allied Group, Inc. was the Company's cover. It was a holding company that did business as TAG Photographic, Inc. The owners were listed in the NY State organizational book – none of whom we knew or who were active in the business. In reality, a small government unit called the Central Intelligence Agency or the CIA owned the Company.

TAG Photo was an import/export operation for photographic equipment and accessories. Its business plan was to introduce 35mm photography to amateur and professional photographers. Its hidden mission was intelligence gathering. The idea was to get cameras into the hands of as many people as possible – to increase the number of photographs taken. The more people travel, the more information is gathered. It was a simple terrific cover.

In the early fifties the main press camera was still the 4" X 5" Speed Graphic Camera made in Buffalo, New York. This was a clumsy, heavy, single shot camera with little appeal for amateur photographers. Some of the Speed Graphics had multi-shot backs but the normal operation was one picture at a time.

For the amateur, Eastman Kodak of Rochester was busy selling its Brownie and Retina cameras. The idea was similar to that of Gillette's Razor Company: give away the razor and sell the blades. Kodak's approach was to sell an inexpensive camera at almost cost and sell the film, processing and printing at full price. That philosophy served Kodak well for many years.

Magazines such as Life and National Geographic were already using smaller format cameras like the German Leica 35mm rangefinder camera. The 35mm cameras allowed lightweight and quick picture operation with a variety of lenses. The Speed Graphic was a bear to use – and its one-at-a-time picture operation made it difficult particularly when used in sports photography.

In these days you had to know your sport well, have great anticipation and timing to get that special picture. In other events you needed to plan your photographic picture way in advance to get a meaningful shot. With a 35mm camera you could shoot 36 exposures in no time and have a picture selection so you could select the 'pick of the litter.'

Luke Albert recruited me to the Company at a job seminar two years earlier when I was finishing my degree in mechanical engineering at New York University – NYU. I was unusual for an engineering graduate because I was more interested in sales and marketing than sitting behind a drawing board.

I worked my way though college selling from behind the counters of camera stores. The camera capital in the United States was a short block of 32nd Street between Broadway and Seventh Avenue. Willoughby's, Fotoshop, Minifilm, Penn Camera Exchange, 32nd Street Camera, Olden Camera were all available to the consumer within one city block.

When I first met Luke Albert I thought the job was strictly to sell the camera lines that TAG represented. That was how it started. After six months of sales in the office Mr. Albert's confidence in me was upheld by how I did my job - Albert decided to tell me the actual mission of TAG Photographic. Now almost two years had past and I have become familiar with the Company's cover operation. Albert thought it was time to take me to the next stage of development in the Company.

Albert's office seemed like a mausoleum done in dark walnut paneling. His large mahogany desk was at the far end of the office with two dark leather-covered side chairs in front and two very large windows in the back of his desk chair. The rest of the room held an enormous conference table and a couch with a coffee table in front, standing on an expensive oriental rug. The sofa had two comfortable looking chairs facing it. Albert's office was imposing – to say the least.

I cautiously knocked on his office door and walked in at 11:00 AM. He pointed to one of the side chairs by his desk. I sat down, as Albert was finishing up some paperwork with Doreen who was in the other chair. Albert looked up and said to Doreen "I think it is time for Robert to graduate and become a full member of the crew. Do you agree, Doreen?" "Yes sir," she replied. Albert went on "Robert, when we first met I told you that we did some interesting work in TAG. I also said, some of it might have a difficult explanation but I think you are here long enough to understand what we do." I replied, "Yes, I think I do." "Then it is done – your pay package is $20,000 per year and you will be taking on new duties."

When he presented the idea of "graduating" I thought he was kidding - that would have been a completely incorrect assessment. Albert was a cold fish with what appeared to be no sense of humor. He had dark black eyes that seemed to pierce your skin and look directly into your heart that made him look anything but docile or light hearted.

I thought it got awfully warm in the room; my palms were sweating as I rubbed my hands together. What was I going to do? I recently married Deborah Davis and as Mr. and Mrs. Robert Schein we were in the process of starting our family. $20,000 was a small fortune. I really didn't have any choice - on the spot I said, "Thank you for showing your confidence in me."

"Good," Albert said. "Let's move on to your first

assignment as a field operative." Albert opened a folder. "You will go to a training site on a horse farm in Virginia to be trained in various weaponry, tactics and your mission. This is a two-week crash course to give you the basics and enough information for you to be able to handle this assignment. This is neither a dangerous nor a high level assignment. It is one to give you a chance to get your feet wet."

"After training you will fly to Tokyo on a buying trip for TAG Photographic, Inc. You will visit the Nippon Kogaku, K.K. – Nikon - factory and examine their new '35 mm single lens reflex camera.' They want to bring this camera to the market in the United States this year or next year. The camera is called the Nikon 'F'. The F stands for focal plane shutter."

"In the evening, in the Starlight lounge of the Imperial Palace Hotel you will meet with Navy Lt. Robert Claypool, a limited duty officer, with a U.S. Navy photographers mate background. He will brief you on what, if anything, he has learned that might affect your mission. He also has access to many military assets should you need them. You both will decide on your next steps to take to complete your mission."

Albert continued, "You leave tomorrow on a flight out of LaGuardia to Roanoke, Virginia at 0715 hours. Have a good trip – oh, we need you to report in to Doreen at about 1700 every day for a verbal update." With that his eyes went to some other paperwork as if both Doreen and I weren't in the room, and we departed.

As we closed the door I heard Albert's desk phone ring. I excitedly exited, almost knocking Doreen over, went quickly to my desk to call home and tell Debbie of our good news. A promotion with more responsibility and more money – who could ask for anything more? I totally ignored the heat and the sound of the fans as I dialed my number and couldn't wait for

Debbie to pick up and say hello.

Albert picked up his phone and said, "Yes, (pause) no he will do very well. He will need some watching but I am confident he is the right choice. Anyhow, Claypool is a long term operative, knows how to use his assets and will watch over him and take him in hand if he has to" - without saying anything further he hung up.

I heard "hello" and I said "hey Deb, lets go out to dinner tonight, I got some good news for us. We got a promotion and the job pays $20,000. That's a $5,000 increase how about that? "Great" said Debbie "when did this come about?" "Just a few minutes ago" I replied." Debbie then said, "Would you mind terribly if we didn't go out? We have dinner in the fridge and I'm tired of walking in the morning heat to my clients." (Debbie was a freelance fashion illustrator) I said, "That's OK. There are some points about the new job I have to discuss with you." "What kind of points?" she asked. "Oh nothing unusual or things we can't handle," I lied. "But there will be longer hours, international travel…" She interrupted "How much travel?" "I'm not sure" - I said "but travel will be a factor."

Debbie then said – "well, maybe its time for us to buy our house?" "I don't know," I said, "We will ask our accountant." We both smiled because our accountant was Debbie's father – Fred Davis. "OK" I said – "when I get back, in about two weeks we will pose the problem to your Dad." "Whoa, where did this two week trip come from?" she asked. I said, "I have to go for some training in Virginia then take a business trip overseas. When Luke Albert offered me the new position, I didn't want him to think I couldn't make a decision. I wanted him to feel comfortable with his decision. So I said yes on the spot. I hope you don't mind that I didn't consult with you." Reluctantly Debbie said, "OK – I guess I will get the details over dinner." As we hung up she said "I love you" and I responded "the same here – bye."

7

CHAPTER TWO
On To Virginia

After a bumpy hot ride in a yellow cab I hailed on the corner of Church Avenue and Flatbush Avenue in Brooklyn I arrived in LaGuardia Airport at about 6:30 AM to board my flight to Roanoke. I was now in my business uniform – blue blazer, grey pants and tie plus a camera bag over my shoulder. As I waited on a line that seemed endless, to get to the Piedmont Airlines counter to check in, I had a strange feeling – like a chill – that someone was watching me. I was sure it was my imagination working overtime but the feeling persisted.

I quickly scanned my fellow travelers and saw nothing that I thought was irregular – except in the corner of my eye I caught a glimpse of a short Asian man in a dark blue suit reading a newspaper standing next to the rentable lockers. When I turned toward him he turned away and quickly stepped to the escalator and disappeared to the second floor. I thought it was strange but again I also thought it was my over active imagination leading me on.

Sweating profusely now – the heat was getting to me – I finally checked my bag, got my seat and gate number from the attendant and walked to the escalator to get a cold drink and find my gate. The Nedick's concession sold a tall orange juice over ice that saved my life. Cup in hand, I started to window shop on the way to my gate in the crowded corridor when I saw a reflection in the store window. It was the same Asian guy peeking out from behind his paper watching me.

This time I was sure he was looking my way. I froze and he sensed I was on to him. He turned and quickly stepped away into the crowd. I tried to pick him up again but with no success. My mind was a jumble of questions – "What the hell was going on? Why was this guy following me? Was Albert not giving me the whole story? Something seemed left out but I didn't know what."

I found my Piedmont gate #35 and just as I arrived they started boarding the plane. Now my senses were working overtime, I started watching everyone in the area and I was ready to spring into action, though I was not sure what that action might be. I think I was sweating more because of nerves rather then the oppressive heat. I boarded the plane, got seated and after looking around and finding no one looking suspicious I felt relatively comfortable and more or less safe in my window seat. We took off and much to my amazement I dozed off.

The Martin 404 started its descent and I awoke to the loud noise and jolt of the wheels locking in place. The 404 was a very reliable and safe propeller aircraft much like the workhorse of the industry, the DC-3. We made a one-bounce touchdown landing and rolled up to the Roanoke terminal.
As I walked down the stairs of the plane I scanned the

people waiting behind the fence line outside the terminal. I spotted a beefy red headed guy dressed in an over shirt and slacks with a military haircut who I figured was the person sent to meet me. As I approached him he said "Bob Schien?" I said "yes" and he introduced himself as "Lt. Red Haggerty at your service." Red was a jovial guy who splattered his conversation with colorful curse words to make his point.

Cornelius 'Red' Haggerty was a thirty-year veteran who entered the Navy as an enlisted man and worked his way through the ranks to Chief Petty Officer. He was a photographer's mate and served aboard the Intrepid in World War II. Equivalent to a Warrant Officer in the Army, Red was offered the Limited Duty Officers – LDO rank of Lieutenant if he re-enlisted. Red had little family and said, "Fuck yes!" and re-upped for another five years.

As we walked to the baggage arrival area Red asked, "How was your trip?" I replied "I fell asleep on the plane but that was after a little anxiety." "What do you mean?" he asked. "Well, I could have imagined it but, I thought someone was following me in New York before I boarded the plane". Red looked at me and said, "Was it one of the little yellow bastards?" "How did you know?" - I replied. Red went on – "Every time we send someone to this facility those sons of bitches just seem to know." "Wait a minute," I said. "What are you talking about? I don't even know what my mission is yet – how could anyone know about it - right?" Red looked back and smiled as we picked up my bag. We walked to his car and he said nothing further until we arrived at 'the complex'.

The complex surprised me. Other then security cameras that I could pick out here and there - there was nothing else to indicate that this was a government facility. It just looked like a horse farm. Fanny Fink, the wife of Commander Billy B. Fink met us at the door. As I walked in Fink stuck his huge paw out and shook my hand. He said, "Welcome to our little nest, I am sure you will have a rewarding and informative stay. For now, let's have a cool drink and then some lunch." With that Fanny slipped off to get the lemonade and prepare lunch.

Cdr. Billy B. Fink was a Navy pilot who flew everything from Goony Birds (kind of a DC-3) to the latest jet planes. He landed on strips of land that would make you close your eyes and pray, to landing on aircraft carriers in bad weather. He was a pilot's pilot. He seemed to be a pleasantly cheerful man who had a barrel chest. From just looking at him you knew he was one guy you didn't want to fight with unless he was on your side. Bill came from a farming family in Iowa, enlisted in the Navy right out of college, became a carrier pilot and flew more than 36 successful dangerous missions in Europe; that made him an Ace and a hero.

Fink flew nighttime missions over France using experimental cameras and strobe lights to get the best possible photos of munitions plants for the next day's bombing raids by the RAF and the US Army Air Corps. His co-pilot on those missions was the famed scientist Dr. Harold Edgerton. Edgerton was the only one who felt confident working with the new technologically advanced strobes that he personally developed in his laboratory in MIT. The two, Fink and Edgerton, made a heck of a pair. One was a hell raiser and the other highly intelligent and introspective. They met in Alexandria, Virginia at the Naval Photographic Center and formed a friendship that would last a lifetime. This is how a Navy pilot got to Europe and did work for the Army. It all happened by chance.

Bill Fink was also an accomplished photographer's mate and an excellent intelligence gatherer. He worked on many intelligence missions in past years and now was in charge of training and preparing the new members of the Company.

CHAPTER Three
The Training

After lunch Cdr. Fink took Lt. Haggerty and myself into his study and laid out the routine for my next eleven days.

 0530 Hours – 2 to 3 mile run, PT exercises for forty-five minutes.
 0630 Hours – Tour of training facility; start learning about mission and necessary weaponry
 1230 Hours – Lunch with trainers
 1345 Hours – Special Language Training – Japanese
 1445 Hours – Mission briefing.
 1600 Hours – 2 to 3 mile run, PT/Judo exercise for forty-five minutes
 1800 Hours – Dinner
 2100 Hours – Lights out

 Cdr. Fink said, "This schedule will be strictly adhered to and I want you to promise me that you will do everything within your power to finish it." I gulped and said – "I didn't bargain for this. Are you sure you've got the right guy? I don't know anything about this and frankly you're scaring me to death - figuratively speaking of course."

Fink and Haggerty laughed and Fink said, "It can be a little overwhelming but obviously you are the right guy because some very trusted people have spoken for you and that is good enough for me." I then blurted out "I was never told about the mission or that there was any danger. On top of all that I am so out of shape I don't think I can last a mile, much less do 2 to 3 miles and PT for 45 minutes. You have got to be kidding."

Fink held up his hand and said – "Enough!" with a finality that I have rarely heard. I meekly said "OK." I couldn't believe what I said but that is how I officially got into the spy business.

At first I said to myself, "Hey this is what kids of all ages dream about - I am young, the adventure all seems romantic and naturally I am interested in the increased money. What the hell – I'll give it a try. If I don't make it then - there it is – I don't make it. I'm done. If I do make it then I have to deal with my wife and friends. That might be easier said then done but I think I am getting way ahead of myself. Let's take it a step at a time."

0500 Hours Haggerty was shaking me and I wasn't responding so he flipped my bed over. I got up and we started the grueling day. I ran about a quarter of a mile and fell to the ground and said, "I can't go any further." Haggerty reached down and picked me up like I was a paper doll and said – "You didn't die, you are still breathing so get the fuck off your ass and start the fucking run again – God damn it! I don't want to hear anymore about this can't-do shit. We get through it together – you understand?" And we continued.

The tour of the 'facility' was next on the list. We entered one of the barns that made up the beautiful horse farm and went down a concrete flight of stairs. We went through a steel door and a whole underground world opened up. Punch card and tape controlled computers all over the place. You would think this was where we launched the first man to orbit the earth. It was overwhelming. Time zone signs were hung from the ceiling with a listing of the various countries on the signs in those zones. There were small groups of people looking at oscilloscopes or sorting punch cards in each area. It was a maze of cubicles that seem to go on endlessly.

I was directed to a side room where I heard a constant sharp cracking noise of weapons being fired. It was a soundproof firing range. This was now getting interesting I thought. I was given a set of 'earmuffs' and my very first weapon. They chose a standard .45 caliber military issue pistol for me. It had a clip of six bullets plus one round in the chamber or could fire seven shots. Fully loaded it weighed three pounds. The safety was a slide lever on the left side of the pistol. You pulled it back and the .45 could single shoot until it was empty. This was to be my weapon of choice – not the most accurate pistol in the world - but it hit its target like a charging rhinoceros. It had impact.

For the next couple of hours – until I couldn't hold my arms up – I fired the pistol at a body outline. I was then shown how to clean the pistol and then fired some more. My shooting result wasn't a tight cluster like Haggerty's but I didn't miss the outlined target that often. They said in a week's time I would be proficient with the weapon.

After lunch it was on to Japanese class. A Japanese woman named Mrs. Wakajima was my instructor. She was dressed in a dark blue everyday kimono with a white obi or sash. Her purpose was not so much for me to be a proficient speaker of the language but to be able to understand what was being said. If the party interviewing you felt you didn't understand the language then they would talk amongst themselves more freely. When we met she said "konichi-wa – hajimaymashti - Wataksi wa Wakajima San." I said, "Whoa – hold it a minute. I don't understand a word of what you are saying." She said, "That is all right for today but in a week's time if you say that to me then we have both failed." She then started to break down what she said in English. She said – "Good afternoon, how do you do? My name is Mrs. Wakajima."

My mission briefing seemed simple. I couldn't understand why all the secrecy. Then Fink explained. "You will be dealing with the 8-B periscope that is aboard most nuclear and diesel boats in our submarine fleet. The 8-B periscope is considered one of the most important weapons, right alongside the fire controls, which are responsible for the various weaponry stored onboard like Nuclear Polaris Missiles.

The periscope, besides being the eyes of the sub, is a major visual reconnaissance device for looking at the 'bad' guys. For example, before the D-Day landings submarines photographed the shores of Normandy. The reconnaissance was also backed up by a team of Navy Seals going ashore from submarines to get a close-up look and take samples of the sand so the Allies would know what they would be up against for the landing.

"The periscope, manufactured by Kollmorgan Corporation of North Hampton Massachusetts wasn't designed for photography. It was an eighteen-foot long tube filled with lens elements and nitrogen. When looking through it everything appeared clear to the human eye. However, when taking a photograph the result was poor. All of the optical color planes of the periscope – blue, green or red – did not focus at one point or on one plain. This made the photographic resolution of the Kollmorgan periscope very questionable. In simple language, it meant you can't take a sharp picture through the 8-B periscope.

"At the end of World War II the Japanese fleet was destroyed. After a period of time the Japanese Navy requested that the United States lend Japan 'retired' ships - kind of a Japanese Lend-Lease-Program. Japan is an island nation and is very dependent of the seas for imports and exports, security and survival.

"One of the vessels we lent the Japanese was a diesel submarine, World War II vintage. The Japanese Navy renovated and fitted out the submarine to their needs. The main renovation was a Nippon Kogaku – Nikon – Periscope." Cdr. Fink said, "We have seen the picture results from this periscope and they are outstanding. The best our reconnaissance people have ever seen."

He went on, "TAG Photo is the distributor of Nikon camera products and instruments in the United States - that gives you entry into Nippon Kogaku. Your job is to go to the factory and learn as much information as possible about Nikon's optical shipboard range finders and submarine periscopes.

"Additionally, we have learned through our intelligence about some radical technological advance involving digitizing an image and taking photographs through an extraordinary periscope. Mitsubishi Heavy Industries is experimenting with this equipment. Nippon Kogaku sits on the board of directors of Mitsubishi. Mitsubishi is a large holding company and owns many Japanese companies such as Nikon, Kirin Beer, Mitsubishi Ship Building, etc. Many of their ventures have been integrated and are working together on different projects. By doing this they get the best look at different technologies.

"Luke Albert has organized, with the management of Nikon, a demonstration of the new system at the factory during your visit. Pick up as much information as you can. We have to determine how important the new system is and if we have to employ further resources to partner with our friends. This is the heart of you mission.

"Jet Propulsion Laboratories - JPL - and Texas Instruments are experimenting with digital photography but we haven't seen good enough results or the opportunity to package it small enough for use aboard a submarine. We are interested in what the Japanese are doing. While you are here we will make you an optical expert on periscopes and range finders. We will also review your technical photographic knowledge to make sure you have the necessary information to successfully complete your mission."

Every day at 1700 Hours (5:00 PM) I checked in with Doreen. It was a very short telephone conversation that went something like this –"Hi Doreen, this is Robert – I'm checking in is as requested." Doreen said, "Anything to report? We already received today's summary of your work from Cdr. Fink." I said, "I guess I have nothing to report other then I am working the schedule." Doreen ended the conversation with "Fine – goodbye – I will speak to you tomorrow" and hung up.

Later in the evening I called Debbie. "Hey Hon, how are you doing?" She said "Great! I am doing some work for a new agency – McGreevy, Warring and Howell we're doing a catalog for E.J. Korvettes. Just run of the mill stuff for now but it promises to be more interesting when we get to the more expensive clothing." I said, "That sounds super! I now know I will be home Friday in the late afternoon. Let's go out to dinner to celebrate and talk." Debbie asked "Where do you want to go" and I said, "We will figure it out later. In the meantime, I miss you very much. I am looking forward to seeing you." "Me too" she replied and I said, "I have to get going" and said "goodbye." Debbie said, "I love you" and I said, "I love you too." We hung up.

There was no question about it, as the eleven days passed, I felt better and way stronger. From my PT/ Judo training I was feeling pretty good about myself – certainly more confident. I must have shed twelve pounds and firmed up like I can't ever remember. My .45-caliber pistol felt like a friendly appendage in my shoulder holster and I was very confident that my target shooting would always end up in a nice round cluster.

Japanese is a tough language. Fortunately it has over 150 English words in it such as camera, milk, car, glasses etc. that helped me understand. I could now speak in phrases to get directions or go shopping. Phrases like - Ikura des ka? – How much is it? Or Wataksi-wa Schein San – I am Mr. Schein. It was all very basic but I did notice that I understood a good part of a conversation Wakajima-San had on the telephone with her husband. I inquired about it afterwards and found that I comprehended just about everything she said. I guess we accomplished our goal but I certainly did not feel comfortable yet.

Finally, with all the information that was drubbed into my head I felt as though I couldn't absorb another fact. I was at my limit and looking to get home. I would be home for only a short time before going to Japan. I would be given a few days to catch up with my office work and with my family. I was physically and mentally exhausted. I was happy the eleven days were over.

It was time to leave – Commander Fink and his wife saw me out the door and Lieutenant Haggerty punched me on the shoulder with the strength of a bull and took my breath away. He said "That's a reminder you bastard – you can't and won't ever quit no matter where the fuck you are – right?" I caught my breath, nodded and got into the car to take the long ride to the airport.

CHAPTER Four
A Short Trip And Stay At Home

When I arrived at LaGuardia my senses were as sharp as I have ever experienced. I looked at everyone and glanced back and forth checking him or her out. Sure enough, sitting on a bench was an Asian in a dark suit seemingly minding his own business behind a newspaper. No one came to him and he didn't get up to retrieve a bag or get a taxi. He just sat there behind his paper.

I decided to stroll by and maybe even catch him in a face-to-face confrontation. I walked over and curiously he didn't move. I got alongside the bench he was sitting on and peeked behind his paper. He was staring and appeared propped up by the arms of the bench. He didn't move and his head was at a strange angle. He was dead. I continued walking away from the bench trying not to draw any attention to myself.

Just as I was about to exit the building Debbie was walking

in and we immediately hugged and kissed. As we were leaving, a woman sat down next to the dead man and screamed, which caught everyone's attention; Debbie and I continued to exit the building. I kept on looking over my shoulder, I'm about 6'2" and Debbie about 5'2" so I had a pretty good view of everything. I couldn't see anyone who might be stalking me but I had that eerie feeling that I was being watched as people were running to the dead man.

We got to the parking lot and drove off in our new Renault Dauphine. Those days the Dauphine was the rage. Everyone spoke highly about it and honked their horns as they passed each other. However, it was a car that had more electrical problems then anyone wanted to deal with. Everyone lied – no one wanted to admit they made a bad purchase and we fell right in with the crowd. I was unhappy that we didn't buy a more reliable vehicle like the Volkswagen Beetle.

As soon as we got home I jumped into the shower and tried to make something out of the mess running around in my head. A guy watches me take off over a week ago and them I find him upon my arrival sitting on a bench, dead. I need to somehow find out what was going on. I got dressed and while Debbie showered I called the office and related what happen to Doreen. She promised to look into it ASAP. I told her I would be in the next day – Saturday - she said "fine - you will be leaving for Japan on Sunday. Sorry for the short notice but we are moving up our schedule because of the incident in the airport. Better be safe then sorry" and she hung up.

I told myself "that sly old bird must have known about the killing in the airport before I talked to her. All my plans got into motion at a very fast pace. My God, what am I into? It is the beginning of August, I have been on the 'new' job for a couple of weeks and everything has gone by so fast I feel that I have been doing this for years." With that Debbie asked "are

21

you ready" and off we went to dinner.

We decided to go to Luigi's for some Italian food. We walked from our apartment on St. Paul's Court to Church Avenue and three blocks later we were in Luigi's, directly across the street from the Freddy Fitzsimons Bowling Alley. We were warmly greeted by the maitre-d' - this was a hangout for us during our courting days. I thought it was an appropriate setting to tell Debbie what was going on. First, a sumptuous dinner of baked clams, pasta marinara for Debbie and lasagna me; over espresso I started to fill her in.

I told her a little about my training and the good shape I was in and that I felt so good. I then slipped in the fact that my trip had been moved up and I would be leaving for Japan. She seemed startled about this because the last eleven days was the longest period we have been apart since we got married. I explained that "there was travel involved and I didn't have much choice of when to do it but to accept it - unless we wanted to give up the 'extra' money that we needed." Debbie swallowed hard and shook her head yes.

I didn't fill her in about the danger or gory part of the job. Actually, I left my pistol and shoulder holster in my briefcase so she wouldn't see it. With that I leaned over and kissed her on the lips and accidentally brushed by her breast with my left hand. She shuddered - I knew it was time to get the check and go home.

As we walked home arm in arm - every now and then I would feel her buttock and she did the same to me. This was the person I wanted to spend my life with – it was an exciting and loving time. As we walked we talked about the house we wanted to purchase and she told me her father said "even if you have no money left in the bank when you move in – go for it." She said that she would "pass that on to Robert."

We got home, not a second too soon, as we picked up our pace across the lobby of our apartment building and as I fumbled with the keys we quickly got inside our apartment and passionately kissed. She was warm, I breathed in her aroma and she felt wonderful in my arms. We wildly undressed each other and made our way to the bedroom where we sat on the edge of the bed teasing each other to the point I thought I would explode. I got a little nervous that I just might do that so I laid her down, mounted her and we made passionate love that we felt would last for a lifetime and fell into a peaceful sleep.

After a while, I felt my wife's hand on my stomach and as she started to rejuvenate me I started to do the same to her. Slowly we revived each other, and then hugged as tightly as we could until we couldn't breath, kissed again and again and made love once more. The night was still young and we both didn't want to see it end and again dozed off into a relaxing peaceful sleep.

I dragged myself out of bed at about 7:30 AM and got into a steaming hot shower. I must have stood under the shower for twenty minutes. I felt great but spent. As I quietly dressed to slip out and go to work I looked at Debbie while she was sleeping and I realized how lucky I was that she married me.

The train on Saturday was almost empty. I made the walk from 14th Street in no time. I seemed to be walking on air. I was happy and felt great. Because it was the weekend none of the buildings air-cooling system was on so we had to depend on open windows and electric fans. Doreen was already in the office - I wonder if she ever left - she was on the phone and reading some paper work. She waved at me to come over to her as I walked in the door. She cupped her phone and said that I should go to Mr. Albert's office as soon as I got settled.

23

I pushed the paperwork around my desk, checked my messages and went to see Albert. We were both dressed down in golf shirts and chinos. Albert was very complimentary of my work these past couple of weeks. He said, "You did an excellent job and made a very good impression amongst the staff. Well done!"

"Now," he continued, "We have to give you information to make you a creditable buyer from TAG Photographic, Inc. Here is a copy of our next six months of planned purchases including the copies of the purchase orders. Next is a report of our sales projections and business plans for the next two six month buying periods. You will see that each of the companies we represent is included; Nikon, Fuji, Mamiya and Tamron."

Handing me four additional folders he said - "These are summaries of all of our contact people and the board of directors in each of the companies we do business with. Some time during your stay in Japan you will visit with each factory and most likely have dinner with their directors or a couple of key members of the president's staff."

"You are to plan your meetings in the order I have listed them. Our largest and most important line is Nikon, next is Fuji and so on. The pecking order is very important. The Japanese are very conscious of position and their importance to our company. It would be a marketing blunder if you saw or gave preferential treatment to Tamron and not to Nikon. Orderly business is very important in Japan."

"You have met all the export representatives of each factory in the last couple of years through their visits to TAG and the various trade shows we attend. They will be in Japan to guide you in their respective factories."

He then paused and said, "It is expected that the hot item we are looking at on this trip is the new Nikon 'F' camera. It is a single lens reflex that is supposed to turn the industry upside down. I am told it is a little like the left-handed German Exacta camera that Doc Wirgen has been trying to promote since the war." (Editors note: Doc Wirgen was an escapee of a German concentration camp and through his German network tried to import the Exacta SLR Camera. He was unsuccessful primarily because of funding and the awkward operation of the camera.)

"This new 'F' camera system is planned to have a full compliment of lenses, it is said to be very consumer friendly and is to have top notch strong quality control during its manufacture."

"We haven't seen the camera yet but if it is anything like what they are talking about then we have one main suggestion that you must get across - Service. The camera's success globally will depend on how well we can service it. The factory should plan on sending technicians throughout the world to stay for a year and train our people - side by side. This is to be the first major quality item in our industry from Japan. Quality is the key word. If we can convince the public that this is a well-built, serviceable camera we will be successful."

"Finally, we have an export broker who represents TAG Photographic in the Orient. Nothing can be exported from Japan without a broker involved. His name is Alex Triguboff. Triguboff is a displaced Russian Jew who escaped communism before the war by walking from Siberia to the Bering Straits and then taking a dangerous open boat ride to Japan. He married a Japanese woman named Miyako and survived World War II in Japan because he was married to a Japanese national. I'll leave it to Alex to tell you all his stories when you meet. I am sure you will find them entertaining.

Alex's offices – TAG Photo Far East Trading - handle all of our export/import paperwork. The office is available to you should you want to use it. The office also has a secure telephone in case you require one."

"Alex will contact you on your second or third day in Japan. I believe Alex can be trusted and he is only involved with our photographic distribution business. He knows nothing about the information we are seeking and I suggest you do not reveal any of your activities regarding the periscope business - unless you find yourself in difficulty and have no one else to turn to or any other choice." That last remark sent a chill up my spine – what the hell did that mean, I thought. I sat quietly trying not to show any sign of weakness, distress or concern.

"Robert," Luke said, "you have been trained by the best, you have been briefed of your mission and you now know your business and agency contacts. We are counting on you to bring this trip to a successful conclusion – Godspeed and I look forward to seeing you in a couple of weeks."

My briefing and audience ended. I collected my airline tickets and cash advance from Doreen and was issued a Company American Express card. I then turned in my revolver for I was to receive one when I arrived in Japan. I decided to go home early to pack, review everything that was going on in my mind and try to memorize whatever I could of the paperwork that was handed to me.

I was also looking forward to spending some time in the evening with Debbie. Last night was so fantastic that I just wanted it to continue. But when I arrived home the golden moment had past and all we did was hold each other because I was going away again for another two weeks. Debbie cried when out of my sight and I must admit I was a little teary too. This was a big step for us.

CHAPTER Five
Japan - For The First Time

I boarded my Pan American flight #001 to Japan at 5 o'clock Monday evening. This was a first class flight on a Boeing C-377, 4-propeller engine, Stratocruiser. The plane had two levels with a spiral staircase near the front. The new jet planes like the Boeing 707 were just coming into the market and were making the Stratocruisers obsolete. But the Stratocruiser was pure luxury in flight. The service was wonderful on china plates with sterling silverware. The amenities were extraordinary: When you wanted to retire you climbed the staircase and went to sleep in your pajamas on what looked like a comfortable cot in a small draped off area. It was the only way to fly in its day.

Our route was New York to San Francisco to Hawaii and then Japan. The winds were very heady and that required us to land in Guam to refuel. This added another hour and a half to our twenty-eight hour flight.

Since this was the buying season I met a number of people aboard my flight from the camera industry. Fritz Scheonheimer of Intercontinental Marketing Company – IMC – distributor of Yashica and a new product brand named Minolta; Irving Roth of Raygram, distributor of Pentax, and Al Bernard, a self promoter who tied up all exports from Hong Kong with a powerful business associate known as the 'Dragon Lady' – Madame Chang.

The camera industry was made up of Jews who escaped from Germany before and during World War II. These resilient people were entrepreneurs of the first class and quickly established a place for themselves in the fledgling photographic industry. Because it was the buying season I was sure to meet many of the executives from the industry during the trip.

One of these individuals – Al Bernard – carried German and Russian passports addition to an American one. Bernard easily went from country to country without being noticed. Bernard's parents were divorced, his mother still lived in Russia and his father lived in Germany; he somehow emigrated to Germany, obtained citizenship, and then got to the States where he established residency and after five years was granted American citizenship. Bernard always puzzled everyone he met. You never seemed to have a straight conversation with him; he always appeared to be hiding something. He was an enigma.

Bernard became very chatty with me during the flight, which I thought odd. In the past when we met at various trade shows he ignored me. Suddenly we were the best of friends. Something bugged me about this relationship and I was on guard. The conversation became uncomfortable when it got around to optics. He was either trying to get information on the new Nikon camera or knew something about my mission and was on a fishing expedition. We started talking about long lenses and that he had a manufacturing source in Hong Kong that I should tell my contacts at Nikon about. I chose not to get into the discussion and said, "I'm tired and I think I will lie down for a while." I broke away and found my way up the staircase where one of the stewards found a place for me to undress and stretch out and sleep.

After twenty-nine hours or so we started our descent to Haneda Airport in Tokyo. This was my first time in Japan so it was an exciting moment when I glimpsed a clear view of Mount Fuji in all its majesty. About thirty minutes later we landed and cleared customs. As I walked out of the customs area I noticed small groups of people waiting to meet the passengers.

Almost by surprise I recognized Miyahara San, Export Director of Nikon. He vigorously shook my hand and introduced me to his party of three people. He whispered that the Nikon limousine driver will be out front and would make sure my luggage got into the car. He then pointed out the Fujica group, the Mamiya group and finally the Tamron Group. Just as Luke Albert said, I thought. All I have to do is follow the pecking order. It was all set up. I visited a few moments with each group and begged my apologies and said, I was tired and my car was waiting.

As I left the terminal I noticed that each of the people I traveled with went through the same ritual with their groups of people. On an overhanging balcony I saw a man shooting pictures of the crowd and I was certain that the camera was looking directly at me. That unnerved me and I walked over to Miyahara-San and said, "Let's get on our way."

Haneda Airport is just outside of Tokyo, maybe a twenty-five minute ride. As we were moving along I marveled that I couldn't read any of the signs on the buildings because they were all in Japanese characters.

29

The Imperial Palace Hotel, a luxurious hotel, was designed by Frank Lloyd Wright in 1923 and had massive columns in a huge lobby. I commented about the columns and Miyahara told me that they were specially designed and were seated in a bed of mud to withstand earthquakes.

The Hotel lobby had a Mayan theme of stone, green carpeting and dark teakwood appointments. On many of the walls were tapestries of American Indian scenes that were actually woven in China. The perimeter lighting gave the traveler a feeling of being in a different part of the world – in the jungle. Additionally, there were many Japanese floral displays throughout the lobby that enhanced that feeling. The Imperial was one of the tallest and most prestigious buildings in the Japan. Though it had a respectable height – five floors - it wasn't able to view anything in the Imperial Gardens where the Emperor lived. That happens to be one of the building restrictions in the area surrounding the Imperial Palace.

I checked in and one of the managers, dressed in a morning suit accompanied by a uniformed bellhop, showed me to my room. As they bowed out of the room – not accepting my offered tip – I started to size up the luxurious sitting room and beautiful bedroom in the two-room suite. There were three telephones in the room. I couldn't believe it - we had one for our entire apartment in Brooklyn. One was in the sitting room, another in the bedroom and one in the bathroom - this was true luxury. The bathroom was in light tan large porcelain tiles and had golden faucets with a mirror that covered the entire wall – ceiling to floor. It was twice the size of my bathroom back home.

I decided to call Debbie and tell her I arrived safely and about my luxurious room. I asked the operator to place the call to New York for me and she said "Mr. Schein it is 4:00 AM in New York, I will call you back as soon as I get a line available." I said, "Whoa – wait - cancel that. I didn't realize what time it was, I will call later." "As you wish" and she hung up.

That hit home, I was on the other side of the world, a day plus thirteen hours ahead and I was alone. I called the 'floor-attendant' for a drink of Chives Regal and water over ice and decided to take a nap even though it was about 5:00 PM. I wanted to acclimate myself to the time as quickly as possible. I put in a call to be awakened at 7:00 PM in time to dress for dinner and drifted off into a fitful sleep wondering about the photographer on the balcony, the dead man in LaGuardia airport and being followed

The phone buzzed and I immediately awoke, perspired and alert. As I moved my feet I kicked a box. I sat up, looked around and checked the door, bathroom and closet. I hadn't double locked the door - maybe that was it. It was unnerving to find someone had visited you while I was sleeping.

I cautiously opened the box. It had no address or note or wrapping but it seemed solid – nothing was loose when I tried to rattle it. After carefully ripping open the tapped end of the box I saw it was a revolver in a holster. The revolver was a .45 caliber military special and came with a box of shells and an extra clip. I operated the pistol in my hand to check the chamber, which was clear, and the clip which was full. Out loud I said, "I'll be damned" and went off to take a shower. As I started walking I reach back for my .45 – at this point I didn't want it to be very far from me. I put it on the bathroom vanity and got ready for dinner.

CHAPTER Six
My First Full Meal In Japan

Dinner was an experience in the Imperial. All the guests and visitors were dressed in suit, tie and white shirt, while many of the women came dressed in kimono with a simple obi, white tabi (socks) and slippers, or zoris. The hotel had some of the finest foreign food restaurants (American, French, Italian and Chinese) in Japan. It also had two of the best Japanese restaurants in the area serving shabu-shabu (raw beef you cook yourself on your table) or tepan-yaki (beef cooked on a grill with a show put on by the chef directly in front of you) and a very expensive separate sushi bar.

The pricing on the menus was much higher then I expected even at ¥360 (Yen) to the U.S. Dollar. You could easily spend between $40 and $50 per person for dinner. I was a little floored with what I was reading.

I had to remind myself TAG Photographic was paying the bill and they did everything first class when they sent their people to the Orient. If they did it any other way TAG would lose face. You can't play it on the cheap with the Japanese. It was important to fly to Japan first class so there would be no embarrassment when the factory people met you in the airport or picked you up at your hotel.

Japan is a status-conscious country. Executives live on large company expense accounts while many of them live in Company owned housing. If you do business in Japan you do it first class if you want to make any long lasting relationships.

After my stroll around the block-long mezzanine and reading all the menus I chose the Chinese restaurant for my first meal in Japan. As I walked in Al Bernard, who had just sat down to have his dinner, hailed me. He asked if I would like to join him. To myself I said "Not really but, I will do so remembering an old saying – 'hold your enemies close'. I was not sure if Al is my enemy but he is a competitor. I accepted. Al suggested he order for us and who was I to argue when he was recognized as Mr. China in the industry and we were in a Chinese restaurant.

The dinner was sumptuous. We started with a delicious corn soup, then had Peking duck skin wrapped in a rice pancake with vegetables and hoisin sauce, a plate of hot green string beans with pork bits, as well as four giant shrimp that were grilled in a light breading. The meal was delicious. For desert, we had a special serving of fried bananas; the bananas were mashed together into the shape of a ball, then dunked into hot boiling honey and immediately dipped into ice-cold water. The crunchy sweet taste was wonderful, unlike any desert I had ever tasted in a Chinese restaurant.

All through dinner Bernard kept the conversation going and

33

I grunted response between bites. Then he said, "Are you here to view the new Nikon Camera?" Whew, I thought, "He is not an agent." Then he said, "Why would TAG Photo send an agent to view a new camera." My heart sank; I guess he is involved in some way. I replied, "Why would you say that? I am on a buying trip just like you and, yes, we are hoping to bring the new camera into the States."

Bernard quickly came to the point – "the bulge under your jacket gave you away." I continued the charade and said, "I wear a pistol for protection." "Sure" he said, – "In the safest country in the Far East - maybe even the world – that makes a lot of sense." I was being cornered – "Yes, Japan is a safe country," I said. "But this is an old habit from when I was helping my dad; We would regularly transport money in dangerous New York neighborhoods from jukeboxes and pinball machines in bars and grills.

"He carried a gun and all through college I carried a permitted gun when I assisted him." (The gun part was a total fabrication for my involvement. However, my father did carry a pistol – a .38 caliber - just for those reasons – he was a mechanic and money collector for the jukes and games that were located in very poor neighborhoods.)

Bernard put his hands up and smiled and said "O.K. – I give up - I am interested to see how this will play out." He didn't know it, but so was I. I waited for the check, which Bernard took care of and said "you're my guest tonight." I then thanked him for an excellent meal and said, "I thought I would go for a walk on the Ginza to stretch my legs and get a feel of the excitement of Tokyo." He said "Goodbye, maybe we can do this again some time during our trip – have a good walk," I nodded and left.

CHAPTER Seven
The Domestic Crime Agency

I walked out of the side door of the Imperial Hotel toward the railroad tracks with the Imperial gardens at my back. Under the tracks in the tunnel started the many stands that sold food, clothing, electronics that made up the American Arcade. After you passed under the railroad tracks you were three blocks shy of the Ginza.

    I started to walk when someone in back of me said "Schein San" and I stopped in my tracks; my left hand went beneath my jacket and felt the steel of my pistol. I slowly turned around and saw that a Japanese man about five feet tall in a dark suit said, "No need to worry - Hiro Sacho-San would like to talk to you." Sacho-San was an indication of respect. It meant boss, president or chief. "Who is Hiro San?" – I asked, "Why does he want to speak to me?" - I slowly started to ease my arm to my side. He replied, "Hiro San is the Chief of Police in charge of the Domestic Crime Agency. I do not know why he wants to see you – just bring you to him were my instructions." "Well" I said, "We all have to follow our instructions – O.K."

I followed the little man to his car and sat in the passenger side of the front seat rather then take the offered back seat. I figured this way I could watch my escorts hands to see if he was legit. He started the car, turned on his lights and we took off through the traffic. We drove to the Yotobashi District and arrived at a modern office building. My driver stopped in front of a building where another short man in a dark suit met us and he directed me out of the car - escorted me inside the building. The car drove off.

We took an elevator – down – and after a few moments the doors in back of us opened and we entered what looked like a World War II bunker. The walls of the place looked massive. The ventilation hummed and the lighting was as if we were on a Broadway stage. It was very bright. The hallway or corridor was not active with many people but from time to time, during our walk to Hiro's office, we passed some young people. As we passed them, they would turn their backs to the wall and bow as we walked by. I thought it felt like an honor guard.

At the end of the corridor we came to a steel door and my escort pressed a button and the heavy door quickly opened – right to left. I stepped into the room and the door shut just as quickly as it opened, leaving my escort outside. This office was larger then Luke Albert's. It was done in a tasteful lightwood, and it had an overall bright appearance. There were heavy leather chairs on one side of the room and beautiful open Japanese shoji screens that served as room dividers. Wonderful Japanese touches like dolls, paintings and statues were throughout the office. The floral display on the large western style glass conference table was extraordinarily dramatic. This was a beautiful office.

A tall thin Japanese man in an expensive light grey beautifully fitted Saville Row suit with a dark silk tie – probably Liberty of London - walked across the room and stuck out his hand. In perfect English he said, "Welcome to Japan." I said "thank you" and he led me over to the leather chairs where he directed me to sit. He sat opposite me and said, "I am Ichiro Hiro, Chief of Police dealing with domestic crime. My agency works directly for the Prime Minister and of course the Emperor. We are described as an elite police unit with military training. In fact, the training takes place in The United States. Our people are continually being shuttled to and from Fort Bragg, North Carolina where your Special Forces people train them."

He continued, "Luke Albert is a friend of mine and we have worked together on several special cases for our governments. He is a very good operative and I have the highest regard for him. I heard he was involved in an incident that took him out of the field and put him behind a desk. I am sorry to hear that - please mention my name when you contact him." I shook my head yes and wondered why this man of obvious power was engaging me in this conversation.

"Whenever the C.I.A. or its cover companies are sending new people into the field and they are expected to work in Japan we get an official heads up from Washington. We get a rare chance to watch them before and after training. From time to time we are even invited to see these potential agents while they are being trained. Neither Washington nor I would want to receive an agent who we didn't think would be acceptable in our community. We have watched you for a few weeks and are impressed with your abilities to learn and to perform."

Hiro stopped for a moment and said, "Pardon my manners but would you like some tea?" Knowing it would be bad form not to accept his offer of refreshment I said, "That would be very nice." Hiro pressed a button somewhere on his chair and a girl in a white kimono appeared and put down a teapot and two cups. She then poured a cup for me an one for Hiro and quietly slipped away.

Hiro reverently picked up the cup of tea and placed it on the palm of his right hand. With his left hand on the rim of the cup he turned the cup clockwise until the painted symbol of flowers was facing me and then sipped at the tea. Before putting the cup down he repeated the process and turned the symbol counterclockwise away from me and then placed the cup on the table.

I was thankful to Mrs. Wakajima - she taught me the ways of the tea ceremony and here, in this modern office a good part of how to handle the teacup was being enacted. I copied Hiro San as best as I could. I think Hiro was testing me. This is the first time we had met and I guess he was confirming his peoples' assessment of me. As Luke Albert said, "These are very orderly people."

"Before you arrived in Japan," he continued, "There was a robbery that caused us to rethink our protocol, and that is why I am talking directly to you."

"First I should make it clear that it was our man who was watching you in LaGuardia; it was our man whose neck was broken in the baggage area of the airport; and it was our man taking pictures of you and others in Haneda Airport. We have other moments where you did not recognize our people, but the ones I have mentioned were the ones that were reported. We have a very thorough group and they do their job well."

With this admission, Hiro went on, "you are here to find out business information on periscopes and optical shipboard range-finders from Nippon Kogaku, K.K. This is a business discussion strictly between Nikon and TAG Photographic. Nikon will most likely have to ask the Japanese Defense Agency for permission to hand over any information and or documents on these products."

After a sip of tea Hiro continued, "We are aware of your Navy's efforts to improve the 8-B periscope. The Kollmorgan periscope does not allow you to take good pictures."

"Mitsubishi Heavy Industries has developed a digital recording periscope with an image enhancement attachment that, it is said will revolutionize photography aboard submarines. The construction of the new periscope design will also assure the safety of the submarine from being discovered." "That is a bold statement," I thought.

Hiro continued, "If the information on the new system got into the wrong hands and they developed it further along before we had an opportunity to develop it we could be at a serious disadvantage.

"Last week, when you were returning from Virginia, a specialized 5" floppy disc was stolen from Mitsubishi's experimental laboratory in a building located in the Nikon Ohi Machi factory in Shinagawa District. On the floppy disc were stored all of the passwords an entry codes to fire up the new digital periscope camera.

"Fortunately, the Mitsubishi engineers had the foresight to make a back-up copy of the disc and store it in a safe. We are certain that a couple of employees were involved because this had to have been an inside job. These people have not been arrested yet and are under our observation hoping to see where the disc will be moved.

"As you can imagine the security around this system is

high and we have yet to learn how the disc was removed. However, we have reason to believe that one of the Americans who arrived in Japan with you – you included – will be contacted by one of the perpetrators or their agents to try and take the disc our of the county.

"We know that you were sent to find out all you could about the possibility of a new periscope camera as well as the new Nikon 'F' 35mm amateur camera. You can still expect to have your demonstrations of the new equipment at the Ohi Machi Factory the day after tomorrow.

"Your government has no idea how far along we have come with the digital periscope and camera. We are very concerned with this break in our security methods. We must stop the perpetrator(s) as soon as possible. Because the robbery occurred and we have not recovered the disc we are willing to share our information with your country. We need to find the missing disc before it leaves Japan and before copies are made."

Hiro continued - "I am laying it all out as openly as possible. This digital camera development is a major scientific breakthrough that will miniaturize digital equipment in the future. We will show you all of our information throughout your stay in Japan."

"In summary, this will be an immeasurable loss for both our countries should the disc fall into the wrong hands. Mr. Schein, as a member of your government, you happen to be in the right place at the right time. We need your help." I was stunned; all I could say was "Yes, of course I will help. I will do whatever I can to assist recapturing the disc."

I asked, "A 5" floppy disc is a fairly new technical development. I think it will be hard to make copies much less view it because there can't be much equipment available to run the disc." Hiro said "That is correct, but, if people have been clever enough to get their hands on the disc then I imagine they will have thought about how they wanted to handle the back end of the operation."

The Chief was right; I chose not to say anything further because I didn't want to sound amateurish in front of this professional. I said, "I would like to sleep on it tonight to think with a clear head on how to approach everyone in my hotel who might be involved. I am sure you are aware that many more of the camera industry executives will be arriving from New York and will be staying in my hotel over the next couple of weeks. I imagine you do not want any direct conversation with anyone regarding the system."

Hiro said, "The fewer people involved or who know about the camera the better. In fact, I request that you do not even talk to your office about it unless it is on one of our secure telephones."

"When we visited your room to deliver your weapon this afternoon we electronically scanned the room and found a listening device in the bathroom telephone. We left it there because we didn't want to raise any suspicion. If you turn on your room radio that should cause enough background noise that you will feel relatively secure. We will check your room again within a day or two to see if anything has changed." I said "thank you for taking such good care of me."

With that Hiro tersely said, "We really didn't have much of a choice to do otherwise." The audience came to an end. He said his people would continue to watch me and he would make further contact if or when necessary. In the meantime, he handed me an Omega Accutron watch and said, "This is a special wristwatch. It is designed with a direct one-way transmitter to listen in and or locate you. It makes no noise. This is given to you for protection in emergencies. The receiving station is monitored 24 hours a day seven days per week. To activate the signal all you have to do is squeeze the winding key."

We shook hands and he bowed his head. I bowed in return, remembering Mrs. Wakajima's instruction to bow a few inches deeper then Chief Hiro. This was a sign of great respect that I am sure did not go unnoticed. He walked over to his desk, pressed a button, the steel door opened and my escort was waiting on the other side to take me to a waiting car.

As I was being chauffeured to my hotel I reviewed what Hiro had said. My pulse started to beat faster and I began to sweat thinking about all that happened in the last couple of weeks, in the last few hours and finally in the last few minutes. It was all turning into a blur.

At least Hiro cleared up some of the mystery. I now understood who was stalking me. The killing was and other thing. I knew who the victim worked for but why was he murdered? The photographer in Haneda airport and the surprise arrival of my pistol in my bedroom all made sense. I guess I felt that I was not completely alone. To know that I had the Domestic Crime Unit and their expertise backing me up was comforting and I breathed easier as my pulse rate returned to normal.

When I arrived at my hotel, I went up to the lounge on the top floor for a nightcap. The view was magnificent. It was a panorama of the Tokyo skyline: lights everywhere except in the area of the Imperial Palace, which appeared like a black hole in the skyline.

My Chivas on the rocks arrived and as I was making myself comfortable in an easy chair looking out of the glass wall, a tall muscular looking man with a blond close cropped crew cut came over to my area and sat down.

He looked at me with a smile and said "Mr. Schein I presume." he stuck out his hand and announced that he was "Lt. Robert Claypool and I was to contact you this evening." Claypool seemed aggressive, I guess he expected to find me earlier and was cooling his heels until I arrived. The fact is, with all that was going on I had forgotten about the meeting.

"Where were you," he said, "I was looking for you earlier." I replied, "I went for a long walk to stretch my legs." Claypool then said, "I am supposedly your contact and you weren't here to be contacted." I repeated with a little edge to my voice "I went for a long walk". Claypool sat back looked at me and then said, "I am here to help you with whatever you need." In the back of my mind the word "supposedly" jumped out. The good lieutenant obviously knew more then he was willing to say and I had the feeling he wasn't happy baby-sitting me. I guess he was also testing the waters just the same way I was. I said, "Lieutenant" – he stopped me and said, "Call me Bob" and I said, "I answer to Robby." I thought, at least we have the commonality of first names.

We made small talk for a while about my first trip to Japan and my observations on how uniformly the people dress and how it felt to stick out in a crowd because we were gaijen – foreigners – and generally taller then everyone around. Bob seemed to relax and I noticed that the chip on his shoulder disappeared. Claypool was regular Navy having worked his way through the ranks from an enlisted man to chief to an LDO lieutenant. His background also included the training of a photographers mate. I think we finally accepted each other and started to talk about the 'mission.'

I didn't think it was time to enlighten him about my meeting with Chief of Police Hiro until I had some direction from my office. I asked Bob "how do I contact you?" He gave me his business card. I said "How Japanese of you." He laughed and said, "When a Japanese person gives you his - maichi - his business card - he is giving you a piece of himself. The ritual of two hands on the card and a bow of the head was a sign of respect." I said to myself there appears to be a rule about everything a Japanese does in his lifetime.

Bob continued, "I suggest you give the concierge one of your business cards and he will have a couple hundred made for you with your information in Japanese on one side and English on the other. This is another sign of respect. It shows you went to the effort and trouble of preparing your card in Japanese to communicate better". I said, "I will organize the cards before I retire tonight." "Good," Bob said, "Knowing the type of first class hotel you living in I am sure they will be ready for you when you go to breakfast tomorrow morning.

"Robby, let me know how your meeting goes with Nippon Kogaku tomorrow. If all goes well I am sure they will want you to visit with the Japanese Defense Agency." I said, "From what I have learned so far – most definitely." "Good," Bob continued, "When we know that for sure I will organize a meeting through our military grapevine." "Bob," I interrupted, "I am bushed and I am looking forward to my bed." He said, "I can understand that" and we said our goodnights as we rode down the elevator. We then shook hands and I went to the concierge and Bob left the building.

CHAPTER Eight
The Head Office Of Nippon Kogaku, K.K.

In the middle of the night I reached Debbie and filled her in on the luxuries of my room. She said she wished she could be with me and I said, "I wish you could – that would be fun." I told her it was the middle of the night and I was beat. She whispered "I love you" and I did the same and hung up the phone, turned off my radio and rolled over into a deep sleep.

My 6:30 AM wake-up call buzzed and I sat up in bed feeling more refreshed than I expected I would be. I got up and went through my morning rituals including a Canadian Air Force exercise routine I was taught in Virginia to keep my aerobic abilities sharp.

I went down to breakfast at about 7:15 AM. As I opened my door there was a package hanging on the doorknob. Hmm, Claypool was right - there were my freshly printed business cards including a plastic cardholder. They looked super and from what he told me I was glad to have them.

I entered the Orchid breakfast room on the lobby floor. As I looked around the spacious room I recognized eight or ten people having their breakfast. I felt as though I was at a P.M.D.A. (Photographic Manufacturers & Distributors Association) trade convention in Chicago and we were all staying at the Conrad Hilton Hotel. I waved to a few people, shook hands with a couple more as I was shown to my table.

I ordered an American breakfast of orange juice, eggs over easy, bacon, sausages, home fried potatoes, buttered toast and coffee. The coffee tasted superb - it was a great cup of coffee. I think I drank four or five cups. I signed the check and returned to my room to pick up my papers.

After I reviewed my papers and checked my pistol, I decided to go to the lobby and wait for my pickup. As I got off the elevator I notice Irving Roth of Raygram sitting by himself and I decided to join him. "Good morning" I said as I took a seat opposite him. He replied in kind and continued to read the Japan Times - English language newspaper. To my surprise he looked up and said "The Brooklyn Dodgers are doing a heck of a job this season." I replied, "I thought they might even win the pennant." Roth grunted agreement then said – "Yeh – and then they would have to play the Yankees. Maybe they should stop trying and just continue to lose." We both chuckled at that.

Roth then said, "Who are you meeting with today?" He knew it was Nikon but I think he was just making conversation. "Nippon Kogaku" I said. In a fatherly way he asked "did you have a good breakfast this morning?" "I did," I Replied. – "Good," he said, "Now you can be as picky as you want with the rest of the crap they will throw at you for lunch and dinner. I always start my trip with food I know, and then I can eat or not eat the raw fish or ugly stuff they give you."

Obviously Roth was a steak and potatoes man and didn't care for Japanese food. Out of the blue he asked "How did your dinner go last night with Bernard. I saw you two together eating in the Chinese Restaurant." My god, I thought, everyone seems to check on everyone else in Japan. I said, "It was delicious. A great repast."

At that moment a bellhop walked by ringing a bell that was connected to a small sign he was holding that read - Mr. Shine. I assumed the incorrect spelling was the fault of translation and he was looking for me - I waved him down. He informed me that I had a telephone call and could take it by the manager's desk.

"Moshi Moshi (Hello - Hello) Schein San. I am Tanaka, assistant to Hiro Sacho San. He asked me to inform you that the two people we have had under observation for the robbery at Mitsubishi have disappeared. He asked that you take special caution when you leave your hotel and be observant and as guarded as possible when you visit the factory." "Thank you," I said and hung up the phone. The bellhop came over to me to tell me a car was waiting for me. I waved goodbye to Irving Roth and went on my way.

It was a bright, sunny, cool day in Tokyo. As I exited the building I looked around and saw nothing unusual. The doorman said, "Good morning Mr. Schein" and already had the back door of the car open. I ducked in and we took off by driving around the 'U' shaped driveway, made a right turn and headed for the Aksaksa District. In about five or six minutes we arrived at an office building on Mianuchi Street and my driver pointed for me to go in.

As I checked in at the front desk Miyahara appeared, shook

my hand and said "Good morning". I nodded in return as we walked to the elevator. Miyahara continued, "Nagaoka Sacho San was waiting in his office to see you." We arrived on the top floor of the building and entered into a large 'bullpen' office set up.

The Japanese felt it was important that their employees for whom they were responsible be seated very close to them. There were about ten rows of gray steel desks and at the head of each row one desk was situated perpendicular to the row. Behind this desk sat either a Manager or Director of that section. It had a very clear table of organization just from its appearance. The older person was at the head, near the windows. On either side of the desks, the ages of the men got younger as you got closer to the door. Women usually occupied the last desks on each of the rows. Japan is a male dominated business world. You couldn't ask for a more distinctive and clear pecking order.

As we walked through the office I was surprised to see the simple set up that everyone was working in. There was no carpeting, no cubicles, artwork or any of the amenities we would expect to see in an office in the States. This was all work and what appeared to be no play.

On the same floor to the right side of the building I entered the Nippon Kogaku K.K. Administration Area. This part of the floor was carpeted and was more decorative. Nagaoka's secretary got up from her desk and led us into the president's office. The room was rather dark with a large window on one side that was shuttered by vertical blinds. On the opposite side was a long teakwood shelf that had plaques, certificates, trophies, and pictures of Nagaoka accepting various awards. Over the course of time, I am sure he received more awards than could be displayed.

Additionally, there was a small round conference table and a sofa, coffee table and what looked like two comfortable leather chairs. Nagaoka came from behind his desk to welcome me. He stuck out his hand and I put two hands on my business card and slightly bowed my head. He stopped in his tracks, went back to his desk to retrieve his card and then rushing to me did the same.

As he was directing Miyahara and me to the sofa I said "Nagaoka Sanse (Sanse means Doctor), it is an honor to meet you." Masao Nagaoka was an affable man, with a shock of white hair and deep creases in his face, and stood about 5'2", he was 61 years of age. He spoke English haltingly. He said, "Iie – Iie (No – No) it is MY honor." A girl in a Nikon staff uniform brought in a teapot and cups and placed them on the coffee table and bowed out of the room.

Masao Nagaoka was the 'guru' of Nikon. During the war Nikon employed over 30,000 people. The Nippon Kogaku, K.K. factory was the optical supplier for the Japanese military. Nagaoka, through Japan's German allies, arranged to visit the Zeiss Optical factory where he learned how to pour optical quality glass. He brought the technology back to Japan.

Factory workers spoke about how he would camp out on a mattress alongside the curing pot for days so that he could watch the curing process of the glass to make sure it met his expectations. Additionally, Nagaoka was the force behind Nikon manufacturing quality 35mm cameras that looked like the Leica Camera. The Nikon 'SP' rangefinder cameras and lenses were born because of the quality of the equipment Nagaoka experienced when he was in Germany. He was an interesting man, with a good sense of humor, but had one major problem - he drank too much. His drink of choice was scotch whiskey at any time and any opportunity.

Nagaoka asked if my trip to Japan was going well and I replied, "All is going very well." He then said, "After your visit to the Ohi Machi Factory would you be available for dinner this evening?" I said, "Of course, I look forward to it." Reaching into my briefcase I presented him with a bottle of Johnny Walker Black Label Scotch I had picked up in New York Duty Free before I boarded my flight. A bottle of imported scotch in a department store in Japan cost about $100 to $150 US Dollars. I paid $15 in Duty Free. Nagaoka's eyes lit up. He asked if I would like a drink and I deferred by saying, "I would wait until dinner this evening." He grunted and picked up the bottle and walked it over to his desk so he could store it out of sight of any visitors. As he walked back he said he would return in a minute and disappeared out his office door.

I asked Miyahara "Why is it so dark in the room? Especially since all of the office areas I have seen are so bright." Miyahara smiled and said, "Look outside the window behind the blinds." Curious, I got up, walked to the blinds, lifted an edge and peeked out the window. I was surprised with what I saw and laughed out loud. Across the street, on top of the building about the same level of Nagaoka's office was a huge red and white sign that read CANON. If you pulled back the blinds the only thing you would see out the window was Canon - Nikon's arch competitor. I guess they take their competition very seriously in Japan.

Nagaoka's secretary announced – "Telephone call for Schein San". She pointed to the phone on Nagaoka's desk. I walked over, picked it up and heard "Tanaka here. The two people we were searching for have been found. They are dead, dispatched by a samurai style beheading. As of yet we do not know who did it. They were found in an apartment near the Ohi Machi factory. Please continue to keep this information to yourself. I will join you when the Mitsubishi meeting takes place." He then hung up. I tried to hold my emotions to myself as I returned to my seat.

Miyahara asked if all was well and I said, "The call was from my hotel relaying a Teletype message regarding some information I requested." Nagaoka returned. "I took the liberty of inviting Trigubuff-San to dinner if that is all right with you." I replied, "I was looking forward to meeting him." Nagaoka continued, "He will pick you up at about 6:00 PM at your hotel." I nodded and Nagaoka said, "I cannot have lunch with you today and I know Miyahara San is anxious to take you to the Ohi Machi Factory. Have a good trip and we will meet this evening." We nodded and bowed and left to go to the factory.

As we went down the elevator, I was trying to imagine how the death of these two people might affect me and why. It just wasn't clear enough yet I thought. The perpetrators certainly cleaned up their handiwork in an extreme way. If you are a challenge them or represent a weak link to them they just kill you. Crude, extreme - but effective.

As we got into our car I noticed there was a black sedan, idling three cars in back of us. When we pulled out it pulled out. Hiro's men were taking no chances this time – they wanted me and anyone else who might be following me to know that they were there. That was fine with me.

CHAPTER Nine
The Ohi Machi Factory - Shinagwa-ku District

We drove onto a short toll road and in about twenty minutes we exited in Shinagawa District. We went about four blocks and made a left turn into a residential area. The streets were very narrow and tight. It was hard to imagine that a factory was in this area. We made about three turns in eight blocks and finally came to the factory. We made one more right into the gated courtyard. The black car that was following also turned into the courtyard. Miyahara introduced me to my hosts and made the necessary courtesy bows and handshakes.

As I was walking toward the building I heard a "spit sound" near my right foot - then a closer one whizzed by my left side. "I am being shot at," I said to myself. I ducked as one of Hiro's men pushed me to the ground before I could pull out my pistol to protect myself. Hiro's other man pulled his gun out searching for the shooter. It was a tense couple of seconds - it seemed to happen in slow motion.

The moment of the shooting the loud ringing of a bell came over speaker system with a factory announcement that it was time to 'exercise'. A hundred or so people came running into the courtyard and lined up like when we line up our kids in school. Then the music started and everyone started a ritualized fifteen-minute exercise routine. It was bizarre. No one seemed to notice that I had hit the ground or that bullets were flying. I decided to go along with the moment and not say anything.

I peered into a courtyard window and saw that those workers who did not go outside were exercising standing alongside their desks. I couldn't believe it - I was shot at and no one noticed. The people who greeted me on my arrival were going back into the office so they had their backs to me. The only people involved were Hiro's men and me.

The timing of the shooting was perfect and the cover of the exercise period was perfect. The only thing that wasn't perfect was that the shooter missed his target - me.

Before I joined Miyahara I looked across the courtyard beyond the road to see if I could figure out where the shooter might have been located. The Ohi Machi factory building looked like an old sturdy concrete printing plant. The building had three floors and it could obviously sustain earthquakes and – during the war – bombings. I had no clue where the shots came from. The only conclusion I could make was that someone knew my schedule and knew the routine of the factory to have timed it so perfectly.

As I walked up the stairs to the second floor conference room I tried to get a handle on what just happened. If they took me out what do they gain? I don't have any valuable information yet, I haven't enforced anything with anybody – I don't get it. Unless, their purpose was to create confusion,

53

delay and scare me. If an American businessman – in this case me - was hurt or shot that could cause an international incident. The diversion might allow someone to move something (a 5" floppy disc) around a little safer. After taking a moment to think it out that's probably what it was. Well, it didn't work out and I feel pretty good about that. I am still able to walk around.

The conference room was brightly lit, had a gray steel conference table with eight steel side chairs. There was a calendar and a simple wall hanging to soften the appearance. My hosts were all dressed in grey, Eisenhower style factory jackets with the name Nikon embroidered on it. Additionally they each had a round pin with their name written in Kanji characters. They were dressed in white shirts and ties and their trousers were part of the suits that they wore to work. Miyahara was in a dark suit and I was in my business 'uniform'.

Everyone exchanged business cards in the usual reverential way and I learned who my hosts were. Mr. Segawa, manager of the mechanical design, Mr. Nakano, director – camera production, Mr. Wakimoto – manager of optics design, and Mr. Takauchi, manager of the administrative department.

After some small talk lunch arrived in bento boxes. The bento box was filled with rice, cooked unagi (eel), and pickles. Alongside the box was a bowl of miso soup. We were having a Japanese working lunch. The meal turned out to be very tasty and filling. I actually enjoyed it.

All through lunch my hosts were discussing my schedule in Japanese. I continued eating and acted as though I had no understanding of what they were saying. The argument was whether to first show me the factory, go over the numbers, or show the new camera. Wakimoto, who was a happy-go-lucky guy, who had a twinkle in his eye and a smile on is face, only wanted to show the new camera. The deciding person was the director - Mr. Nakano. After listening to the discussion he quietly said "the factory first, then the figures and finally the new products."

Mr. Nakano said to me, "Wakimoto San, Segawa San and Takauchi San will show you the factory. After the tour we will meet again to go over the numbers and projections and if it is all right with you we would like to then show you our new products."

To be a little obstinate and to try to exert some control of the meeting I said, "After the tour is over why not view the new products first before we review our projections and orders? After all, I continued, "The new products might have an effect and change our projections." Nakano looked at his colleagues, and then nodded agreement saying, "That will be fine."

I was not happy going out into the courtyard again and made sure that I walked behind one of my tour guides. As we were walking I continued to search the windows and balconies ahead. Halfway through the courtyard one of Hiro's men got out of his parked car and joined us by walking about five yards in back of me. I guess no one was surprised with the intruder because they must have been briefed at some time before my arrival. I wonder what their cover story was, I thought to myself.

We climbed to the third floor on some well-worn concrete stairs and entered a corridor. Wakimoto opened one of the doors and before us there must have been fifty or sixty young people sitting in teams of three with each team member wildly working an abacus. There was a constant clicking of the beads as they were moved. Wakimoto simply said, "They are

55

working on lens formulas. Each team is working on a lens-grinding angle so that we can prove the formula."

In the far part of the room there was a glass sectioned off area that had a large tape controlled computer. The tape was spinning and men in lab coats were writing numbers on a clipboard. Wakimoto said, "That is our future. We will have to find something else for these people to do when we bring in more computers." He smiled.

The second floor was devoted to assembly. I saw two production lines for the 'SP' series cameras. At each station either a part was added or the camera was being worked or tested and in some cases with the assistance of an oscilloscope. It was impressive to see no one look up but stayed glued to his or her work.

The other half of the floor was devoted to lens assembly and testing. People worked on small lathes with pointed lights reflecting from the lens surface as it spun around. When the light was steady the lens would be 'crimped' into position. This assured proper lens alignment.

The main floor was Segawa's area. It was a floor jammed packed with heavy equipment for cutting, pressing and stamping. It was a high ceiling floor, noisier and dirtier then any of the other parts of the factory. The workers, all male, were in their gray uniforms and again I was surprised that no one looked up to see who was visiting. They just plodded away and repeated their part of the manufacturing process.

The final part of the tour was a visit to the lower floor - the area we would call the basement - where their quality control equipment and lens grinding equipment was housed. The assembly of specialized optics, new product design and new tooling development was also on this floor. A steel door separated a part of the floor - this was where they worked on military products.

We signed in as we passed a guard and I was led into an assembly area where they were manufacturing one-of-a-kind special optical products. I saw a shipboard optical range finder being tested and on a lower shelf, stored like a sailboat mast, I saw a submarine's periscope about eighteen feet in length.

Takauchi San said, "Through Albert San we know of your interest in our periscope. We are not at liberty to discuss it with you until the Japanese Defense Agency gives us permission to do so. From the outside there isn't very much to see and that is why we were allowed to show you this part of the factory. Since your Company has made a formal request we have asked the Japanese Defense Agency to accept a meeting with you." I said, "Thank you" as we left the area to return to the conference room.

We entered the conference room and I noticed that the teapot and tea cups were already refreshed On the table sat the new Nikon 'F' camera with three Nikkor lenses - 50mm f2, 28mm f 3.5 and 105mm f4. Everything was shown on a red jeweler's placemat. The camera looked like a piece of jewelry. I couldn't wait to get my hands on it but restrained myself to wait for their presentation. It would have been rude for me to pick it up and start making comments. I just kept quiet as Miyahara demonstrated the camera.

He stripped the camera down; took off the prism, removed the ground-glass, removed the back and individually pointed out the features. The focal plane shutter traveled 24.5 mm per second across the aperture opening. The flatness of the film is important for sharp pictures. The 'F' was designed to make film flat during picture taking. This is accomplished by the

57

precision tracks and back of the camera. Finally, the 100% viewing area looking through the camera would give you what you see is what you get in the photograph. He then put on the 50mm lens and handed it to me.

It was heavier then I thought it would be. But after that it was perfect. It handled like a range-finder camera with a full size viewing screen. I was impressed and I knew this was a winner. I thought when everyone in my office back home sees it they would agree. I tried the other two lenses and kept on shooting and advancing the camera as I was looking out of the window.

Everyone was very quiet in the room. In fact, since they handed the camera to me no one had spoken. It felt kind of awkward. Then I realized, they were waiting for me to say something. I had to be very careful and chose my words correctly. "Gentlemen" I started, "This is a revolutionary camera. I am more than impressed with what you have developed. I think it will have a terrific market success for many years to come." I held my breath hoping I'd said the right words and they all started to smile. Nakano said, "Thank you and we completely agree with you." He then stuck out his hand to shake mine.

My next question, I thought, might turn everyone off. "When will it go into production and when do you think we could expect to see it in the United Stated" - nothing like putting water on the fire I thought. My question caused the room to go silent. Miyahara started by saying, "That is a difficult question to answer" - that was not a good sign. When a Japanese businessman says "difficult" it means 'no' or he doesn't know. Miyahara continued, "We are developing new materials and have not yet secured the manufacturing schedule. Before you leave Japan Nagaoka Sacho San will try to answer your questions." I chose not to go further and said, "Thank you."

I then handed over my orders and paperwork for the forthcoming six-month purchasing periods. They graciously accepted the paperwork and said they would work with their staff to review them and get back to me in a few days. With that the meeting was over. We went downstairs to my waiting car. As we pulled out they all lined up in the courtyard and bowed goodbye. I also noticed that Hiro's men quickly got in back of my car as we went to the highway to return to the Imperial Palace Hotel.

In the quiet of the car I started to review some of the happenings of the day in my head. A couple of people were killed "samurai style" and I was shot at. The shooter obviously used a silencer and it was a low caliber pistol – maybe a .22. If it were a rifle it would have had more accuracy. The shooter could have been 100 yards away. It kept gnawing away at me – why shoot me? It still didn't make any sense as we arrived at my hotel.

CHAPTER Ten
Dinner With Dr. Masao Nagaoka And Directors Of Nikon

The music was playing softly as I finished dressing and at exactly 6:00 PM my telephone buzzed. A voice said "Mr. Schein there is a car waiting for you at the front entrance." "Thank you – I will be right down" and hung up the telephone. I guess Mr. Triguboff is on time, I thought.

When I walked out the front door there was a blue Buick waiting for me. I got in and Alex Triguboff, a stocky, broad-shouldered man in his late fifties or early sixties, thinning gray hair with a Russian accent, stuck out his hand and said, "I hope your trip has been successful so far. Welcome to Japan."

I had never met Alex - I only heard of him from Luke Albert. Right from the outset, as we were driving to the restaurant, he started telling me the story of his life. He never asked any specific question about my visit to Nikon, which I thought unusual. After all, that is how the man earns his commission. He just rambled on about himself and every now and then a word or two regarding his wife, Miyako.

One of the first things he mentioned was how he survived Japan during the War. Because he was married to a Japanese National and wasn't an American - "I am Russian" he said - he was spared internment in a concentration camp that housed the Giajen. However, he and his wife were banished to the wooded unpopulated area of Hakone. This way the Triguboffs were kept out of the mainstream of everyday activities.

They had to build their own house to live in with their bare hands and practically no tools. When the local military authority visited the house on an inspection tour he realized that Triguboff and his wife were going to survive. Shortly after a government 'servant' arrived. Her job was to spy on the Triguboffs and report their activities to the military once a week. The story became fascinating and my interest in this man grew as we passed the streets on the way to the restaurant.

We arrived at the La Tour d'Argent restaurant on the top floor of an office building. This French restaurant is recognized as one of the top restaurants in all of Japan. When a nation is starved for western items and foreign food it is quite an honor to be one of the best of anything. La Tour had a sister operation and its origins in Paris.

We entered a small room with plush leather chairs arranged in a circle with a round coffee table within reach of each chair. As soon as we walked in the introductions started. Nagaoka and Miyahara introduced us to directors Fuketa, Shirahama, Nakano – whom I had met earlier in the day, Fukuoka and Hirose.

A tuxedo-clad waiter came in and took our drink orders. I was asked first as the honored guest. Alex leaned over and whispered, "Whatever you order make it a double." I looked at him and he winked. I said, "I will take a double Chivas Regal on the rocks." With that each person followed suit and ordered the very same drink.

When the drinks came Triguboff quaffed the drink like he had never seen a drink before. He then whispered, "Do the same." I looked at him a little startled and once again he winked. What hell was he up to? I couldn't figure it out. However, I did what he asked and drank my scotch in one large pull. I came up for air and noticed that each of my hosts did exactly what I did.

Before you knew it we had fresh drinks in our hands and Alex whispered, "Do it again." I whispered back, "I can't if I want to stand up the rest of the evening." He said, "Figure out how to get rid of it." Alongside of my chair was a small tree. Not quite a Bonsai but a miniature. I started to sip the drink and before I put my glass on the table I carefully and nonchalantly dumped the remainder of my drink into the dirt base of the plant.

As soon as I put my glass on the coffee table another fresh drink appeared. I started to see what Alex was doing. In a few minutes our crowd was noisy and feeling no pain. Alex leaned over and said, "Except for Nagaoka the rest of these monkeys can't hold their liquor." Crude I thought, but was probably true and it gave me a laugh.

A maitre d' came in to show us to our table. We marched out of the small room in a procession that appeared to look like Snow White and the seven dwarfs. I started out and single file everyone followed.

The restaurant was done in the style of the Great Gatsby. There was a pond in the middle of the room. There were white flowing curtains surrounding the organist who was playing on a revolving stage in the center of the pond. She would play and effortlessly be moved around and around in a circle. It was a very pretty sight.

Tables were lined perpendicular to the pond. We crossed in front of the water and sat down next to the pond at the far end. The lighting was low, the music subdued and our fourth double scotch arrived. The meal was a planned 13 or 14 course tasting menu. The service started as soon as we were seated.

I have no idea what I ate – each dish had some unusual item on it and as the waiter put the plate down he would announce it. My waiter's English ability was nil but he kept on trying. Through the meal I tried to figure out what he had said. I would eat something and imagine I was eating pigeon or rabbit or whatever. Now added to the food, we were served different wines with each course. Everyone was loud and boisterous – by now we were anesthetized.

When the third or fourth course came around I heard a crash at the end of the long table. I turned to see Fuketa asleep or passed out on his dish of what looked like salmon mousse. With his colleague's head in the salmon on the table, Shirahama said, "Fuketa San had a very tough day of union negotiations. I imagine he is very tired." A couple of waiters arrived and helped Fuketa – almost carried him - to the elevator, then I guess to his car and he was driven home. I am sure I was a little drunk because I almost could not contain myself. I must have had a laughing fit. Alex kept kicking me under the table to stop and pay attention.

Nagaoka kept on putting the scotch away. No wine for him - he just wanted the straight stuff. As the meal continued Shirahama decided he wanted to make a request of the organist. Without saying a word, he got up out of his chair and walked to the edge of the pond. He stood there for a moment. For some reason I was the only one in our party watching him – and then I couldn't believe my eyes.

He obviously didn't see the path to the rotating stage so he got up on the edge of the pond and starting walking, in the water, to the organist. I kicked Alex to get his attention and he immediately caught on.

We were staring in amazement as Shirahama walked six or seven steps in water that was about four inches above his trouser cuffs, to reach the organist. As the circling stage came around, the organist was minding her own business and concentrating on what she was playing. Shirahama tapped her on her back. She was so startled - she jumped up and almost fell off her chair into the water. She was totally shaken that someone would creep up on her in the middle of the pond.

All hell broke lose as the maitre d' and a couple of waiters came running down the concrete path on the other side of the pond to rescue of the organist and Shirahama. The scene was too much, I was laughing so hard inside that I almost peed in my pants.

It didn't quite end there. When Shirahama started to walk back to the table his shoes were squishing – squish/squash – squish/squash - as he walked by me. My sides were hurting. I couldn't stop from laughing and I covered my mouth as best as I could. I was trying to hold it back but it wasn't working. I couldn't make this stuff up I said to myself.

The organist recovered and then out of courtesy to Shirahama she started to play his request – believe it or not the song was Red River Valley. That was it! That sent me over the top; I had to go to the benjo, water closet or toilet - whatever it is called to pull myself together.

When dinner was over we said our goodnights and everyone remarked what a wonderful dinner it was and what a great time we all had. I thanked Nagaoka profusely and we got into Alex's car and he drove me to my hotel. Along the way he asked if I had given our orders and projections to Nikon yet and I confirmed that I had. He said, "Good – now we will see what they come up with. I bet they ask for a lot more. They have to finance the new camera and that will be on the backs of their distributors around the world. Alex was right but I said, "We will wait and see."

I went directly to the top floor lounge to meet with Bob Claypool. He was waiting where we met last night. I said, "Bob, I am exhausted. I am looking forward to my bed. However, I have a couple of things I must review with you." He said, "I am all ears."

I continued, "Believe it or not I was shot at today. The guys who stole a 5" floppy disc from Nikon/Mitsubishi were killed Samurai style. 'Oh' and by the way, we have authorization from Nikon to visit with the Japanese Defense Agency. I think you will agree with me that I have had a busy day." Bob said, "I know about The JDA visit - my office was contacted. The rest is out of the blue. You didn't mention anything to lead me to believe what was going on last night." "I didn't expect this either."

I decided to tell Bob about my visit with Hiro. I hadn't been able to talk to my office and I realized I couldn't do this alone. I decided that I had to trust Bob and try to get some back up instead of going it alone. I explained that I needed his help to start finding out why I was a target and why were these men killed?

Bob was astonished and I think I gained his respect with what I told him. He said, "I have been here for three years; I have not been involved with as much as you have stirred up in two days." I said, "Bob, I think it is only the beginning." Bob put his hand on my shoulder and said "get some sleep and I will start looking into this with the information you have given me."

"One more thing" I said, "since my room is bugged and I have not had the time to get to a secure telephone; please inform Luke Albert of what is going on." "Consider it done" Bob said.

I went down to my room, had a couple of Alka-Seltzers and got ready for bed. As I started to drift off to sleep I was feeling a little better - I have someone working with me and for the first time I think I have covered all bases. Not too bad for a beginner.

CHAPTER Eleven
Thursday - Another Day Has Started

I went down for breakfast and again waved at a few friends just as I had the day before. Breakfast seems to be the meeting time and place for everyone in the camera industry who happens to be in Japan.

Al Bernard waved at me to come over to his table. As I was walking over I noticed that his guest was a gorgeous young Chinese woman. Al said, "Why don't join us?" Looking at this beautiful creature I said, "Of course." She stuck out her hand and said, "Juniper Chang." I repeated, "Juniper?" she smiled and said, "Yes" and I debonairly kissed her hand and sat down. Al continued, "This young lady is Madame Chang's third daughter. Juniper is very active in the photo operation of the family business. I work with her when I am not directly working with her mother."

He then added, "don't let her good looks fool you, Juniper

is a graduate of the Wharton School of Business and has a masters degree from Yale in international economics. She is a very smart lady."

Juniper was about my age, had long black hair with a chrysanthemum flower in it. Her face had impeccable features, her body had full rounded breasts, and a very thin waist and, it was all poured into a full length 'Suzie Wong' style green dress that matched her eyes. While she was sitting the slit on the side of her dress showed off her legs, which were smooth and creamy looking and were perfectly shaped. On her feet was a pair of Italian stiletto heels. 'Wow', was all I could think – she took my breath away.

She had to be one of the most beautiful women I had ever seen up close. In fact, as I looked around the room, I noticed that everyone sitting near her, with or without women at their table, was sneaking a peek at her. Every male in the room couldn't take his eyes off her.

In a nicely pitched even voice she said, "Al has been telling me of your company and that you were going to see the new Nikon camera." She paused and asked, "Have you seen it yet?" I couldn't find my voice then blurted out "err, yes." "Well" she said, "What is it like? Is it everything they say it is?" She waited for my reply. How much could I say? What should I tell her? This woman was radiant and confusing my senses. I opted for caution.

I replied, "I think you will not be disappointed with the new camera. It felt good in my hands and I think most people will agree with me." "How expensive will it be?" she asked? "I don't think we have that information yet" I replied. "Of course not" she said in what I thought was a harsh tone – she seemed to be toying with me. I wonder why?

She then asked me a question that blew me away. "Mr. Schein, my company in Hong Kong is the entranceway to mainland China and Taiwan. We have many contacts and they have developed many interesting products – consumer and military type products. I am sure your company would be interested in them. We would like the opportunity to show some of them to you. Can you arrange such a meeting?"

Now I was on the edge of my seat. "Yes" I said, "I think we might be very interested. However, please recognize that this is not a commitment to see those products until I have had the opportunity to converse with my directors in New York City." She said, in the same condescending tone as she did a moment ago, "Of course, I totally understand. If I heard of such an offer I would want to discuss it with my mother – Madame Chang."

Al chimed in and broke the moment and said, "Well, now that is done let's order some breakfast." I wasn't sure if I was hungry any more after fencing with Juniper Chang. When the waiter came by I said, "Yes, I will have an American breakfast – thank you."

As I was eating I said to myself, it is amazing how everyone knows what everyone else is cooking in his or her pots in this country. Everyone is a Yenta (gossip) and each factory seems to share its information with every other one. The communication hot line seems to work faster then the telephone lines.

A few minutes later a bellhop was walking by ringing a bell and on his sign placard was printed "Mr. Shine." I flagged him down and he said, "Your car is waiting by the front lobby door." I said goodbye to Miss Chang, again kissing her hand, and promised to get back to Bernard within the next couple of days. I left to go upstairs, get my papers out of my room and take the car to the Fuji headquarters.

CHAPTER Twelve
Fuji Photo Film K.K. - Aasaksa District - Tokyo

The Fuji head office had recently opened a new office building, a circular structure with floor to ceiling glass windows overlooking one of the inter-highway toll arteries. Seven floors high, it was one of the tallest buildings in the business district.

Fuji Photo Film was the Kodak of the Far East. Their arch competitor was Kodak Far East Laboratories. Kodak film sales had made strong headway into the Japanese market. On the other hand Fuji hadn't caught on in the States. There was a strong jealousy of Kodak. Kodak marketed as though Fuji didn't exist. Fuji found that hard to accept - especially in Japan.

TAG Photographic sold Fuji's line of film and Fujica 35mm inexpensive rangefinder cameras after a difficult contract-negotiating period. Fuji always thought that its distributors never gave their products enough attention. The distributors, on the other hand, felt that Fuji's products didn't have the features that Kodak had.

Everyone knew that it was a matter of time before Fuji went direct to the consumer market and eliminated the pricing structure of the distributor. But Fuji was tight with the buck and it was thought to be too expensive to sell direct in a vast country like the United States.

I arrived on the seventh floor and Takano, director of international marketing, met me as I walked off the elevator. I had met Takano at a PMDA exhibit in Chicago. Takano said, "Welcome to our head office Schein San. Nakamura Sacho San is waiting to greet you."

Fred Nakamura went to college in Berkley. He seemed more American then Japanese. He was a smooth hard driving individual who was hard to warm up to. The primary reason for that was you didn't feel he could be trusted. You knew he was looking for some advantage to stab you in the back. His reputation was well deserved. He made many deals in the States that he broke his word on. In the fledgling photo industry after the war your handshake was your bond. Things were not always put in writing. Nakamura took advantage of that.

Luke Albert was approached by Fuji a couple of years ago to distribute Fuji products in the States. Nakamura was sent to make the deal. Knowing Nakamura's methods Albert spent most of the two months negotiations with the company's attorneys. Nakamura cooled his heels in New York. Actually he had no other distributor to talk to. He had burned too many of them.

Ultimately he backed into a five-year contract with TAG

Photo. The contract indicated to Fuji's board of directors that they could finally expect to see some stability in the United States market. With the contract in place, Nakamura was soon promoted to president of Fuji Photo. The board felt he was the right person to front for the company. He was always destined for that position but the instability of the U.S. market held him back.

Nakamura was a good-looking man, a little beefy, with slick black hair; he dressed in an expensive grey suit. As I walked in his modest office he came from in back of his desk and greeted me. "It is good to see you again Robert. I hope you have had a successful trip and like our country." I said, "Fred, I am looking at this trip through rose colored glasses. Everyone has been more then hospitable," I lied. To myself I said sarcastically, being shot at is not very hospitable. Fred said, "Good, I am glad to hear that."

Nakamura was not one to spar or delay his conversation. He got to the point. "How are we doing in the market with our product line? I am not happy with what has been ordered so far and I was wondering if you were going to boost your purchases for the fall and spring of next year." I sparred a little with him by saying – "Fred, even if our sales were great – and I don't think they are too bad – you would say you were unhappy, right?" Fred laughed and ignored what I said.

"Robert," he continued, "do you have your projections and orders so I can turn it over to my staff to review?" I said "yes" reached into my briefcase and handed the file to him. Fred then said something that made me sit up straight in my chair.

"Robert, as a friend I ask that you take as much caution as possible moving around in Japan." I said, "What do you mean?" He continued, "We are very aware of the Mitsubishi loss of a tactical floppy disc for a new piece of equipment. We also know of the elimination of the people involved with the theft. This appears to be a very organized thorough group. I'm just saying – be careful."

I let the air out of my lungs and said, "Why me? I haven't learned about anything of value yet." Fred smiled and said "Simple – Who is most interested in the new piece of equipment Mitsubishi is working on? – Your military. If you think these people do not know who TAG really is then you are being naive. Their thought is to eliminate the competition until they have the disc and the technology in a safe place." It was like a light bulb went on. Fred was right. Everything he said made sense.

I continued, "Fred, why are you telling me all this? Why not just let me find out for myself." Fred smiled, "It is strictly business – not personal. If you get killed there will be an investigation. We are trying to do something successful in the States and move forward. An investigation might slow us down for quite some time - even bring our efforts to a complete stand still. We rather not see that happen. We are just being good businessmen, friends and partners by reporting our findings to you."

I almost laughed – the guy I least trust is now my best friend. However, what he has said makes sense; I wondered what Claypool would dig up. I then thought – God – it is amazing how everyone is so hooked up with one another in this place. It is scary!

We then had the obligatory cup of tea and Takano led me into a nicely appointed small conference room where we had a brainstorming session with five members of his staff. When we finished our discussion I was brought back to Nakamura's office where a very nice display of sushi had been set on the conference table for lunch. Nakamura, Takano and I sat around the table picking at the sushi and making small talk. After the lunch a young lady quietly whisked into the room and whispered in Nakamura's ear. He said, "Robert, your car is waiting." I thanked him and Takano for their hospitality and went down the elevator to get my car.

CHAPTER Thirteen
An Air Controlled Room For A Demonstration

The car was waiting and as I approached, my driver in a dark suit and white gloves got out and opened the rear door for me. Before I stepped in I scanned everything in about a 280° slow turn to see if I could spot anything suspicious. I noticed Hiro's men in a black sedan about six cars in back of us and they were getting ready to pull out. Nothing looked unusual. I started to get into the car and caught myself and stepped out again. About a block and a half away a black Volkswagen Beetle was double-parked. It was too far away to be able to see if anybody was inside. I said to myself – I'm getting carried away. Forget about it. I got into the car.

We got onto the highway and the highway ended in the Shinagawa-ku district. We again took the winding streets, this time it appeared via different ones and ended up in the very same courtyard where I was shot at yesterday. I quickly got out of my car and with the door open stood in back of it looking across the street at the factory building. I didn't notice anything unusual. I rapidly walked into the lobby of the factory head office.

Wakimoto, Segawa, and Miyahara of the factory and Tanaka, Hiro's right hand man, greeted me. I was told that Mr. Nakano couldn't make it in because he had a terrible headache. Takeuchi had some administrative meeting he had to go to at the head office and could not join us. I said that is fine, I have no problem with the present company. Tanaka obviously had greased the way and the Nikon people accepted his joining the meeting.

We went directly downstairs of the office building we were standing in. As we came to the bottom landing two guards greeted us and asked for our identification. I noticed at least two security cameras trained on us. I was asked for my passport. After inspection of my briefcase I was given back my passport and without any command or button being pressed the steel door slid open and we walked through.

On the other side we immediately walked into what appeared to be a laboratory. Chemical bottles were bubbling away and strange robotic machines were all over the place. This looked like a science fiction movie. I was immediately caught up in it. There were about 15 people dressed in white lab coats and everyone seemed to ignore us while they were concentrating on what they were working on.

A bald man with dark rimmed glasses in a lab coat walked over to greet us. Wakimoto introduced "Koana Sense." Dr. Koana was a physics professor at the prestigious Tokyo University. Wakamoto declared "He had been my teacher when I was a student in the university."

When Fukuchi, the creator of the digital periscope camera,

mysteriously disappeared the administration of Mitsubishi felt they needed an expert to make sense of what had been done on the project. They replaced Fukuchi with Koana. He was requested to take a leave of absence from the university to consult and assist in the investigation. Koana had assisted the government on other projects in the past - he was the respected expert to call upon in an emergency involving optical products.

Dr. Koana spoke English like an automaton. He was precise and even toned and spoke only when the question was directed to him. We walked through the lab and entered a room that had additional security, where a card was slipped through a reading device. I also noticed another security camera watching us. Wakimoto slipped his card through and nothing happened. He started to laugh and said, "Maybe they don't want me in this room" - everyone joined in with a nervous laugh. He tried again and the door clicked open.

Inside were four large air controlled rooms. We went into the one on the right. I couldn't believe my eyes. There in a mounting that looked like the conning tower of a submarine was a U.S.A - made in America - Kollmorgan 8-B periscope. Wakimoto said, "When we fitted the Nikon periscope onto the submarine you gave us we took the Kollmorgan periscope here for examination. There are many optical problems in this periscope. It was an interesting study. I even wrote a paper on it."

"Please look at what we had done to it." I walked over and noticed another new Nikon 'F' camera in the room – it seemed to be held in a bent piece of metal that had two prongs on each side.

As I looked through the scope I realized I was looking outside the building. I circled – got my bearings and located the factory across the street, the courtyard and some of the residential dwellings we passed on the way in. The picture was very clear

– actually sharp. I took my eye away and I was then shown some excellent black & white photographs that were taken through this particular periscope. It was amazing – nothing that I was shown in Virginia could match this quality. Every picture I saw in Virginia was fuzzy.

Wakimoto explained some of the procedures he went through to get a good result through this periscope. It was wide ranging - from the regrinding of elements to realignment and the insertion of different colored filters to bring all the optical plains to one point was an extraordinary job. The rework was extensive and very expensive.

He then took the Nikon 'F' camera that had a yellow filter on the lens and bent metal mount with the two prongs from across the room and slipped it onto the periscope. Around the eyepiece of the periscope was a mounted piece of metal that looked like the outline of a cat's head with the two ears sticking up. The two prongs on the camera mount fit into this and the camera hung in front of the eyepiece. I looked through the Nikon SLR camera and even though I was looking through the camera with a yellow filter I thought the view was perfect. 100 % of what I was able to see before when looking through the scope was still the same viewing through the eyepiece of the periscope, the camera and the yellow filter.

I became very excited; this was exactly what the Navy was looking for. Wakimoto stopped me in my tracks – he was reading my mind. "Remember Schein San - the single lens reflex 'F' camera is not yet in production. This is only a prototype." My mind was way ahead of him. I said, "We will discuss this in our next production meeting." Wakimoto said, "We can only do that after your meeting with the Japanese Defense Agency."

CHAPTER Fourteen
Another Air Controlled Room And Demonstration

Wakimoto then led our little party into the next air-controlled room. This room was slightly larger and had two reel-to-reel computers in it. Two lab-coated assistants bowed as we walked in. Dr. Koana started to talk in a professorial way explaining what we were going to see.

"We have two missions with this project," he said – "One is safety of the submarine and its crew and the second is to improve the reconnaissance capability of the submarine." He then explained the tactics of periscope use. "When the captain is satisfied that the boat is at periscope depth he elevates the periscope; breaks the surface of the water; takes a visual and in about fifteen seconds then orders the periscope down.

"The periscope is a little more then five inches in diameter at the top –the part that sticks out of the water. If a radar sweep passed the periscope and it was discovered upon the sweep's return (about 20 seconds later) the radar operator would know exactly where the submarine was by the radar hits on the periscope. An enemy could literally destroy the submarine from an offshore battery.

"To solve this problem we have developed a fiber optics device that is about one-and- a-half-inches in diameter that can serve as a reconnaissance periscope. A one-and-a-half inch diameter periscope would be undetectable by current radar systems.

"The next problem was just as difficult: Take a series of photographs and be able to view them immediately. That is a large chore." He walked over to a device about the size of an office desk and picked up what looked like a 4 X 5" Speed Graphic camera. It had a cable connected to the desk-sized device. One of Koana's assistants held the camera up and snapped a picture. We were invited to walk over to the device. There I saw my first digital photograph. It wasn't the sharpest picture I had seen but in a 2" X 3" screen on the camera was a black and white picture of Wakimoto and me.

Koana continued "To understand what we are looking at we should imagine a gray scale showing a range of black and white. Each change in the gray scale has a numerical value. The difference in light and dark numbers is how we take a digital photograph. It gets processed in the device and enhanced just before it appears in the screen. Obviously a print can be made and in a few seconds you will have one in your hands."

As I looked at the print I mentally noted that the print was good. Not 100% or what is called in the industry a "saleable print" but it was good. I thought - this is only the beginning. Digital photography will be something to reckon with in the future.

Koana had one of his assistants uncover what looked like the bottom part of a periscope. It had an eyepiece and the normal two handles that are used for magnification and angle of view. He asked me to look through it. I complied and was surprised to see the same scene, though a little darker, I saw looking through the Kollmorgan periscope. Koana said, "You are looking through a fiber optics periscope."

He then had an assistant attach an item to the eyepiece of the scope. The device was a little bigger then a normal sized breadbox. To this Koana slipped in a 5" floppy disc on the side of the "breadbox." The box was attached by cable to a 2' X 3' X 4' "computer" that had a series of lights on it. As soon as the disc started spinning the lights on both boxes came alive.

Koana said, "Gentlemen you are looking at the first digital camera and fiber optics periscope." Koana once again had me look through the scope, press a button and a few moments later I was looking at a picture result. From what I had learned about this subject this all seemed like a space fantasy. I could not help but be impressed.

Everyone in the room was silent. I was trying to absorb what I was looking at. I then realized they were waiting for a comment from me. All I could think of was "remarkable." They were like children waiting for their guest to say something. They all smiled, so I guess my response was good enough.

Tanaka interrupted the moment and said, "I assume the floppy disc you inserted was the back up copy." Koana shook his head yes and said "Hai". Tanaka continued, "From what we learned Dr. Fukuchi was in debt because of medical expenses. One of his children was dying of a little known autoimmune disease recently named Scleroderma. He was in debt to a loan shark group of Yakuza and couldn't pay it back.

"The Yakuza is the Mafia of Japan" he said. (Yakuza - The organization's origin goes back to the early 1600's. The word Yakuza means 8-9-3. Ya means 8, ku 9, za 3. It comes from Japans counterpart to Black Jack, Oicho-Kabu. Blackjack has a value of 21 points and Oicho-Kabu a value of 20 points.)

"The Yakuza Oyab-un - gang leader - visited Fukuchi and with a little physical persuasion convinced Fukuchi that he could make his debt disappear. All he had to do was identify a certain five-inch (5") floppy disc. Then take that disc out of the laboratory and hand it to one of the guards. It was a simple task." Fukuchi did exactly what he was told. He took the disc, tucked it in his pants as he reached to his back, covered it with his lab coat and walked out.

"Fukuchi was to contact a Mr. Kobi at a local pachinko parlor. Everyone in the parlor would be concentrating on their games and with the noise level in the parlor no one would pay attention. Fukuchi was to pass the disc to Kobi, whom Fukuchi would recognize as one of the guards he passed every day at the entrance door on the way into the laboratory.

"Kobi had a history of gambling. As it happens, Kobi borrowed money from the same Yakuza loan sharks for a gambling debt. He kept on losing and ultimately made a deal with the Yakuza to be relieved of his debt.

"The two people – Fukuchi and Kobi - were called to an apartment complex not far from the factory. The meeting ostensibly was for their debts to be settled. Instead of a debt settlement, they were both beheaded. It is obvious none of the Yakuza members wanted to leave any knowledge about the theft with anyone who they did not trust."

It wasn't necessary to ask how Hiro's people learned this information. They obviously got their information from an informant or a deep undercover agent in the hierarchy of the Yakuza.

Tanaka continued, "The Yakuza are doing this work for some influential individual, company or country. We are not sure yet. Our best guess is that they are working with one of the Communist governments of China, Russia or East Germany. Unfortunately we do not have much information beyond this at this time."

Tanaka then said, "Chief of Police Hiro strongly requests that you keep everything you have seen and learned today as much of a secret as humanly possible. We are dealing with people who have very little regard for life and who are simply dangerous. You must leave dealing with the Yakuza to us. If anyone approaches you - make sure we are your next call. Your life may depend upon it."

I think all of what Tanaka said was directed at me. However, what he said had a very sobering effect with the others in the room. Tanaka took me aside and said, "Hiro Sacho- San would like to organize another meeting." I said, "Whenever he wants to meet I am available." Tanaka said, "Thank you" and left the room.

Everyone stood around not saying very much. I said, "I should be getting back to my hotel" when Wakimoto said, "Not so fast – how about having dinner in a local sushi house with me, Miyahara-San and Segawa-San?" I assume the other people present were busy. No one really wanted to part very quickly after this meeting and I thought it was a good idea. I said, "Hai – Yes" they laughed at my Japanese/English response and it seem to lighten everyone's mood.

Chapter Fifteen
Dinner With Friends In A Sushi Restaurant

We all jumped into one car and drove a few minutes to a local Shinagawa sushi restaurant. The restaurant looked like a Japanese inn. We got out we were met by three kimono clad girls who helped us down a small pathway where at the end we were helped off with our shoes. We stepped into slippers and naturally there where none to fit the huge giajen - foreigner. They all twittered and laughed and I said "my socks would do fine."

We walked into the restaurant and I almost hit my head on one of the low beams. This building had a nice old and simple ambiance about it. There was a large fish tank in the wall that started off a long corridor. The tank was loaded with many fish I had never seen before. I was admiring them when Wakimoto asked, "Which one do you like the best?" I said, "They are all beautiful - it is hard to say. However, that one with the yellow tail is very different from the others."

We continued walking into the corridor and one of the girls got on her knees and slide the shoji screen door to the side and we entered a five-tatami private room with cushions and a rectangular black lacquered table in the center of the room (tatami mats are made to standard sizes. The number of tatamis on the floor of the room measures the size of a room). I was requested to sit in the middle of the other side of the table facing the door because that was the seat of honor. Behind me was a wall hanging of Mount Fuji. I guessed that is what made it the seat of honor.

The waitresses helped us off with our jackets and I folded my pistol and holster in the jacket. They then asked what we wanted to drink. Wakimoto chimed in, - in Japanese - I translated in my head - "from what Nakano-San told me Schein-San drinks scotch" he said to Miyahara - who nodded. – The waitress got concerned and said, "Suntory Scotch is all we have" – Wakimoto grunted approval. A few minutes later, a waitress slid the door aside, bowed and carried in a platter containing glasses, ice and a full bottle of Suntory Scotch. I pick up the bottle and read the label. "I said this will do fine" and everyone seemed to relax.

Miyahara was getting blitzed on the scotch. I said, "Slow down or you will end up like Fuketa-San did last night." He laughed, "I am staying in practice so I can keep up with Nagaoka Sacho-San." "Then I am afraid you are on a losing quest, from what I have seen that is not possible" - everyone laughed.

A course of miso soup arrived with small bowls that were carefully placed in front of us. Looking into one of the bowls - I said "Hello" - I saw small eyes looking back at me. "Grilled shrimp heads." Miyahara said, "When you eat them they will tickle as you swallowed – they are very crunchy."

85

The scotch was put aside as we were now drinking hot sake poured from small decanters. It was rude to pour your own, everyone made sure the next person's cup was filled – at all times. The sake was flowing and we started to mellow out. It felt good and I felt that this is where old friends are made and we will remember this evening for years to come.

The next course was sashimi and sushi displayed on a large beautiful round plate from which we jointly picked. While we were eating four waitresses entered the room to grandly introduce the specialty of the evening - yellow tail oduri. The word oduri had no meaning to me. Miyahara translated – "dancing vivid".

The fish I had admired, as we entered the restaurant, was now sitting before me on the table. – It was displayed with its head looking up and its tail pointing up. What was unusual was that it was moving. It actually was shaking. The backbone and nervous system of the fish were still connected to the head and tail. The belly part of the fish was cut into small sashimi slices.

I looked helplessly at Wakimoto and he said, "Oh - It is very good fish – it is very fresh fish." He leaned over and took a slice from the fish's belly. "Schein-San - try it". I realized the waitresses would not leave until I tasted it. I took a deep breath and grabbed a piece with my chopsticks and quickly swallowed it. I then lied and said, "It was very good". They obviously wanted more – I didn't know what else to say so I said the first thing that came to mind – "The chef must be very skillful to be able to do something like this."

Everyone translated what I said and everyone seemed to be happy with my response – All except for me. I thought I would have to eat more of this poor fish. With that the fish started to shake more violently – Miyahara leaned over and poured some sake down the fish's gullet. Believe it or not, that quieted the fish. It surprised me that I didn't see any of the sake drip down onto the plate. We were all staring at the fish while it was gasping for air when Segawa said, "I have never seen this before." "Neither have I" - I blurted out. Everybody else – thank goodness - took slices and after a while the fish seem to get more noisy and violent again. One of the waitresses reached over and the fish was taken away – Thank God.

The rest of the meal was uneventful with no additional live offerings. The meal was ended with a desert plate of Ichi-Go (literally means 1-5). Ichi-Go was the Japanese description for the most beautiful tasty strawberries. There were four strawberries on my plate and they were large and perfectly shaped. Not one of them had a flaw that I could see.

We all shared another decanter of sake and the meal came to an end. It was about 8:00 PM and I had the feeling my day was far from over. My car was waiting for me; I started saying my goodbyes when two waitresses, one on each arm, led me to the car. Maybe they thought I was drunk. I didn't feel as though I was. I got in waved and as the car was leaving everyone, including my hosts, bowed as we headed out on to the street. We turned the corner and I saw that Hiro's men were still with me.

CHAPTER Sixteen
The Evening Was Just Getting Started

I walked into my hotel and went to the concierge's desk to see if there were any messages. I was given three. Alex Triguboff "needs me to call him ASAP"; "Scheonheimer would like to have breakfast with me tomorrow" – Huh, that should prove to be interesting and Whoa – "Juniper Chang would like to have a drink with me in the Starlight lounge. If I would be so kind to call her room – #543 -when I got in, she would meet me there."

I decided it was safer to call Alex from the lobby instead of my bugged room. I walked over to the manager's desk and asked him to dial Alex's number. Alex immediately got on the phone and said – "Robert, Doreen Parks requests that you use our secure telephone and call Mr. Albert ASAP. There is no one in the office this evening and the secure telephone is locked in my personal office. Please come over early tomorrow, my secretary will help you make your call." I said, "I will get there at 6:00 AM make the call and will still be able to meet my host for breakfast."

"Who might that be?" Alex inquired. "Fritz Scheonheimer" I said. Alex then said, "He is a cagey old bastard. When you shake his hands make sure you get all your fingers back. He will pick your pockets without you knowing it, – be careful." Alex meant Scheonheimer had a reputation for driving a hard bargain when in negotiations.

I made my next call and felt nervous doing it. Juniper Chang is a beautiful woman but I think I was feeling guilty seeing her privately. All I could see was my wife's disapproval. I said to myself, "Hey, get a hold of yourself - she hasn't said was she going to bed with you – all she has asked for is to have a drink with me. Stop being so stupid or romantic - dummy. She is a businesswoman and she wants to talk to you - period".

The phone rang and Juniper picked up and said, "Hello?" I said, "Juniper Chang please" – she laughed and imitated my voice and asked, – "Is this Robert Schein?" I said, "Yes." She laughed again and asked, "How would you like to go out for a bite of late dinner and a dance at the Copa?" This was totally unexpected and took me by surprise.

The Copa was a legendary nightclub owned and run by 'Mama' Cherry. Just about everyone in the photographic business that went to Japan spent a few evenings at the Copa. You could have a steak dinner or enjoy the company of a woman sitting alongside of you for a few hours and watch some garish show. Naturally, the women were on the clock. In some cases, if you paid an additional ¥5,000 (US $138) she might consent to go back to your hotel. You had to be very cautious doing this because first class hotels like the Imperial Palace had very strict rules about 'loose' women.

89

I made up my mind and said, "I have some business to attend to and I will meet you in the lobby in thirty minutes – about 9:15 – O.K.?" She replied, "That will be fine – see you in a half an hour" and we hung up. My heart was racing now. If I was feeling any effects from drinking all that scotch and sake a short while ago it certainly didn't feel that way now. I was stone cold sober and raring to go. Before I went up the elevator I left a message with the concierge for Fritz Scheonheimer that I would be happy to join him tomorrow at 7:30 AM in the Orchid Room.

I arrived in the Starlight lounge on the top floor of the hotel and looked for Claypool. Somehow he was able to manage the same seats where we first met. After saying our hellos I brought Bob up to date to the very moment where I was taking Juniper Chang to the Copa. Bob sat back and said, "When I talked to Albert, per your instructions, he seemed surprised that the mission had become so vital and dangerous. He wanted my opinion if he should send anyone else from the Company or would it be better if he appeared on the scene and took the lead?"

I held my breath for what Bob would say next. "I told Albert I thought you had a handle on the situation and you were doing fine." I let the air out of my lungs. "Thank you, Bob," I said - realizing that this was a political and difficult thing for him to back me up.

Bob waved me off – "This is no bargain" he continued, "We now have our hands full and are expected to 'reel in the fish'. Robby, you somehow have fallen into some sort of international plot. Your information gathering, from everything I have been able to check - is on the money. This is a break we have been looking for, for a long time. We have tried a number of years, unsuccessfully I might add, to do what you have accomplished in a number of days. That is exactly what I told Albert. You have given everyone a new young fresh look at something we were stale with. I recommended we go with you for now and Albert agreed."

Bob continued – "We have an appointment with the Japanese Defense Agency tomorrow at 3:00. Major Michael Picker is our Embassy Military Liaison. He will lead the meeting from our side. We will follow the military protocol that the highest ranking person is the spokesman unless otherwise indicated." "Fine – I will be there – I have a meeting with Iishida of Mamiya that I do not want to miss. He is a legendary businessman in Japan who is a friend of the Company. He might be able to shed some light and have some information that can help us. I am having lunch with him and will leave in time to meet you. See you tomorrow."

I went down to my room changed my business shirt to a sport shirt, jacket and freshened up a bit. I was almost on time to meet my 'date' – for the evening, I said to myself.

I stepped off the elevator and she wasn't there. I walked around the lobby to make sure and just as I was about to turn she tapped me on my back. I turned and peered at this tall, radiantly beautiful woman. She was dressed in tapered pants that clung to her curves; white blouse - open to show the cleavage of her bosom and on her shoulders was a colorful silk shawl. Her black hair was in a bun and this time she had small red roses in it. She took my arm and we walked out of the hotel to her waiting car and driver. The doorman opened the rear door of the Mercedes Benz Model–500 and we got in to go to the Copa.

The Copa was located in the Aksaksa District. The small streets were a montage of lighted restaurant and nightclub signs. There were shills in front of some of the nightclubs trying to entice the customers to walk in. The Copa on the other hand had a uniformed doorman and its building was new when compared to all the other walk-down and walk-up restaurants.

When we went through the door an older, very heavy woman shouted "Juniper Chang – as I breathe and live." The woman creating the scene was none other than the owner - Mama Cherry. Mama Cherry was a successful high-class madam and restaurateur. She truly appeared to be happy to see Juniper. She asked about her mother and how she was doing. Juniper replied, "She is fine and sends her regards. By the way, my escort is Robert Schein of TAG photographic from New York."

Mama Cherry gave me her hand and I kissed it. She said, "Any friend of the Changs is a friend of mine. Oh," she stopped, "TAG – That is Luke Albert right?" I nodded yes. "Is that cute boy back in Japan?" In my wildest dreams I couldn't think of Albert as being a 'cute boy' – I just said, "He did not make this trip." "Well send him my regards – Are we having dinner or just the show?" Juniper said, "A light dinner please."

We were led up a staircase to a mezzanine that overlooked the dance floor and the band. In back of the band was a small stage. The place was gaudily done in red and gold and it was jumping. The dance floor was crowded with what looked like an all-Japanese crowd. The giajen were all on the mezzanine having dinner and intimate conversations with their paid escorts. If breakfast looked like the PMDA convention then this was the planning committee. I must have recognized ten people from the industry including my fellow plane travelers, Bernard, Roth and Scheonheimer.

As soon as Bernard saw us he came over to where Mama Cherry wanted to seat us and asked us to join him. Juniper said, "Not right now please – I would like to talk to Mama Cherry and Robert for a few minutes. Maybe later thank you." Bernard immediately backed away. So Juniper does control her end of the business – she didn't give in to Al Bernard or show any sign of weakness – I thought.

The three of us sat down in a corner. Juniper started, "Robert, what I am about to tell you has to remain at this table." That certainly got my attention. "What are we talking about?" I said. "We are talking about a floppy disc that was 'lifted' from Mitsubishi," she said. That was descriptive enough for me.

"How are you involved?" I asked. "That is not important right now. Mama Cherry has contacts with the Yakuza." She turned to Cherry and asked, "Have they contacted you yet?" The old lady shook her head no and said, "That is not unusual. They have to be feeling safe before they will go outside of their circle. With the beheadings and all the police around I do not think they feel safe enough."

Cherry must have noticed that my mouth dropped. She said. "Don't be so surprised Mr. Schein. A woman can't be successful in business in China or Japan unless she is a madam, or restaurant owner or she is holding some wealthy or important person by his gonads. I happen to be in the position of having all three possibilities available to me." She laughed. "Madame Chang, Juniper's Mother – the Dragon Lady - and I – the happy Mama-San - have done business together many times and our alliance is built on trust and money. Look at us as if we were an organization – The Shina/Nippon (Chinese/Japanese) Women's Mafia. Now that's a thought," she said. "Scary", I thought but did not say it out loud.

Juniper looked at me and said, "The Russians have a vast submarine fleet maybe 300 vessels. You Americans have a number larger then that. The Russians have an interest in this weapon." I chimed in – "It is only a periscope and simple camera. It is not a weapon that shoots or fires at anyone." Juniper scolded me and she was right to do so. "Don't give me foolish answers. Fire control all starts with the periscope." She had the right answer, I thought. She knows what she is talking about – no more stupid comments. I held up my hands and said, "It was foolish of me to say what I did, and I was only testing the waters."

Juniper had her business face on now. There was no sweetness or smile. Her jaw was clenched as she spit out, "$100,000,000 if we get the information before you do." "One hundred million" I stammered. "That is a hell of a lot of money." She said, "Figure it out. A new periscope system will cost between $500,000 and $1,000,000 per submarine - take that times 400 units. All I am doing is adding a cost of $250,000 each. That is not so expensive for the military."

I am not used to thinking in such numbers; especially when I just started making $20,000 per year. However, her reasoning did make sense. I could almost accept her idea. But I said, "How can we be sure that there are no other copies that have been made from the disc." She continued, "I have checked with my computer engineers and they say they can tell if copies were made."

Man, she is at the top of her game. My admiration for her was growing by leaps and bounds. I had no idea that could be checked. That was my biggest fear in this project. I never asked Koana that question because I assumed you could not tell if a copy was made. On my part – that was obviously a very bad assumption - dumb.

Then I said – "You do know we have a back-up copy" – she corrected me – "No, you do not – the Japanese Defense

Agency owns the back-up copy." I said, "Yes, I know that but, we are very good neighbors." She said, "Not good enough. Japan wants to keep this technology, manufacture the product and sell it to the super-powers as a finished unit. You will never see a copy of the disc until the periscopes are delivered to your factories for installation in submarines. Then it will be too late to start up and try to manufacture it."

"I have a meeting with the Japanese Defense Agency tomorrow. I will let you know what they say. Hopefully you are incorrect." Juniper smiled and said, "I can almost tell you the results of that meeting. I don't think you really want to hear them." "Nothing ventured nothing gained I always say - I will talk with you tomorrow evening about my results. If you are correct, I then need to get some direction from my office to find out how we might be able to work a deal."

"By the way" I continued - "Can I now assume I will be off your hit list? A dead negotiator will be hard to close a deal." "Robert, we didn't shoot at you. We had no reason to. We want you to be our customer. We do not control the Yakuza. They get their orders and direction from other sources." "Well, I guess I am still fair game then." (How the hell did she know I was shot at?) Mama Cherry chimed in, "let's have a drink and some dinner. Why not drop the business talk and enjoy what is left of the evening."

I was no longer in a mood to be seduced. I had to confirm what Juniper said and I had to call the office in the morning. I asked, "If we might return to the hotel after our small repast." Juniper said, "by all means - we can leave now if you wish?" I said, "No, no please have something to eat and drink." She then said, "I am sorry but, I had to discuss this in a public place where I know, no one is listening."

"I completely understand." I said, "We do not have to leave

95

right now." She smiled at me and that gorgeous glow that I had admired returned to her body language. We ate and drank without saying a word and left as soon as we were done.

When I got back to my room I said, "I might as well start organizing everything in my mind for tomorrow mornings call." I think I was a little down in the mouth. This has been a heck of a day. I decided I wanted to hear a friendly voice and placed a call through the operator to my wife.

As I was changing into my pajamas the phone buzzed and I picked it up. – The operator said "Your party in on the line" and clicked off. "Debbie?" "Robert" she replied all excited. She continued – "You have got me in the middle of the catalog. It is very interesting now because I am drawing full length fashion figures with fur coats and expensive dresses." "That sounds great" I replied. She said, "What is the matter Robert. You don't sound like yourself. Is something wrong?"

She was very perceptive, I thought. "No, I am in a ton of meetings and I hardly have had any time to myself. I just have been very busy and tired – but – no everything is fine" I lied. "I can't wait to show you some of the stuff I am doing. I am really happy how it is coming out." Debbie kept on chirping away about her work and all of a sudden I felt exhausted. I could hardly keep my head up.

I said, "Deb, I have a big day ahead of me tomorrow and I think I better get into bed." She said, "From what you sound like I think that is a good idea. When do think you will call again?" she asked. "The way things are going; don't expect to hear from me until the weekend – OK?" "OK – I love you" I replied in kind and the line went dead. I got under the blankets that felt so soft and comfortable I don't remember closing my eyes. I slept the sleep of the dead.

CHAPTER Seventeen
Secure Telephone Call With Luke Albert

The telephone buzzed - I picked it up and the operator said, "It is 5:00 AM your wake up call - Mr. Schein." I hung up and dragged myself out of bed. I didn't feel too bad I thought. A hot shower will revive me. I then spent the next fifteen minutes under the hottest shower I had ever taken. I felt much better, quickly got dressed and went down the elevator.

I decided that Alex's office was only three blocks away, halfway to the Ginza. I thought a brisk walk would do me some good and get the juices flowing. I went out of the hotel's side door and started walking toward the Ginza. I didn't get ten feet when a black car drove up and a man jumped out of the front seat. He then pointed to the rear of the car and opened the door.

I said, "I think I would rather walk." The man dressed in the traditional dark suit held up his hand and in broken English said "Iie – Iie - No Chances. Hiro Sacho-San not approves." I got the message. Mr. Hiro was not taking any chances with me. He has instructed his men to baby-sit and correct me whenever I get out of line. I consented and we drove off.

We arrived in a couple of minutes and I entered the building. I kept thinking to myself. They knew everything I was going to do. What time I would get up, what time I would leave the building, where Alex's office was. I stopped, "Huh, they knew my destination; I never told them where I was going. I wonder who is bugging whom?"

TAG Photo – Far East Offices - was on the fourth floor. I got off the elevator and noticed that the office door was ajar. I put my hand on my pistol and slowly opened the door. Out of nowhere came a very chirpy voice that shouted, "Come in, come in. I left the door open for you. At this hour there is no one here." From behind a partition a middle-aged American woman with wild reddish hair, large rimmed glasses and dressed like she just got out of bed said, "Linda Hockberg" and stuck out her hand. I said, "Robert Schein of the New York Office." "I know" she said, "Doreen Parks and I had a discussion about you yesterday." "I hope it was good?" "It was fine. Doreen and I know each other a long time."

I am Mr. Triguboff's administrative assistant. I understand you need to use the secure telephone - it is all set up for you in his office. All you have to do is wait for the tone and dial 319 and the automatic system will connect you directly to Mr. Albert."

I went into Alex's office, which was a mess of paperwork all over his desk and piled on a couple of chairs. There was nothing fancy in the office but it felt and smelled like a lived in room. Ashtrays were filled to the top. The garbage pail was clean only because Linda was carrying it in after the cleaning staff took care of it. "Mr. Triguboff always keeps his door locked when he is not in the office. I am the only one who has a master key." She began emptying the ashtrays while she was talking. I said, "I will make my call now" and she left room closing the door behind her. I picked up the phone and listened – there was static, a number of beeping noises and then a tone – I dialed on the rotary dialer 319 – almost immediately the phone rang and was picked up by Luke Albert. His voice was very clear – "Robert – I have been expecting your call." "I just got to the office sir, sorry I made you wait." – "Not at all, let's get down to business," he said.

I started out by reviewing everything that happened since I boarded my flight in New York. It took me about twenty minutes to go over as much detail as I could remember. Albert said nothing while I was reporting – I don't think he wanted to interrupt me for fear of throwing me off course. I finished my wrap-up with almost exactly – word for word – what I could remember of my conversation with Juniper Chang and Mama Cherry. I stopped and waited for his response.

"Just a moment, Robert, I want to make sure that Doreen had no difficulty in recording your report." There was a pause and I said to myself "I hadn't thought he was recording this conversation. He was right to do so, this way he will be able to review it after I have hung up."

"OK, Robert – everything is copasetic. I think Claypool is correct: You seem to have a handle on everything. I want to go back to a couple of points. The Nikon 'F' periscope camera appears to be one of the quickest interventions we can make to upgrade our reconnaissance capability. - Correct?" "Yes," I said, "But the Nikon 'F' camera is not yet in production. Without the camera I don't see how it can work."

Albert almost ignored what I said and continued, "This is

what I want you to offer the factory. We will pay for the entire first production run, at a very large premium. That alone will finance the future of the Nikon 'F' camera. They will not have to go to Mitsubishi or Sumitomo banks to borrow money using their distributors purchase orders as collateral. This purchase will be guaranteed by our Government.

"We will come to an agreement that will allow them to introduce and sell the new camera in the Japanese domestic market so that they do not lose any competitive edge. All of the rest of the first production will go to the US Navy. The military nomenclature for the camera system will be the KS-80."

"But sir", I said, "The Kollmorgan periscope is a lousy lens. It will not take a sharp picture." "Zenji Wakimoto did not tell you about a paper he wrote on the 8-B periscope – did he," Albert asked, "He did but I did not get anything from it" – I said. "Wakimoto stated, without new lenses or manipulation of the elements in the current 8-B periscope you can focus on one optical wavelength and take a very good black and white picture.

"We tested his theory in Dr. Harold Edgerton's laboratory at MIT. Wakimoto was absolutely correct. We used a yellow filter, blocked out all other wavelengths and were able to take good black and white photographs. All we need now is the recording system. That is where the 'F' comes in.

"We also would like to know exactly what did Wakimoto do to the periscope he showed you in the laboratory yesterday. We have taken the 8-B periscope apart a number of times, realigned it, tried different lenses and still have been unsuccessful in improving it. I am sure it has to do with the magical art of optics with very heavy emphasis on factory knowhow.

"The second part of our conversation will deal with the amazing information you related on the combining of digital photography and fiber optics in a periscope. I can't imagine they let you take the pictures they showed you out of the lab – did they?" "No Sir, they did not," I replied.

"This periscope camera system can be one of the most revolutionary developments in photography since the development of film. When we learn to miniaturize this type of equipment the opportunities can be mind-boggling. I understand why a super-power would want to get a jump with this technology. It can be very useful."

"I must admit," he said, "My computer knowledge is not very good. I also do not know if you can tell that a copy was made from an original 5" floppy disc. That is a key here and we will have our technical services people look into that. In the meantime I do not want to discourage our relationship with Miss Chang. Tell her we are checking into technical questions regarding the disc. However, let's turn it into a 'Persian Market' and see what happens. Offer her 50 million. I am curious to see if she negotiates further or goes to another buyer. She then will pit one buyer against the other if she has takers."

"Finally, Robert your business with Chief of Police Hiro is very important. Continue being as open as possible with him realizing that we are playing with an economic time bomb."

- "If the Japanese lose the disc and it falls into 'enemy' hands, we will lose billions of dollars annually.
- "If they are forced to share the technology with us, they make less money but their business community can still capture a good part of the market. Japan will still make billions of dollars.
- "However, if they can handle this whole matter without

anyone else like us involved, then they make hundreds of billions of dollars.

"As I said before – this is an economic time bomb.

"Robert, we are impressed with how you are handling yourself and how successful you have been to date. I compliment you on the job you are doing.

"I must warn you that we do not have any reliable contact with the Yakuza. They are very difficult people to deal with. We have tried to work with them in the past but were unsuccessful." "I understand," I said.

"Do you have any feeling at this point who might be in direct contact with the Yakuza or whom they might be involved with to get the disc out of the country?" "As I said, Hiro is pretty confident that it will be Bernard, Roth or Scheonheimer. I am expecting to meet Scheonheimer after this call. Maybe I will get some better feeling at that time. Right now, I haven't the slightest idea who it might be. I have suspicions but truly, I have no idea. Roth and Bernard have relatives in Russia and Scheonheimer has relatives in East Berlin. Pressure could be applied to any one or all of them. I have no clue yet."

"We are going to check out some things here for you. When do you think you can get back to us?" "Having to use a secure telephone each time is a problem, so I am not sure. - In the meantime, I will ask Claypool to report to you regularly – every other day

"I may be able to get back to you by or on the weekend." "Fair enough – stay safe and good hunting." With that we both hung up. I had been on the phone with Albert for a full 60 minutes. – "Phew!"

I walked out of Alex's office and Linda Hockberg asked if all went well. I said, "As well as can be expected – thank you. Please tell Alex that it might be a good idea that he joins me at the Nikon meeting tomorrow morning. We are going to discuss purchase orders for the new Nikon 'F' camera system and I think it would be wise for him to be present." "Will do," she said as I was leaving the office. I had a few minutes to get back to the hotel in time to meet with Fritz Scheonheimer.

CHAPTER Eighteen
Another Breakfast Meeting In The Orchid Room Of The Palace Hotel

I walked into the Orchid Room and Scheonheimer was already seated and looking at his watch. I walked over and said, "I am sorry for keeping you waiting but I was on the telephone with my office and just couldn't break free." He didn't answer, "He stood up, all 6'4" and stuck out his hand and said, "Good morning Mr. Schein." I said to myself, "Very formal, very cold and very European. - OK - let's go from here and see what is going to happen."

While we were looking at the menus I asked how his son Pierre was (I had spent a couple of evenings with Pierre Scheonheimer at the last PMDA in Chicago.) "Pierre is fine, he is minding the store," he replied in his German accent. We both ordered an American breakfast with rolls and jams.

While we were waiting he asked if all "was going well with my trip." I said, "I had no complaints." "Any news about the new camera?" he inquired. "I have seen it," I said and "I believe it will be a good product for the market." "Is it everything they say it is" "Yes and even more then we expected." "Good," he said, - "It is about time we get a new innovative quality product from Japan." I was a little surprised with all this small talk. I am sure he is leading up to something - I can't imagine what.

"Mr. Schein" he said and I interrupted - "please call me Robert - My father is Mr. Schein." "Humph" he grunted, "Robert, my company - IMC - is the representative of Yashica in the States." "I am aware of that," I said. "Of course," he said and continued - "During my last trip to Japan I made arrangements with Minolta to handle their product line. We came to an agreement and started to import their products."

"Well, Yashica is very unhappy that we made this agreement. They have threatened to pull their product from our company - cancel our contract. Yashica represents 40 % of our total sales, this would be a large blow to our revenues and to the shareholders." "Huh," I thought, "This has got to be very difficult for the old man. He prides himself that everything works efficiently and correctly in his company and he maintains good relationships with his vendors."

"Naturally, I ask that you keep this confidential until I work something out with both manufacturers." "Of course", I said. He then asked if - "TAG Photo might be interested in representing Minolta. This way there could be an orderly transition in the States and no one would be the wiser." I also thought, "He would get his money out this way with no blemish to his reputation."

"I will have to talk to Luke Albert about this and I plan to speak to him over the weekend. I will tell you what our position is sometime next week." "Time is of the essence" he

105

said, "If this is to be a successful and we are to have an orderly transition we must watch the clock." I said, "I agree and understand."

A commotion occurred at the entrance of the restaurant - My goodness, it was Juniper Chang - radiant as ever in a white dress that accentuated her figure and - of all people - Mama Cherry! Many of the men in the room went over to kiss Mama Cherry's hand as if royalty were being escorted to their seats. It was quite a scene.

As our meal was being served I glanced at Scheonheimer and he didn't take any notice or make any reference to what was going on. He started to eat without looking up - I thought that was odd. I decided to find out why. "That Juniper Chang is something to look at," I said. "Yes" he said, "I noticed you got a close look last night." "Not really – but I wish I did. All I did was act as her escort her for a light meal at the Copa - I had never been to the renowned Copa." "Uh-huh" he said, "You, Chang and Cherry. I thought that fat bitch didn't get out of her bed before noon." "Whoa," I thought, "Where did this come from? What happened to all of that European grace and style?"

"Do you have a problem with Mama Cherry?" I asked. He blurted out, "I am doing some business with her and she is a most difficult person to deal with. She has not accepted a generous offer I have made. To get her way and try to convince me, she has applied some unnecessary pressure from her ungodly friends to force me to up my offer."

My mind started racing, the offer was for what? - I wondered - "The 'ungodly' friends were most likely the Yakuza," - A light bulb then went on in my head - "Mama Cherry was lying last night. She had the disc all the time and was trying to sell it to the highest bidder. I'm just one of the bidders. I'll bet that Bernard, Roth, Scheonheimer and me have been put into the "Persian Market" as Albert referred to it. That can only be the reason why Cherry and Chang are making an appearance this morning. It is to put pressure on all of us - to make a point that she has the disc or knows where it is."

Scheonheimer didn't appreciate all the attention the ladies were receiving. He took note when individually Roth and Bernard went over to their table, sat down and leaned over to whisper a few words to them.

While the ladies were holding court we finished breakfast. I thanked Doctor Scheonheimer for his hospitality and said, I would get back to him on the Minolta situation as soon as I got word from New York. He nodded his head, stood up to his full height and shook my hand as I was leaving the table. On the way out of the room I caught Juniper's eye - or maybe she caught my eye - and waved and blew her a kiss. She smiled and I exited the Orchid Room.

CHAPTER Nineteen
A Short Meeting With Chief Of Police Hiro

I was walking to the elevator when Tanaka intercepted me and said, "Hiro Sacho-San is in the manager's office waiting to meet with you." I nodded and followed Tanaka. I walked through the office door while Tanaka took at his post outside the door. Hiro was seated on the couch in the office and his hand showed me he wished for me to sit in the chair to his right. We said our good mornings and Hiro got down to business.

"I believe you already have talked to Luke Albert and you are now familiar with the products and the players whom we are dealing with." I said, "Yes and I think I am starting to put some of the pieces of the puzzle together." "For instance" Hiro asked. "I believe the three Americans who were on my plane and I are in a bidding war for the disc." "Have you made a bid yet" he asked. "Not formally, I am waiting to learn if it can be detected that copies were made from the master disc." Hiro simply said, "Yes, we can clearly tell if copies were made from the master disc. From the original footprint of the disc we can also tell how many copies were made. Anything else?" he asked.

"I believe that Mama Cherry and or Juniper Chang might know where the disc is." Hiro then said, "We have been watching Mama Cherry for some time. We know of her Yakuza contacts and have tapped her home and business telephone lines. We have a 24-hour surveillance team watching her as well. We have not detected any contact with the Yakuza or the Yakuza's known affiliates."

Hiro then asked, "What is your opening bidding?" "US $50 million" I said." "What did they originally ask for?" "US $100 million." Hiro continued, "We have to assume everyone is bidding within those numbers. I imagine the Yakuza know the value of keeping the disc clean and free of copies. We probably can depend on that."

"Someone who has excellent computer skills and inside information of the factory's products is advising them. The Yakuza have obviously been planning this for many years. They either have a mole in the management of Mitsubishi or have an employee they have been able to nurture and turn. This is not the way the Yakuza usually works. I think they are getting advice from someone they trust outside of their world."

I then asked, "If I am a bidder do I still have to assume my life is on the line?" "Yes" Hiro said. "We will continue our surveillance on you and we will keep it out in the open so that people know you are being covered. Robert, whoever is in back of this does not really want to sell the disc to the United States - or Japan for that matter. They would rather it went to someone not as scrupulous as we are. I expect those people to bid higher."

Hiro then said, "OK - we have a better idea where the disc might be and who is flogging it. We are working to find the 'mole' or employee who is involved. Our surveillance will continue on Mama Cherry, you and I think we will add the activities of Juniper Chang. She seems to be a bigger player then we have given her credit for.

"Tanaka will stay in touch with you with anything that develops. You will be able to reach me at all times through your Omega watch should you encounter any emergency. I think that brings us up to date Robert - do you agree." I said, "Yes." This is no turkey shoot I thought - I really have to watch myself - I don't think I really believed that I was actually shot at a couple of days ago. I have to wake up and smell the roses if, I want to continue to smell the roses - I chided myself.

I walked out of the room past Tanaka and went to the elevator to get my stuff and wait for the Mamiya limousine.

CHAPTER Twenty
Michicho Iishida The President Of Mamiya

It was about 11:00 AM when I arrived at Iishida's office. Michicho Iishida was the president of Mamiya Optical K.K. Osawa Trading, K.K. was the holding company or financial group that controlled its destiny.

Iishida was about 70 years of age and was considered a traditionalist of Japanese mores. His office had a low conference table on tatami mats with cushions around the table for about ten people to sit as comfortably as possible. His desk was at the far end of the room and that is where he directed me to sit. I had met Iishida-San in New York and spent a couple of days with him. Despite the large age difference we seemed to get along, and I considered him a friend. He spoke in a hoarse voice that seemed to come from his abdomen.

"Good to see you in Japan" - Schein-San. "The pleasure is all mine" I said. He continued, "I have been following your activities - they have been very busy." I said, "Iishida-San, I am amazed that when something happens to me everyone knows the how, when and what. What kind of intelligence method do you have to get all this information out as quickly as you do?" - I laughed and meant it as a light comment but Iishida took it seriously.

"There is no intelligence method – it is all about old friends visiting regularly with each other - maybe twice a week. During the war the optical industry was centered on Nippon Kogaku. All military optical equipment, from cameras to binoculars to larger items was manufactured in one location. At that time NK employed almost 35,000 people.

"After the war during the occupation, General MacArthur broke up the large monopolies and manufacturing facilities. He didn't disband them but he set limits on how many people they could employ. NK was allowed to keep 3,500 people. Everyone else was let go. That is how the Japanese Optical Industry really began in Japan. In just about every optical house there is a graduate of Nippon Kogaku. We have all stayed friends and share information so that all of us can be successful. We owe our livelihood to NK and to General MacArthur."

I sat in amazement, "That made a lot of sense", I thought. Iishida's explanation cleared up quite a bit. "This is how everyone knows to line up at the airport in the right order; this is how everyone knows what is stirring in everyone else's pot. The Japanese are a very orderly group of people."

We talked about business and Mamiya's remarkable twin lens reflex camera with interchangeable lenses. It was the only camera of its kind in the world. It looked like a slightly larger version of the German Rolliflex twin-lens reflex but the Mamiya had the ability to change lenses. The camera had just started to take off in the States particularly among the press photographers. I handed my folder of orders and projections to Iishida who transferred it to his secretary for review.

Iishida said, "I would like to make a visit to the Aksaksa Shinto Temple to make an offering for your visit and then have some lunch in a small restaurant where I ate when I was a student in university." I said, "Please lead the way, it sounds like a wonderful schedule." We left his office and were accompanied only by his driver whom I gathered was his chauffeur, outside escort and bodyguard. Iishida never directly addressed the chauffeur nor did he have to. He just knew what it was that the old man needed, anticipated his moves and always - though a couple of steps in back - was at his right side.

We drove away from the office and almost immediately the chauffeur - in Japanese - said, "We are being followed." He was awaiting instructions when I chose to reveal that I understood what he said. "Iishida-San - that car is my escort compliments of Chief of Police Hiro." Iishida grunted and we drove on without further conversation.

The Aksaksa Shinto Temple is in the middle of Tokyo in a busy business district. The driver let us off at the major torii (arch) that signified the entrance. Before you reached the temple you had to walk through a large corridor of vendors on each side of the path. Iishida asked, "How is your Oku-San (wife) and is she doing well?" I said, "She is in good health and is very busy." He grunted and said, "I want to buy her a gift." I started to object and he held up his hand. "My choice" he said and started looking into the stalls of the vendors as we walked past them.

Just them his chauffeur got in step with us and I noticed Hiro's men were not far behind. Iishida spied a teapot with four cups that made up a beautifully decorated Imari tea set. He pointed at it and I walked over – Ishida missed a small step - slipped and abruptly leaned over in front of me and a shot rang out - Iishida went down to the ground. Iishida's bodyguard pounced on him to protect him - I got down on a knee and drew my pistol. All bedlam broke out and the people walking or in the stalls starting running away. I couldn't find the shooter.

Just them Hiro's men started running past me. They were onto something. I asked Iishida's man – Iishida-San ikaga des ka? (Mr. Iishida - how is he?)- Hai Genki des (OK – Good health) he reported and I took off after Hiro's men. That shot was meant for me and Iishida just got in the way, I thought.

The Police arrived and got into the chase in between Hiro's men and me. I stopped, holstered my pistol and I walked back to where Iishida was.

I saw him sitting on a chair in the teapot vender's stall. Everyone was making a fuss over him. I walked up and said "domo sumimasen" (I am so sorry); "Iie – Iie" (No - No) he replied and in English with a smile "I haven't had so much attention in a very long time. It is only a flesh wound on the side of my shoulder. It is nothing to worry about." "That might be true but we are going to get you to the hospital." He held up his hand and said, "No - not until we make our offering in the temple."

As the ambulance and medics arrived, Iishida and I started for the temple. His bodyguard headed the medics off and they got into step with us as we all walked to the temple entrance. Iishida washed his hands in the open fountain and instructed me to do the same. We then walked over to the Buddha and stared at it for a couple of moments and then he sharply clapped his hands together and bowed his head. I did the same.

On the way out he put an offering of money into a red box. I tried to do the same and he stopped me - "I took care of that," he said.

The ambulance was waiting for us by the exit. Iishida gave instructions to his chauffeur then boarded the ambulance and with the sound of a ringing bell they took off.

On the way to Iishida's vehicle one of Hiro's men came up to me and said, "We could not find anyone - ...- he disappeared in the crowd." I was driven back to my hotel. As I was getting out the car the driver stopped me and handed me a large box wrapped in a kerchief. It was Iishida's gift for my wife - a tea set.

CHAPTER Twenty-one
The Japanese Defense Agency

At 3:00 PM I arrived in the building that housed the JDA, which was very close to where General MacArthur had his offices during the occupation. In fact, his offices were across the moat and road from the Emperor's palace. MacArthur's offices are now a museum. People visit the general's office very reverently because this was the man who accepted the surrender of Japan and made the Emperor appear as just a man. He viewed the Emperor as a common man but allowed him to keep his title, prestige and figurehead position. For this, the Japanese people were very grateful and respectful of General MacArthur.

Major Michael Picker was in his late forties and dressed to the hilt with a chest full of his campaign ribbons. I was a little surprised when I walked in and saw both Picker and Claypool dressed in uniforms all gussied up. Claypool's uniform was straight Navy with gold lieutenant bars, a couple of rows of campaign ribbons and two gold bars at the end of each sleeve. I was just in a simple conservative dark business suit with a red tie.

We said our greetings in the lobby of the building. I asked the major if he was fully briefed on our visit and he replied flatly "Yes." A little curt, I thought. You would think he would ask a question or two to confirm what we were trying to accomplish. When I started to offer information he looked at his watch and without any prelude or formality said, "Let's get this over with." We signed in and followed him to the elevator. I didn't have a good feeling about this meeting.

I caught Claypool's eye as we got off on the third floor and he shrugged his shoulders – and didn't indicate he had any clue about the major. We were led into a small simple conference room by a petty officer and were asked if we wanted anything to drink. I said "Tea will be fine" and both the major and Bob said, "Nothing – thank you."

My tea came very quickly but our hosts didn't come into the room until twenty minutes later. I thought this was very unusual and very un-Japanese. The Japanese are very prompt people. Finally, a door on the other side of the room opened and an admiral dressed in his dark blue uniform, understated with no campaign ribbons and two officers came into the room.

The admiral was about 5'5" and was a stocky, strong looking man, maybe in his fifties with a pock marked face. His two aides – one an ensign and the other a commander with the admiral's braid on his right shoulder were both slight in build and shorter then the admiral.

The introductions were completed and the admiral started a conversation with the ensign in Japanese. The ensign was the translator and looked scared to death of his superior. There was a lot of Hai – Hai (Yes – Yes) by Ensign Nomura who hadn't said one word in English since he walked into the room. The admiral's name was Moto and his aide was Cmdr. Uchi.

Moto was telling Nomura about a desalinization water purification station that they were having trouble with. The US Army recently delivered it and the army engineers were not helping to solve the problem. He wanted Nomura to be particularly strong with Major Picker regarding this problem. "Whoa, I said to myself, we are going to be here for some time."

Nomura translated directly to Picker and Picker responded by saying, "We have not finished the spare parts agreement and until then there is nothing I can do." When that was translated to Moto I thought he would take poor Nomura's head off. Moto grunted out his words to Nomura and said, "He expected the US Army to stand behind their products and rectify the problem within the week." Moto further stated, "Our part of the paperwork was completed months ago – this hold-up is strictly from the major's side."

Picker objected when Nomura translated and said, "There were procedures and he had to follow them as any good officer follows his orders." With that, Moto said in English directly to Picker, "Nonsense – this is a stupid answer and a stupid problem!" Picker got on his high horse and said, "Admiral, who the hell are you calling stupid. If we are so stupid then who the fuck won the war – you or me." Moto spat out – "Neither of us major – other people smarter then us and they were not paper pushers like you and me."

Admiral Moto then looked directly at me totally ignoring Picker and Claypool and said, "Mr. Schein, I am so sorry for my bad temper and manners. We have a foolish problem to work out with the US Army."

He continued, "I understand that you would like to discuss our fiber optics periscope, new digital camera and modifications to the Kollmorgan periscope, is that correct?" Major Picker interrupted – "We would like to work out an agreement to manufacture and partner with Japan - particularly regarding the new items – periscope and camera. The Kollmorgan modifications do not have the same priority as the other two."

I objected – "Major, I think the priority is equal for all three products including my business negotiations regarding a new camera with Nippon Kogaku." The major turned to me and said – "Would you please refrain from participating in this conversation – my orders come from the Pentagon."

Moto sat back and smiled as we argued in front of him. This is a complete no – no in etiquette. It is a total loss of face. This just doesn't happen in Japan. I said, "I don't care where your orders come from – you have no rights in this conversation." Moto liked what I said and stopped us from talking and making fools out of ourselves by further digging a hole – "Gentleman, I enjoy your earnest conversation but this is not getting anywhere."

"Mr. Schein, you have posed a very difficult problem for us." There is that word - "difficult" - I thought. The answer is not going to be to my liking. The admiral went on, "We have discussed this with the highest military and political authorities in the country. We have unanimously agreed that the technology should remain in Japan. We will help you with the Kollmorgan periscope but concerning the other two items the discussion is closed. We still have the problem recovering the missing disc. Until that is solved there can be no further discussion."

Major Picker blurted out, "How can you say this to your

closest friendly nation regarding something so militarily important. We are allies aren't we? We did rearm you, we did give you ships to organize your navy again ..." He was stopped by the admiral in mid-sentence, "This is an economic decision as well as a military decision. As you said before Major Picker, you were only following orders. Well, others have to follow orders as well."

The admiral and his aides got up, bowed and left the room. The audience was over. I turned to Picker and called him an ass and he muttered back something I didn't hear and left. I turned to Claypool and said, "That went well - ha - ha." Bob just said "yeah – very well."

We left the room and went down the elevator. Bob said he had the answer about being able to detect if copies were made for an original disc and I said, "It can be detected - chief of police Hiro told me so." "Well, I can positively confirm what the chief told you is correct." We decided to walk back to the hotel and over my shoulder I saw one of Hiro's cars keeping pace with us as we walked the four blocks.

When we walked into the hotel lobby I went to check my messages. There was one from Mr. Iishida's secretary. I placed a call from the manager's desk and talked to her for a few minutes. I learned that Iishida's wound was more serious then originally thought. "A low caliber bullet was taken out of his shoulder after being in surgery for about an hour." She said, "Mr. Iishida is doing well for a man of his age and the doctors do not anticipate any complications. He will be staying in the hospital at least for tonight."

I replied, "Thank you for calling me and please send him my regards. I am so sorry that this happened and I apologize if being in my presence has put him in harm's way." She continued, "He is an old soldier and I am sure would not want to hear any of that. Quite frankly, I have been around him for many years and I think he is enjoying the attention he is getting." I chuckled, we said goodbye and hung up.

I thought for a minute – 'low caliber bullet' that must have been the same shooter who took a couple of shots at me the other day. I then placed a call to Alex Triguboff. I filled him in and asked what I could send Iishida while he was in the hospital? "We will send him a display of 100 cranes - that will bring him good luck" - said Alex. "Cranes – not flowers or chocolates?" I questioned. "Yes – origami cranes. I will take care of it."

CHAPTER Twenty-two
A Fifty Million Dollar Offer

Bob and I sat huddled in the Starlight lounge reviewing the day and trying to plan how we were going to handle our offer to Chang and Cherry. I filled Bob in about Fritz Scheonheimer's request for TAG to handle Minolta. I asked him to discuss this with Albert and tell him my opinion: "We should not get involved. I think it would take too much effort to launch and promote Minolta at the same time we are launching the new Nikon camera system. I think the Minolta deal is being offered to TAG at the wrong time."

I reviewed the shooting of Iishida - I said to Bob, "I was convinced the shot was meant for me. I couldn't help but be impressed with Iishida by the way he carried himself throughout this ordeal. Not only did he complete going to the temple to make our offering, he had the presence of mind to instruct his driver to take me back to the hotel and make sure that my wife had her gift. He is an amazing man. He certainly lives up to his reputation of being a legend in the industry." Bob and I just shook our heads in wonderment.

We started planning how we were going to approach Chang and Cherry and how to protect me. We decided that it would be better to make the offer in a public place like the Copa. "Do it out in the open and present it" – as Juniper said – "where no one else could listen in."

Bob said, "Before we offer anything we might want to make sure they have the goods. I am sure there are markings on the disc that will make it identifiable as the original. We want a look see – don't you think?" I could try that but I am not so sure they will go along with that type of request. I will ask Koana if there are any identifiable markings on the disc – he would know."

"Now" Bob continued, "If they are willing to show you the disc then they are going to make you jump through hoops before you get somewhere safe enough for them to feel comfortable to show it to you. My Seal Team will try to stay on you throughout the ordeal but we could lose you and that is the reality."

"I think not," I said. "I want to play this as straight as possible without getting killed. Here is what I want to do … I outlined a loose plan that included Bob calling Hiro on a secure phone and informing him of what we are planning. I looked at Bob's Seal Team and Hiro's Domestic Crime Agency as the Cavalry. Everything else was in the hands of Chang and Cherry.

I called Juniper Chang and she was not in here room. I decided to write a message for her and leave it in her key box. It was about 6:30 PM. I thought I should grab some rest, a shower and a change of clothes and get ready for the evening.

No sooner had I put my head on the pillow the phone buzzed. I picked it up and it was Juniper.

"Robert," She said. "I got your note and will be happy to meet you at the Copa at 9:00. I have some business out of the hotel and it will be easier for me that way. – Is that OK with you?" I replied – "9:00 o'clock it is – see you then." We hung up – "it was strictly business – no foreplay" I thought.

At 8:30 I went to the lobby, looked around, saw no one I recognized and had the doorman hail a taxicab for me. The rear door opened – you don't touch the doors in a Japanese taxi because the driver from the front seat operates them by a lever.

I slid over in the immaculate taxi and said – "Copa – mada ida kudisai." (Please take me to the Copa). The driver responded – "Hai" and off we went. I peered at the rear and side view mirrors to see if any of Hiro's cars were following me. They were not – "I guess he got the message" I said to myself. We arrived within fifteen minutes and I paid the driver and stepped into the Copa.

I got a big greeting from Mama Cherry – all hugs and kisses, - after all we were 'close' friends now. She indicated that Juniper had not yet arrived. I requested a dinner table and she guided me upstairs where it seemed that the same crowd that was there yesterday was there today. Except Scheonheimer, Roth and Bernard were missing. I thought that odd but maybe their factories were entertaining them this evening.

Mama Cherry suggested that I order and eat because she didn't think that Juniper would be along for about an hour. I said, "Fine, what do you recommend." She said, "Corn soup and Matsusaka Beef. It is better then Kobe beef. These cows are kept in a barn and are massaged and given beer as part of their diet. The result is the best tasting beef and leanest beef in the world." There was no question about it she was a heck of a saleswoman. I said, "Fine – I will have the recommendation of the house." She said, "Thank you Schein-San" and off she went.

The corn soup was the best I had ever tasted and the meat melted in my mouth. I didn't have to use a knife to cut it. It was the best steak I had ever had. The show went up and it was an imitation of the high kicking and shouting of girls you would see in Paris doing the Can-Can. It was loud and everyone seemed to be having a good time. I looked at my newly acquired Seiko watch and it was 10:30 PM and still no Juniper.

I looked up as she was coming up the stairs in a short red dress that look painted on her. Her heels were high so she towered over everyone in the room. She arrived with a thin Chinese man and brought him over to the table. She introduced him as Commissioner Cao from Hong Kong. Juniper explained that, Mr. Cao was in charge of economic development for Hong Kong. We shared business cards and indeed that is what his card said. Juniper apologized for her tardiness because she had some business negotiations that she couldn't get out of. I said I understood and we all made small talk for a while.

A few minutes later Mama Cherry had a beautiful young Chinese girl on her arm and suggested that Cao might want to dance with her. He stood up before Mama Cherry could say the words and walked off with the young girl. Cherry said that Rosalie would keep Cao busy for a while. In my mind I repeated her name – "Rosalie? Where did that come from?"

Mama Cherry ordered after-diner drinks for us and while we were waiting for them Juniper said, "Have you decided to meet our price, Robert?" I said – "Well, yesterday you indicated 'if you get the item before I do' tells me you do not have it in your possession." I'm not sure I can bid if you don't have it." "Oh, we have it" she said." "How can I be sure you do?" I asked.

Juniper took a deep breath, and before I realized it she was holding a small handgun in her right hand and it was pressed in my groin under the table. "I'm too close to miss you this time." Pain and all - I coolly said, "Use a higher caliber pistol and you might not miss." Her position reaching under the table - was uncomfortable and I was in a bit of pain. I said, "Look, I'm not running anywhere, I am here alone, you can remove your weapon and we can talk like adults." She removed her pistol.

She said, "Once we agree that you are going to make an offer that is acceptable then we will show you the disc. You will be in our custody until we feel it safe to let you go." "Juniper, I can't just disappear and not raise some questions. My business people will start searching for me – they know I'm here – if I don't report in they will come after you." "We are not suggesting keeping you off the street for any period of time other than tonight."

"If that is it - I agree to your terms," I said. "My offer is US $50 million." "You Americans must have fixed the prices before you got here" she said. "I'm sorry, but I don't understand." "All of our bidders have started with that number" she said. I laughed out loud and she put her pistol away in her pocketbook.

Juniper was now very serious. "Robert, you will give me all of your metal before you leave the Copa. Everything; – tie tack, watch, wallet, change, lapel pin, belt, shoes and your weapon. If we detect any slip-up or contact with the outside world you will be killed.

You will exit the Copa through Mama Cherry's apartment on the top floor, and then you will be blindfolded until the morning. You will see the disc early in the morning and then you might want to reconsider your bid. Our business will be finished early enough for you to make your appointment with Nippon Kogaku tomorrow morning.

"How will I know I am looking at the real thing," I asked? She took out a folded copy of a picture from her handbag. It was of two men and the man on the right was holding a disc. She said. "Dr. Fukuchi is the man on the left and Kobi on the right with the disc.

Look closely at the disc.- it had a Japanese chop (red ink symbol) on it and the name Mitsubishi/Nippon Kogaku and a name of the discs purpose in English – 'Digital Camera Startup'." "Very impressive" I said.

"Juniper, this is a very dangerous business. What if chief of police Hiro and his men arrested you right now – what would happen?" "This is a free country and Japan has adopted a constitution similar to the one you have. In fact it is based entirely on your Constitution. What reason do they have to arrest me?

"I have no association with anybody involved with the theft of the disc or the beheadings. Neither does Mama Cherry. There is no evidence of any wrongdoing. This evening is the closest Hiro would have anything to hold us on. If he did arrest us our lawyers would have us free and on our way home in no time.

"If you gave us up, we would say it was all hearsay evidence, two [Cherry and Chang] people against one. Hiro hasn't anything concrete to touch us with." She made some sense – I then asked, "Why did you shoot at me?" "That was to keep you in the game. I didn't want to hit you, just put you on edge enough to make sure you would bid. That clod Iishida slipped and fell in the path of my bullet and almost got killed – the fool!" "You weren't shooting to hit me?" "No" she said, "I wanted to hit the teapot directly in front of you."

CHAPTER Twenty-three
A Night Spent In Darkness

When our conversation was over I climbed two flights of stairs to Mama Cherry's apartment. I obviously was expected; there was a short man in a gray worker's uniform wearing a hat and a surgical white mask covering his nose down to his chin. Many people in Japan wore these masks if they had a cough, cold or felt they might be infectious. Japan is a country of good manners and this was just showing good manners towards your neighbor. The mask also effectively hid who you were.

I took off my belt, emptied my pockets of all change and keys, took off my tie-tack, company lapel pin, Cross pen & pencil set, wallet and passport, took off my shoes and finally took off my shoulder holster and pistol. I put everything into a large plastic shopping bag that had printed on it "American Arcade." The short man did not speak; he then walked across the room and indicated I should put my hands up. He then searched me, very intimately I might add, from head to toe. Satisfied I did not have anything that might be out of order he then directed me to follow him.

As we were leaving the room, through floor-to-ceiling glass doors that led onto a balcony, Juniper said - "Have a good evening - I will see you tomorrow." There was a ladder on the side and we climbed down the equivalent of one floor to another balcony. The railing of the balcony had a board that crossed the alley to the next building. It was about ten or fifteen feet to the other building. I got up on the railing and I felt I was walking the plank. We gingerly crossed the board and started walking quickly. I was being shoved and ran down three flights of concrete stairs wearing only socks on my feet to a waiting car and driver.

I was shown the passenger's seat in the front and my escort sat in the back. The driver wore a surgical mask and hat so I could not make out his face. As soon as the doors were shut he took off without a word being said. We drove about five minutes making many turns constantly monitoring if anyone was following us. We drove up to another parked car in an alley. I was instructed to get out. I started to get into the second car when my escort, who was in back of me, put a cloth bag over my head and pulled a drawstring around my neck and tied it tightly closed. I was pushed into a car and we took off.

We drove for maybe another ten minutes – no one talked. I felt - hey, I could breath, I wasn't terribly uncomfortable, if this is the worse it gets I can live with it. Suddenly my escort said, "migi" (right) and we turned to the right. We drove a few moments - I then heard "migi" again and we made another right turn. The driver slowed down and I heard, "masugo" (straight ahead) and finally I heard what sounded like a garage door opening. We made a left turn and after a few seconds we came to a stop and I could hear the garage door being closed. I could clearly hear one of the men pulling on the chain.

I was pulled out of the car. With my elbows being held on both sides I was walked about 150 steps straight ahead, made a left turn and up a flight of fifteen steps then through a door and about 20 more steps. I was turned around and pushed down onto a couch. I could tell the room was lit by the slight glow I could see through the bag.

I wasn't sure how many people were with me but I figured there must be as many as three or four. No one was being difficult, no one was yelling at me or hitting me - in fact - no one said a word. Everyone was very quiet. If my guards were talking they must have been using sign language. I did not hear a peep. I remember Juniper saying, "We will detain you for one night." It was not quite the way I imagined being detained by Juniper Chang - I smiled - I guess it will just have to do.

I started thinking and reviewing everything that had happened in this short week. Some of the mystery was slowly being cleared up. I hoped Iishida was recovering without any complications. It surprised me how upset Juniper was when she announced she had accidentally shot him. Well, I only hope Bob is able to live up to his end of the bargain.

I thought it was ridiculous sitting up – I imagine that is why they put me on a couch, - I felt for the end of the couch, put my head on the arm - swung my legs onto the couch and stretched out - eventually I fell asleep.

I was being shaken and I sat up. Everything was dark, I reached for the bag over my head and someone slapped my hand. I then fully awoke and realized where I was. I could still see the light through the bag so I assumed nothing had changed. I guess I really didn't sleep very long.

I was being pulled up - two people were pushing me by my elbows. I started counting steps, 20 to the door, fifteen steps down and they stopped. The pushed me to a sitting position on a step. They handed me a shoe. I was surprised; I could feel the tassels of my loafer. One by one I slipped them on. They pulled me up and I started counting about 150 steps or so and they pushed me into a car.

The garage door was opened, the engine of the car started and we were on another trip. It was still dark - I didn't read any light through the bag over my head when we left the building. I had no feeling of how much time had passed or any idea what time it was. I was going to ask my escorts but figured they wouldn't answer.

I tried to concentrate on the sounds of my trip - there was a bus about five or eight minuets into the trip, and an ambulance passed just about the same time, I kept trying to visualize anything I could recognize in case we may have to find where they kept me. I was concentrating so hard that I practically forgot to breath. I would close my eyes and held my breath so I could hear everything possible.

Strange, I did smell - yes - it was 'Old Spice' cologne from someone in the car - most likely the driver. That would be an expensive taste for Japanese.

I lost track of time - there wasn't much traffic but I would say thirty minutes passed. We started to slow down and came to a stop. Someone from the back seat untied the knot around my neck and the bag was snatched off my head. I was in an area I had never seen before. Hundreds of people in gray uniforms were wheeling all sorts of fish. That's it: we are in the Fish Market.

My escort opened my door and motioned for me to get out.

I saw a clock that said 4:30. So, we are at the beginning of the day for the market. We started walking, as we entered the huge open pavilion, I looked back as the car drove away. My escort still had on his surgical mask - in fact, many of the people we were passing had their masks on. I didn't know if they did that for health reasons or to help block out the smell of fish.

This was a fascinating place and I surely would have liked to have been a tourist viewing the activity but I had other business. I couldn't imagine why we were in this particular location. We passed stands selling octopus, shrimp, eel, yellowtail, and some fish I had never seen before.

We walked about 100 yards to where the tuna was being auctioned. Skids of frozen and fresh tuna were being bid on by about eighteen or twenty buyers. I was led to the right side of the group. After the auction of a skid was completed the group would move up one or two skids and start bidding again.

I was directed to stay put by my escort. One of the skids was passing me and someone wearing the gray worker's uniform - with a surgical mask covering his face - threw a gutted tuna on top of the skid and the skid stopped in front of me. He turned the fish and separated the two sides of its belly and showed me a plastic bag. Inside the clear plastic bag was the same 5" floppy disc that was in the picture I saw last night. All the markings were identical. I nodded, scratched the back of my head with my left hand and just as I was about to say something to the worker a whole crowd of new bidders entered the area and literally pushed me aside.

I looked around and my escort was not to be found. I looked back to where the worker and the tuna were and there were different people in that spot. The skid that had been stopped in front of me was no longer in the area and I had no idea where it had been taken. There were hundreds of skids all looking alike. It was the perfect getaway.

Well I guess I am on my own. Fortunately I had my paper money in my pocket so there would be no problem to get a taxi to take me back to the hotel. I started walking toward the front of the pavilion when I spied a vendor selling what looked like a fish stew. I realized I was starved and decided I wasn't in any rush. So I had a hot bowl of the vendor's stew, sitting on a stool among the workers and started to relax and reflect on what had happened.

CHAPTER Twenty-four
Another Breakfast And More Information In The Orchid Room

I got back to the Imperial Palace Hotel in about a 30-minute taxi ride. I was surprised to be able to get a taxi so early in the morning. It was 6:00 AM and I had a whole day ahead of me. I checked at the desk and there were no messages but I had a package. I waited for it and there was my American Arcade shopping bag. All my belongings were in the bag and I turned and went up the elevator to my room.

I have to say, I give Chang, Cherry and the Yakuza kudos. They have planned everything out and have shown they are very organized. Now, if we can put a finger in their eye with what I worked out with Bob last night - maybe we can get ahead of the game.

My phone started to buzz and I picked it up - "Schein here," I said. The voice said "I kept my promise, you will be on time for your meeting at Nikon this morning" - it was

Juniper Chang. "Yes you did" I replied. Remembering that my phone is bugged I said, "Too bad we had such a short time together last night." "What" she said and then recovered, "Yes and I hope to make it up to you tonight." "Fine - what time would you like to meet?" "Say around 7:30 in the lobby?" "See you then ..." and we both hung up.

I took a shower, changed my clothes, put my laundry and cleaning out and decided to have a light breakfast before meeting with Alex to go to Nikon. It was only 7:00 in the morning – the sun had been up for about a half hour. I walked into the Orchid room Al Bernard waved to me.

I walked over to his table and he said, "Had I heard the news?" "No," I said "what news?" "Irving Roth is missing. He didn't pick up his key or messages yesterday and one of his staff members tried calling his room most of the evening. Finally, the staff member prevailed upon the manager to open the door to Roth's room. They found the room clean and the bed hadn't been slept in. "That's curious," I said – "I imagine he didn't check out either." Bernard shook his head no. "I wondered what could have happened to him."

I said, "I will be back in a few minutes" and quickly walked out of the room to the manager's desk. I had the operator connect me to the number of the Domestic Crime Agency and asked to speak to Inspector Tanaka.

"Moshi – Moshi" said Tanaka. I said this is Robert Schein. "Ah-so" Tanaka said. He immediately launched into our project update that we had worked out last night with Bob and chief Hiro. He said, "Everything is going according to plan and we have our eyes on the merchandise."

"Did you know that Irving Roth disappeared from his room?" I asked. "Yes" Tanaka said, "He is in a Yakuza safe house."

"I wonder why they have abducted Roth?" I said. Tanaka replied, "Hiro Sacho-San believes that the weakest link in the bidding was Roth. By taking Roth out of the picture, showing that 'foul play' might be involved, the bidders would look at each other thinking the other party did it. The Yakuza and whoever else is behind this wants to bring this to a quick conclusion."

I asked if he had he heard from Robert Claypool yet. Tanaka said, "Not since 1:30 AM this morning." I said, "I don't expect to hear from him today – if by any chance he contacts you please reach me and tell me what is going down." "We will do that" - we both hung up.

Claypool went undercover with a Navy Seal team. They have been following me throughout the evening. Claypool's job was to keep me under surveillance until I made contact with the disc. When that happened I was to signal by scratching the back of my head with my left hand.

They had placed men on every building around the Copa. The building roofs were like tenement buildings in New York City. You could jump from one roof to the next without too much trouble. If a car was able to turn at an intersection the Seal Team had eyes on it. Once the car was committed in a particular direction the team took up positions of all the possible routes in that area. There were only a few streets that were near the Copa. A vehicle had choices where to turn or where to go but they were few.

When the team recognized the vehicle I was in, they took positions further away from the Copa. They kept advancing that way until they could determine my location for the evening. Once they were able to determine the evening's route and felt I was camped out for the night - Hiro's people were contacted at - 1:30 AM. Bob must have pressed the winding key on the Omega watch I gave him and reported our status.

In the morning they planned all possible routes from where I was being held with the help of the Domestic Crime Agency and had people on buildings and employed bicycles, motorcycles and scooters to follow me.

I returned to the Orchid Room and went over to Bernard's table and he pointed at a chair for me to join him. The waiter came over and I ordered a croissant, coffee and juice. Bernard asked if that "was going to hold me for the day?" I said, "I had eaten very early this morning." Bernard asked, "What do you make of the Roth thing?" "I'm sure he is all right," I said. "I imagine he forgot to tell his people that he had to go to Osaka, Hakone or someplace else." I lied.

Bernard was having none of it – "It may have something to do with a project we were both working on." "Like what," I asked. Bernard looked at me a few seconds and said, "Never mind, I'll find out later."

"Interesting" I thought. "He and Roth could be working together. The Yakuza would have known that and might have decided to put pressure on Bernard by threatening the life of his partner - maybe a long shot. Wouldn't Juniper have known that? After all, they do a lot of business together. Well the only thing I can say for sure is Bernard is very upset this morning."

Bernard finished his meal and before I could say anything he said, "Sorry but I have an early appointment – I hope you don't mind – oh, I took care of the check." "Thank you but that wasn't necessary." He left room in a hurry.

CHAPTER Twenty-five
Planning The Nikon 'F' Introduction

I was driven as planned to the Ohi-Machi factory by Alex Triguboff. The same group I had started with - Wakimoto, Miyahara, Nakano, Segawa and Takeuchi - met us. We walked up to the modest second floor conference room and were served the obligatory cup of tea. I stood up for a moment and looked out the window overlooking the courtyard. All of a sudden the tea sloshed over my hand and to stand more firmly I spaced my feet further apart. Over the speaker system I heard, "Earthquake - Earthquake!"

Many of the workers came running into the courtyard and looked around, gesturing at each other. I guess they were identifying friends. Some of the workers were laughing and they appeared to be talking loudly. Soon the all clear sounded and everyone docilely went back to work. This was my first earthquake and it felt as though I was on the deck of a sailboat. I wondered how often these things happen. Then as if nothing had interrupted us the camera and lenses were brought into the room and the meeting began.

I started the meeting by saying; "TAG Photo and my government would like to assist you in getting the new camera system into production ahead of your schedule. Please tell me how much funding you need for full production, tooling, new materials, bonus fees for your suppliers and how many camera bodies are planned for the first production run. Additionally, if possible, what are your production plans for the first twelve months?"

I seemed to have caught everyone by surprise. There was a furious discussion amongst them in Japanese regarding why I was asking this and did anyone have any information regarding what I was asking for. It was interesting listening to them. The leader was definitely Nakano. He was calm throughout the storm. The most passionate arguments came from Wakimoto. "We are NK" he said, "We don't have to have outside assistance; we must do these things ourselves." Miyahara was the voice of reason, "If we don't have to go to outside financing then we will be a much healthier company and be the leader - once again - in Japan."

Nakano had enough. He held up his hand and all conversation stopped. "Schein-San, You are asking questions that this small committee cannot be expected to answer. Can you please explain why you are asking these questions?" "It will be my pleasure," I said.

I went into the importance of the Nikon 'F' camera in conjunction with the Kollmorgan 8-B periscope for our Navy. "It became particularly interesting for us when our Pentagon people reported on Wakimoto San's paper explaining how he thought a good picture could be taken with the current 8-B periscope. Dr. Edgerton tested the 8-B in his MIT laboratory as Wakimoto-San suggested. Everything Wakimoto-San suggested proved to be correct." With that statement an ear-to-ear smiled spread across Wakimoto's face.

"TAG Photo and our military want to work closely with you to manufacture the first 300 to 500 cameras so we can immediately upgrade our present periscope systems. We will use about 50 of the cameras allocated for the US market for advertising and press promotional purposes.

"We will beat all of the competition's efforts - whoever they might be - and establish this camera as the first of its kind from Japan. We assume you would need 100 to 150 units for your distributors and domestic market to be able to make a similar announcement throughout the world.

"We will hold no ownership of the camera. What we are looking for is the quickest delivery possible. We will place a blanket order for whatever number of cameras you require. For placing an order of this magnitude all we request - - as our payback - is that we receive the lowest price per unit between 5 and 7% below then what you offer any distributor in your world distribution network.

"Finally, we need a commitment from you that you will send about twenty engineers - repair technicians - to live in the States for one or two years. They will train our technicians and will work in our repair shops. We will pay all of their expenses including housing.

"Schein-San," Nakano said, "I must bring this to our board of directors before we can comment on your generous proposal." I was thinking: "The key word or tip off is his use of 'generous'. I believe Nakano likes the offer - I embellished it a little more then I think Albert would have preferred but I am here and he is not."

While I was talking Alex did not say a word nor did he try to interrupt me. He kept starring at the faces across the table trying to be as inscrutable as they were. He whispered in my ear and said, "That is a good offer and I think they will go for it. There are many financial issues about being able to produce this camera in quantity. They need the money - I don't see how they won't go for it."

That comment made me feel a lot better. I then leaned over to Alex and said "I need to talk to them privately for a few minutes - without you being present – OK?" "No Problem. I will take Nakano aside and tell him I have an appointment back at my office. They will make sure you will be transported to your hotel." "Great - thank you Alex."

After Alex left, I was asked if I would like a traditional cold soft summer drink. I said "sure." In came bottles shaped like beer bottles but I had to read the label at least three times. It said, "Kal-Pus". I wasn't sure what it tasted like - the closest I could think of was the milky looking drink was Milk-of-Magnesia. It was cooling but I wasn't sure if I liked it.

I then said, "I would like to talk a few minutes about the digital camera and new fiber optics periscope if I may." Nakano said, "Within the limitations of what you were told by the Japanese Defense Agency. - That would be fine."

"Gentlemen, we are obviously very interested in this system. We also understand what it could mean economically to the factory and to Japan. At this early stage in your research do you have any idea when a completed product could be tested aboard a submarine and when production might begin?"

Again a heated discussion erupted. I was even surprised to hear Takiuchi get involved in the conversation. He usually didn't say a word. Nakano apologized for talking in Japanese while I was waiting for my answer. Finally, Wakimoto said, "To give you a better answer we should really talk to Koana-Sansei. My guess is we would test it within five or six years and produce it within ten years." "That long?" I asked. - All Wakimoto said was "Hai."

I had my answer - If we wanted this system faster we needed to get our hands on the original disc first and make a partnership with Japan as Hiro suggested. This conversation strengthened my resolve to follow through on the bidding for the system and or try to pluck it out of the Yakuzas' hands using Bob Claypool and Hardwick's Seal Team.

The group was getting antsy about discussing this project with me. They kept on referring to the JDA throughout their discussion. The JDA is obviously one of their largest customers. I decided that we should move on. I said, "Thank you all for being so up front with me and I think I would like to return to my hotel."

Takiuchi asked me if I wanted to join the factory employees in the general cafeteria for lunch or might we go out for lunch. I said, "I thought it would be interesting to see how everyone lives each day. The factory cafeteria will do just fine." Everyone seemed surprised I chose the cafeteria but they were happy I did. Takiuchi then said, "Please do not expect too much." I said, "Please, you have no need to worry."

We went to the courtyard and entered the cafeteria, which was brightly lighted. It had long tables that sat groups of ten people. We got on line with everyone else and now that they were not working they were gawking at me. I guess I was one of the first gaijin to eat in the cafeteria.

143

I started to read the specialty of the day. - tonkatsu - breaded pork chop served with string beans and mashed potatoes. "What more can you ask for?" When we sat down with our trays at one of the long tables I thought the meal was actually delicious.

After lunch I said my good-byes and asked if the driver might go by the hospital that Iishida was in for a few minutes. The driver was given instructions, everyone bowed and off we went.

Iishida was in a private room in a hospital that brought to mind a dozen old movies. It was clean but ancient and it needed a paint job. All the carts and beds were probably purchased before the war.

Iishida was sitting up in a chair and a couple of his young people were meeting with him. There were a few displays of origami cranes and a few bouquets of flowers spaced around in the room. When I came in his assistants stood up and bowed. Iishida shooed them out of the room. Before I could say anything Iishida said "I am fine, they just want me to stay another night to make sure of that." I said, "You look great." Iishida continued, "I do not want you to fret about this - it was an accident for all I care."

"I know who did it and I am convinced that it was an accident. You were not the target. The shot was to tweak my interest in obtaining the infamous disc that was stolen from Mitsubishi." "Ah-so - hanto des ka?" (Ahh - is it true?) "Hai" I said. The old man said "That is good news."

We then talked about New York when we met. That was the last time we had seen each other. I thanked him for my wife's gift and he apologized for such a small gift. This is the Japanese custom to say what he gave me was small and unimportant. The thought was in the giving. He was happy I came to visit. I stayed a little longer, then said my good-byes and reminded him he owed me a lunch at his favorite university restaurant - we waved and I walked to my waiting car.

CHAPTER Twenty-six
The Set-Up Before The Bidding Gets More Interesting

Walking into the lobby of my hotel I notice Al Bernard, Juniper Chang and Economic Commissioner Cao in an intense discussion. The last time I had met him we were in the Copa and he seemed very involved with his paid escort. I was watching the group and almost ran down Fritz Scheonheimer. He grabbed me before I walked into him and asked, "Do you know what is going on over there?" - pointing in Juniper's direction. "I can't say that I do" I replied. Scheonheimer went on - "They are talking about Irving Roth." "How can you be so sure," I asked.

"Al told me he was going to talk to them about Roth to see if they had anything to do with his disappearance." I continued to play my part - I knew nothing of what he was talking about. "Why would they know where Irving Roth was? They do not usually do business with him." "Are you serious?" Scheonheimer asked. "You can stand there and tell me you don't know what is going on?" "Yes I can" I said - and he stormed off toward the elevator realizing he was not going to get any answers from me.

Before I went to my room I checked my messages and found one from Claypool. I had the manager dial the call and he handed the phone to me. It was Bob's answering service - I said, "Please have Mr. Claypool call Mr. Schein - I am in my hotel."

"This has been a very long day and I am not halfway through it," I thought. "I better take a few winks now so I am sharp enough to handle myself this evening. As the Green Bay Packers Coach Vince Lombardi says, 'Tiredness will make cowards of us all.' - Yes, the bed is very inviting."

It seemed to me I just put my head down when the phone began to buzz - I looked at the clock over the night table and it said 4:30 PM - "My God I must have slept for two and a half hours." - The phone continued to buzz. I felt refreshed, raring to go and picked up the phone. Bob said, "Meet you in the Starlight in ten minutes." I quickly got dressed in slacks, open shirt, blue blazer and loafers. I made it to the lounge just less than ten minutes.

Bob was in our usual seating area and had tall, 6'2", good looking black man with him. I walked over and Bob introduced me to Lt. Cmdr. Andrew Hardwick. Hardwick had a firm grip when we shook hands, an athletic appearance and the posture of an officer. He was a guy who immediately gave you the impression you wanted to hear what he had to say. You had confidence in him as soon as you looked at him.

After the introduction Bob said - "Glad to see you survived the evening's ordeal." I responded, "It wasn't so bad - Just a little uncomfortable." "Good," he continued, "Andrew is the team leader of the Seal team off of the aircraft carrier Enterprise. They have done a heck of a job sticking to you like glue." "I appreciate that," I said. "Just taking care of business," Hardwick said.

Bob continued: "Our plan, so far, has worked well. We asked Hiro's men to back off and they did. We spotted you as you came out of the building onto the balcony. We put two and two together and focused on the car that you would end up in. That was easy because there were no private cars in the area - only limousines and taxicabs. It almost became a problem when you changed vehicles. We got a lucky break when we spotted a car in an alley. We guessed that was the one they were heading for and it proved out. It was reported over the radio when they put the bag over your head and you were pushed into the car.

"Much to our surprise they did not take a lot of precautions to get you to your destination. They were cautious but did the trip directly without another change or stop. A little loose, I thought. This morning's trip was much easier. We had bikes, scooters and cars following you. There was no traffic so it was easy to see you but difficult for us to remain hidden. When we realized your destination was the fish market we broke off and reorganized our team in the market ahead of your arrival.

"When you gave the signal - it was very cleaver how they created a disturbance and got away in the crowd - so they thought." Bob seemed to be relishing the telling of the story. "Andrew, why don't you take it from here?"

In as low bass voice Andrew Hardwick started to recap what happened after I signaled. "We immediately got an eyeball on the skid and ignored the crowd and skid movement. We also had a team member tail your escort - who I might add ended up in the same spot where you spent the night. The skid was stored with the other 'sold' skids. About a half hour later one of the gray suited workers snatched one tuna off of the skid and walked it to the back of the pavilion. The pavilion on the rear side is a dock where the boats tie up."

"While this was going on we contacted Chief of Police Hiro and brought him up to date. The Chief anticipated that they might use water transportation to move the disc. He had pleasure boats close by where they could observe the boat carrying the tuna and disc. The boat traveled about a quarter of a mile north and pulled into a dock. The tuna was hacked into a number of pieces and dumped over the side."

"Three men emerged from the boat - two in suits and one in a gray uniform. One of the suits was carrying a Halliburton metal case. We are confident the disc is in the case."

"Finally, while waiting for the man who escorted you to emerge from the building; another car drove up with a man in the back seat. We couldn't tell who he was because he had a bag - similar to the one you had on your head - over his head."
"Irving Roth" I said.

Andrew said, "Obviously, this being Japan and all, our people can't legally make any raid or arrest. We have to leave that in the hands of Chief of Police Hiro and his Domestic Crime Agency - But" he added, "We have scores to settle with the Yakuza and my guys are itching to mix it up with them." Albert's words of 'we haven't been very successful with the Yakuza' came to mind. "Sorry" I said, "Not this time around. The stakes are pretty high and I don't think we could afford an international incident."

I thought a minute and said, "I am going to go to my meeting tonight and when I am with the negotiating parties I suggest that Hiro turn his men loose and make the arrests and recapture the disc. Andrew, I assume you will be present when the Domestic Crime Agency goes for the disc - correct?" "That is OK with me" he responded. "Bob I think you and I will attend the meeting and hopefully have some fun with our two ladies - that is only if the disc is recovered. Andrew - we need one of your men to bring word to us in the Copa of the disc's status.

"If the disc is recovered then we have to worry about an American citizen - Irving Roth - who is in the hands of the Yakuza. In this case commander, with the Domestic Crime Agency, you can mix it up with the Yakuza as long as you bring Mr. Roth out alive.

"If the disc is not recovered - Roth should be safe for a while – then we have to start figuring out how to complete the deal with the negotiating team of Cherry and Chang. Did I leave anything out?" I asked. They both responded "'No".

"OK – let's organize what has to be done and go out and get it done. Bob, why don't you and I hang out here and leave for the Copa around 7:15. Andrew, you go to Hiro's headquarters and make sure everyone understands what we are doing and that you put yourself in a position to observe the recovery the disc. We have to know that for sure." Bob and I ordered a couple of drinks and Andrew Hardwick left.

CHAPTER Twenty-seven
Face-To-Face Negotiations

Claypool and I put our heads together to come up with a plan for the evening. He was going to play 'bad cop' to my 'good cop.' Bob was going to be the negative bidder to see if we could ferret out what the other bids were. If and when we got positive word on the disc recovery we would still play the game to learn what we could.

It was 7:10 PM we decided to get started for the Copa. I said, "Juniper is in for a surprise - she didn't expect me to bring company." We went down to the lobby and as we started to look for a place to wait for Juniper the bellhop was passing ringing his bell and the placard read Mr. Shine. I flagged him down and he gave me a note.

"Robert," the note read, "My car is waiting to take you to the Copa. I have been delayed and will meet you there – sorry – Juniper Chang." I showed the note to Bob and we left the hotel and found Juniper's Mercedes. The ride was short and uneventful. The luxurious car made the trip feel even shorter.

We arrived at the Copa and were surprised we didn't receive the traditional loud but warm greeting of Mama Cherry. One of her people said that Mama Cherry was out of the building and will return shortly. I said, "We will have dinner when she arrives. In the meantime we will wait upstairs and have a drink." We climbed the stairs and were seated in what I assumed was Mama Cherry's reserved table.

Fritz Scheonheimer walked over to say hello and wondered if I had any news regarding the Minolta distributorship. I introduced Bob as my TAG colleague and said, "That it didn't appear that our manufacturers would be happy with a decision for TAG to take on Minolta." He seemed unhappy to hear that but I think he expected that decision. He then inquired. "Had I'd heard any news regarding Irving Roth – I said, "No." We shook hands and he walked back to his table to join a very lovely paid escort.

The music was playing, the customers were dancing and the atmosphere was generally upbeat. Still, I had a feeling of doom. I had to get myself out of it if we were going to be successful this evening. Bob and I made small talk in case anyone was listening, had a couple of drinks and ordered some dim sum to keep us busy. It was now 8:00 PM - still no sign of Juniper Chang or Mama Cherry.

I knew where Roth was, Scheonheimer was in the room but Bernard was missing. I wondered if that was the reason why everyone was late. Bob thought it was a definite possibility. We speculated that Bernard was the front-runner in the bidding race.

I checked my watch again and it was 8:15 PM – by now

Hiro's men had made their raid. I hoped they were successful. Bob and I started to constantly peek at our watches and I said out loud, "This won't do. Bob, if you were observing this table you would notice that we were anxious about something. Let's make an effort to ignore the clock." Bob agreed and we tried to make casual nonsense small talk until the action started.

Just then Mama Cherry appeared in all her glory, right after her - Juniper Chang. She was a sight to behold dressed in a black short cocktail dress with a white magnolia flower in her jet-black hair - beautiful. Behind Juniper there was Cao dressed in his traditional tan Mao outfit buttoned to his neck. All three came over to our table.

Juniper and Mama Cherry were all apologies for being late – Cao said nothing but stood beside the ladies. I was sure Cherry would organize an escort for him shortly. I introduced Bob Claypool as a colleague of TAG Photographic and Bob passed out his business card which had the title of Director on it. That is a powerful title in Japan.

Everyone including Cao sat down at our table. Juniper explained that, "Mr. Cao is a special participant in our conversation and will be joining us. Cao is Commissioner of Economic Development in Hong Kong and what we are discussing is in his purview." A light bulb in my brain lit up – of course, Red China, which controls Hong Kong, then still a British Colony, is in back of this and they are the ones financing and directing the Yakuza. Chang and Cherry are just brokers or pawns in the game.

The Chinese do not have the submarine fleet that Russia or the United States has. They're throwing their weight around to force the two super-powers to bid against each other. China's object is for Russia and the United States to have something else to be angry about in the Cold War.

153

Juniper appeared to speak for the group. She started the 'negotiations' by saying, "Robert, you are going to have to do a lot better then what we originally discussed." I replied "That is why Mr. Claypool is here. We are here to make a decision and come to a conclusion. He knows the limits that our board of directors has authorized."

She then asked, "Are you satisfied that our people have the disc?" Bob and I had previously decided I would continue as spokesman. "It appears you have the same disc that was pictured with Dr. Fukuchi and Mr. Kobi. We would naturally want to set up some control to make sure it is the correct disc and no copies have been made. Other then that we are reasonably satisfied that you might have the right disc."

She asked, "Reasonably - might? Come now – we either have it or we don't." "Juniper – there is no black and white here – we are willing to discuss the project further; that is all I have to say. We are talking a lot of money and in something like this it would be nice to be one hundred percent positive." She said, "Once we agree on the figure an arrangement can be made." "Thank you" I said.

She continued, "What did you have in mind?" "I told you what I had in mind. If you want to counter that - that is strictly up to you; accept my offer of fifty million or say something else." She laughed and said, "I already have a higher offer. We have to do better." "How much better" I asked.

At that moment a tall lean young man with a very short crew cut in a dark suit walked over to Bob and handed him a note, whispered in his ear and walked away disappearing down the stairs across the room. Juniper responded to this interruption by asking sarcastically, "A note from home?" "No," Bob said, "Just confirmation of our negotiations that we have the go-ahead." That was my signal that all was well.

Now, I was very confident I was on the winning team. I thought I could give away anything I wanted to without actually having to give anything away. I smiled and said – "You will tell me you have a bid for 90 million and I will say 60 million; then it will go back to you and you will say 80 million and I will respond with 70 million. I am going to make it easy for you - anticipating the disc is in good condition and can be proven that no copies have been made from it – our final bid is $75,000,000.

Juniper smiled and said, "That is a generous offer. If I may, I would like a few minutes alone with Mama Cherry and Mr. Cao before we go any further." In the meantime, Mama Cherry chimed in and said, "I have ordered champagne for the table to drink a toast." Cao said something sharply in Chinese to Mama Cherry and Cherry seemed to be rebuffed. Juniper answered strongly to Cao and he said nothing further, just tightened his lips and jaw-line. Cherry and Cao were both looking at each other as if they were going to claw out the other's eyes.

When they walked away to go to Mama Cherry's office Bob leaned over and gave me the note that read three words – Disc In Hand! Bob then said the ensign also reported that Mr. Roth has been recovered unharmed. "Good" I said, ripped and crumples the note and put it in my suit pocket.

"Now – they obviously are going to talk to their contacts in the Yakuza. They might be trying to contact the very people holding the disc. When they come back they may know they do not have the disc. I think we continue to play our part, as I am sure they will play their part. I can't imagine them saying they do not have the disc or can't complete the deal."

A half of an hour must have past and they still hadn't returned to our table. I said to Bob, "They have got to know.

155

Once this information gets out I am sure the Yakuza will cause a problem. They are the recognized 'bad guys' in this country and they certainly will have difficulty with a loss of face. It will show weakness. I imagine they will strike out at someone or something. Maybe we should ask Hiro to strengthen the security around the Palace Hotel and its guests." Bob said, "Knowing the thoroughness of Hiro and his people I am sure they have already taken care of that."

Finally the negotiating team returned to the table. Juniper looked a little tense but Mama Cherry and Commissioner Cao showed nothing but their inscrutable demeanor. There was no apology for making us wait. Juniper just started – "We have talked to our 'partners' and they have accepted your offer of 75 million US dollars. We wish to make the trade the end of next week." I said, "Fine – please remember that we need time to verify the disc. How do you wish for the transfer of funds to proceed?"

She said, "We will organize everything from our side and will request that the actual trade happens with the transfer of funds into a Swiss bank account. The routing numbers for the bank will be given to you once the disc is verified. When the money is confirmed in the account the disc will be handed to you" "Good" I said – "That gives us enough time to bring a computer engineer here and to organize the money."

I then tried to lighten the mood by saying – "I am starved, talking about money makes me hungry - how about some dinner?" Bob said, "That sounds good" and picked up a menu. The others declined and said they were going back to Mama Cherry's office and would join us after we had eaten.

Bob and I ordered a couple of Kobe beef steaks, with baked potatoes, butter and sour cream and the vegetables of the day – peas and carrots. The meat could be cut with a fork it was so soft and delicious. We were having coffee and a cordial when Juniper came back. Mama Cherry was doing her restaurant welcoming work and Cao was nowhere to be seen. She sat down and it was obvious I was looking for the rest of her party when she said, "Mr. Cao left the building to go to another meeting."

Juniper seemed more relaxed now that she wasn't in business mode nor had Commissioner Cao around to watch her. It was just after 11:00 PM and I was eager to get back to the hotel to talk to Hardwick. I wanted the details of the raid. I was concerned with who might have escaped – if anyone. I was certain the Yakuza would strike somewhere – and eye-for-an-eye mentality is difficult to deal with.

Juniper asked if I wanted to go to a little nightclub that is starting to do something that will eventually be a craze in Japan – Karaoke. The music plays, the words are projected on a screen and you sing the song. I said, "I don't think so, I am bushed but I will take a rain-check."

She replied, "Then how about a dance?" "I'm not that bushed, let's go." Just then a Nat King Cole song started up – I couldn't believe my ears – "Night and Day." A Japanese singer with a crooning voice – who sounded identical to Nat Cole – was singing. The young man, I am sure, did not speak English - he learned the song by hearing it over and over a couple a hundred times. He was good – it was a good imitation, he sounded fine. Bob excused himself and said he was returning to the hotel.

Juniper and I went down the stairs and held hands as we got onto the dance floor. She smelled delicious – I think of magnolias like the flower in her hair. I was tentative to hold her – I was treating her like a China doll. She pulled my arm tighter around her and her thigh was in my groin. I got nervous; I thought for sure I would embarrass myself. I didn't want things to get out of hand. I tried to step a little back but

157

she wouldn't let me. We were dancing very closely and in my deep thoughts I said, "How do I explain this to Debbie?"

I sighed and said to myself "I was grateful to have my wife's image in my mind." I think Juniper took my sigh to mean something else. She seemed to get closer. Her eyes were closed and we were moving on the dance floor as one person. My God – what is she thinking? With that thought in my head - she said- "Why don't we return to our hotel?" I guardedly said, "OK."

I went to the doorman to tell him to signal for Miss Chang's car while the hostesses were putting on her wrap. The car was in a line picking up people who were leaving the Copa. We decided to walk to the car instead of waiting for it to pull up.

As we walked on the street a black car came whirling around the corner at a high speed and a man was sticking out of the window with a gun – I shouted "Down!" I went to grab Juniper and the shooter started firing – it was the distinctive sound of a Russian AK-47. Maybe a whole clip was fired. We both were hit – my leg gave out and I fell to the ground with a burning sensation in my inside thigh: I was bleeding profusely. Before I passed out I saw Juniper hit the ground like a sack of potatoes. She went straight down to the ground and there was no movement. I stared at her lifeless face and everything went black and the sound of people yelling disappeared.

CHAPTER Twenty-eight
Awake And An Update

My eyes were closed, I was hearing people talk; one of the voices was Bob Claypool's and the other – yes – was Andrew Hardwick's. They were talking about a raid or something like that. I fought to open my eyes and once everything came into focus I felt better. Then I heard, "Well look who is amongst the living. How do you feel?" It was Bob leaning over the bed – "Thirsty" I croaked. Andrew leaned over the bed and said, "Here drink this" – I sucked on a straw and swallowed. I asked, "What the hell happened?"

I tried to sit up by propping up my pillows; I noticed that I didn't feel too much pain anywhere. I then saw a heavy sandbag on my thigh. "What's all this" I asked. Bob said, "I'll try to fill you in. When you started walking to get your car another car came zooming around the corner. Eyewitnesses said that a man was half hanging out of the car with a gun. From the shells and bullets we can tell it was an AK-47. He sprayed the area and hit you another person and juniper Chang.

"The innocent bystander had a hand wound – nothing too serious. On the other hand you had an almost serious thigh wound. The quick reaction by the doorman of the Copa saved your life. He took off his belt and tied it above the wound as a tourniquet. He stopped the loss of blood until the ambulance arrived.

"Juniper Chang's wounds were fatal. The AK-47 stitched her across her chest. One of the three bullets that hit her found her heart and she died instantly. We believe the gunman's main target was Juniper Chang. The Dragon Lady – her mother – is not going to be too happy with this. I wouldn't want to be in that gunman's shoes and have someone with her connections in the underworld looking for me."

"When did all this happen? I mean, I haven't been out of touch with the world for a long time - right?" "Don't worry, Robby, this only happened late last night around midnight. "What time is it now?" – Bob looked at his watch and said "3:00 PM." "OK – when do I get out of here?" "Whoa buddy – let's talk to the doctor first." "Bullshit – I want this sandbag off and I want to be patched up as best as possible and get out on the street." "What's the hurry?" Andrew asked.

"Simple – if the Yakuza do not make a play for the disc again they will most definitely make a play for the people who were directly involved in the negotiations and I am a sitting duck in here. From what different people have told me, the Yakuza would knock off their own family to create a distraction if it got the target they wanted. This is a dedicated and tough group of killers." Bob and Andrew were silent letting what I had said sink in.

A nurse walked in and said, "Time to get sandbag off" in

broken English. I said, "Can I speak to the doctor?" "Doctor fine" she said. I said "No, I'm not fine until I can speak to the doctor" Bob got into the mix and said – "I think what she means is the Doctor says you are fine." "Oh, if that is the case get my clothing and let's get the hell out of here." The nurse ran out of the room as Bob and Andrew started to reach for my clothing.

The doctor came into the room soon after and said, "We would like to keep Mr. Schein overnight. What are you doing?" "They are getting me organized to get me out of here. By the way Doc, tell me about my wound please." The Doctor said, "It is a flesh wound that just nicked your artery in your thigh. There was no difficulty in closing your wound, we gave you a pint of blood and you have a few stitches that should come out next week." "So, I am good to go?" "If you don't put too much weight on the leg you are OK to go. You should really keep your leg up for a day or two." "Thank you"

I was then wheeled out of the hospital and carried crutches in a wheelchair to Bob's awaiting car. I figured if I can get into his very small sports car - a classic MG-TD - I wouldn't have any trouble with anything else. I gave the crutches to the aide and said "Goodbye." Andrew was going to meet us at the hotel; he wanted to get an update from the team who recovered Roth.

"Bob, I think we have to check in with Luke Albert. Let's get to Triguboff's office and use the secure phone." Bob said, "I have already done that while you were taking your 'nap'. Albert was ready to fly here and he still may do that. He is the boss, so I have no idea what he will do. I reported everything that went on – I gave him a complete debriefing. I told him that I thought you were going to be all right." Albert wanted to know if you should be sent home and I said, "I didn't think so. I think he can finish the job."

Bob's next comment was interesting. "Albert said for a rookie in the field to get this involved on his first assignment is unheard of. I think we have the right guy in the right place this time around." I said, "I agree."

"Robby, I think you have done a heck of a job and you have been extremely lucky. I think I'm going to ride your streak a little further." We arrived at the hotel and I struggled to get out the little car. With a little twisting and some pain I got myself out and with a noticeable limp walked into the hotel unassisted.

There was a big commotion at the manager's desk with a large party checking in. A lot of bowing and many bellhops lined up. A sad regal looking Chinese woman dressed in black with a string of pearls around her neck that had to be the largest pearls I had ever seen.

There was a young lady with her who was also dressed in black and was wearing a black hat with a large brim. She had her back to me but something was odd - her body looked familiar. She turned around and happened to look in my direction - I saw her face and became weak-kneed and almost fell. The young woman beside the regal looking older lady was Juniper Chang? That's impossible - she's dead - I thought.

Just then, Bob came beside me and saw my distressed look. He looked over at the manager's desk and whispered in my ear, "That is Madam Chang and her fourth daughter the identical twin sister of Juniper Chang. Her name is Hyacinth Chang."

"Bob" I blurted out, "She looks and carries herself so much like Juniper I thought she was reincarnated. I couldn't believe my eyes." "I know" Bob said as I hobbled toward the elevator.

CHAPTER Twenty-nine
The Debriefing

I was rather shaken seeing Hyacinth and needed a drink - badly - something to soothe my already weakened nerves. We went to the Starlight Lounge and found our usual seats. I ordered a double Chivas on the rocks with a glass of ice water on the side. I sat there for a few minutes, not saying a word, just staring out of the windows at the skyline.

Things happen in strange ways I thought - I could have gotten into a difficult romantic attachment with Juniper Chang if she were alive. I would have felt extraordinarily guilty doing so. I am sorry she is dead but I am happy that I didn't have the opportunity to be an unfaithful husband.

I don't know if I could ever tell any of what has happened to Debbie. It is going to be hard enough to explain my thigh wound. I don't think she would understand everything I have gotten involved in. At this point I'm not sure I understand everything. The one thing I am certain about is my training, this trip and what has happened to me has changed me for the rest of my life.

Andrew Hardwick arrived. He sat next to me and we immediately got down to business. He said, "I thought Hiro's men were real professionals. They handled the raid of the small house like a swarm of ants. I had two of my men with me and we watched the raid unfold. They surrounded the house, placed their marksmen in strategic locations and slowly crept up to the house. Everyone was dressed in black against the dark sky.

"At the signal for attack a couple of stun grenades were thrown into the house. All entrances of the house were immediately charged. Firing ensued and after only about a couple of minutes everything was quiet. The all clear was given and we went into the house.

"Two of the Yakuza were killed with pistols in their hands. Their bodies were tattooed with large designs from their backs to their chests. They were sleeping when the attack started. The third man was not to be found. The Halliburton case was found between two sleeping bags where the victims lay. The bomb squad to make sure it was not booby-trapped carefully opened the case. The disc was inside.

"I then wrote my note for Bob - Disc In Hand! – and sent Ensign Hunter Held to the Copa. I told Held I would check the Roth situation and by radio we would tell him what it was. As planned, Held changed into his civvies. We wanted him to be able to fit in with the Copa crowd."

"The raid to capture Roth was a little more complicated. It was in a residential area and there were more people around who might get hurt. Hiro's men quietly evacuated the buildings along side of the targeted garage. The sharpshooters took up their positions. They had an idea about the inside from your description of the steps you counted when you were taken into the building.

"The garage was quietly surrounded. Front and back entrances covered. Through a back door Hiro's men slipped into the building. They climbed the fifteen steps you described and waited outside the office door. One of the team members slipped a tiny periscope mirror under the door and found that there were two Yakuza in the room plus Irving Roth.

"They crashed in the door and took everyone by surprise. One of the Yakuza tried to point his weapon at Roth and was shot and killed. The other one surrendered. As soon as the all clear was given Lt. Ian Siegel personally checked Roth, saw that he was unhurt then radioed me with the news. I radioed Ensign Held and I reached him just as he was parking his car before going into the Copa."

I asked, "Are they sure that both of the men were Yakuza?" "Yes, their bodies were well tattooed on their backs and chest." "Were they able to get any information from the captured Yakuza?" "Not sure" Andrew said." The captured Yakuza from what Hiro's men knew was a kyodai (second level boss) and we were thinking that the Yakuza believes they were sold out. We guess that is why they retaliated by killing Juniper Chang."

A bellboy was passing ringing his bell and the placard surprisingly said Mr. Schein. It was spelled correctly this time. There were three other names on the placard as well - all people from the photographic industry; Abbott, Berkey and Scheonheimer. I waved the bellboy over and he gave me a note. It was a formally prepared Invitation to a memorial service for Juniper Chang. It was to be held in one of the catering halls in the hotel the next day at 10:00 AM. I showed the invitation to both Bob and Andrew.

"I guess Madame Chang feels that many people from the photographic industry are present and this is as good a time as any to make a tribute to her daughter. It will also give Madam Chang an opportunity to address everyone at one time." Smart lady, I thought.

The three of us decided we would like a light dinner so we stayed in the hotel and went down to the lobby and ate in the Orchid room. We all had some corn soup because I recommended it. We had different fish dinners whether it was grilled, fried or broiled. We all skirted the dessert pastry tray, had some coffee and called it a night.

I went to my room and decided to call Debbie and tell her a little about what happened to me. Ultimately, I lied to her and said that I got hurt in the factory when I ran into a piece of steel that was sticking out in the aisle. She was very solicitous which made me feel good. I told her the wound would be around for some time because I nicked an artery in my thigh. She got very concerned and asked if I was coming home so she could take care of me. I said I was fine, I am walking OK and there was no need to worry. We said our good-byes hung up and I fell into a dreamless deep sleep.

CHAPTER Thirty
In Memoriam

I had a 6:30 AM wake up call - got out of bed feeling refreshed, showered, changed my dressing and re-taped it as securely as I possibly could. Before getting dressed I called Alex's office to make sure he would be attending the memorial service and for TAG to send the appropriate flowers.

The phone rang and Linda's chirpy voice said "TAG Photo - Far East Offices." "Linda," I said, "Is Alex in?" "No, but I was going to leave you a message about the Juniper Chang memorial service. Mr. Triguboff assumed you will be attending and has sent a floral display on a stand from TAG." "Thank you, that is exactly what I wanted to confirm. Goodbye" and hung up.

It was very quiet in the Orchid Restaurant, a sea of black or dark colored suits. No one waved to me or even looked up. I felt as though I knew more then fifty percent of the people in the room. A nod of a head here or there was all I got. I was led to my own table; I walked trying to disguise my slight limp and sat down. I ordered a full American breakfast with coffee and orange juice.

Everyone seemed to finish at the same time. As we were filtering out into the lobby Scheonheimer approached me and said, "That was a nasty business last night outside of the Copa. Were you close to Miss Chang when she was killed?" I said, "Yes". "Was she in much pain - did she suffer much?" "The Doctor claims she was killed instantly." "Good" he said, "Better not to suffer" and walked off. I thought that everyone wanted to ask me that question since I was with Juniper and was the last person she saw on this earth.

Alex arrived about a half an hour before the memorial service was to begin. As we walked into the room there was a receiving line of Madame Chang and Hyacinth Chang - they were in the front row and Mama Cherry and Al Bernard a step in back of Madame Chang forming a second row. As the people came up to Madame Chang, Cherry or Bernard would whisper the name of the arriving person and his/her association in Madame Chang's ear. There were a couple of other people in the line a few steps further in the room and they were executives of Madame Chang's Photo Company in Hong Kong.

When it was my turn to offer my respects, Madame Chang said "I understand that you were the young man who was with my daughter when she was killed." I replied, "Yes - I was." "Was she in any pain before she died?" She asked what any mother would ask I thought. "I am certain she felt no pain. She most likely was dead before she hit the ground. I am sorry." "We are going to have a light lunch at about noon and I invite you to join us." I said, "I would be honored." She said, "One of my men will give you the details." "Thank you"

I replied and moved on.

Many of the factories the Changs dealt with as well as their competitive factories sent representatives to the service. It was the place to be seen in Japan this morning. The Chang photo empire also supplied many parts to all of the manufacturers in Japan. Cheaper labor has forced the manufacturers to seek assistance from people like the Changs.

The gathering was a who's who of the Photo industry. Kowa, Konica, Miranda, Nikon, Canon, Mamiya, Bronica, Bolsey, Stecki, Yashica, Pentax, Fuji, private label manufacturers and many more. There must have been over 400 people present'

The austere room was set up with a couple of tiered tables symbolizing a shrine along the wall as we entered. Flowers in rosette forms – on stands - blocked out the entire wall. In the middle of the wall above the tables was a 40" X 60" black and white picture of the beautiful Juniper Chang. On top of the tiered table was a statue of Buddha and in front of the statue - a step down - a large decorated urn holding Juniper Chang's ashes. The rest of the room was set up schoolroom style with a twelve-foot gap between the first row of seats and the shrine.

I nodded to many people walking in and Miyahara sitting next to Nagaoka lifted his hand and indicated he had saved seats. Alex and I got into the aisle and I sat next to Nagaoka. There was a program on the folding chair that indicated what was going to happen and a brief biography of Juniper Chang with a smiling picture of her. I stared at it a moment and the ceremony started.

Chinese and Japanese Buddhist priests and their cadre walked in clashing cymbals, blowing horns and banging drums. The ceremony lasted about twenty minutes. The

Chinese style - more flamboyant than the Japanese style, was exhibited. Offerings to Buddha were presented and the ceremony part was over.

Madame Chang was to make a few short comments in Chinese, Japanese and in English. She went to a small podium to the right of the room, adjusted the microphone and started in Chinese.

I listened to her comments in Japanese - I thought I understood most of what she said but I didn't think I got the full gist of the meaning. It was time for her comments in English. She did not read these comments from any paper. This came from the heart. She started by making a short statement of Juniper Chang's life and the success and joy it meant to her, her sister and the family.

She went on and said, "Her twin sister cannot express the depth of our loss. Hyacinth knows that the rest of her life she will be compared to Juniper and will always hold a place in her heart for her twin sister. While Juniper was educated in the States at Wharton College and Yale University, Hyacinth was educated at UCLA and Princeton. Today I declare that Hyacinth Chang - my fourth daughter - will fill the position of trust and power that Juniper held."

She went on "I have five daughters and three adopted sons. They are the foundation from which I get my strength. I state here today - loud and clear - the people who upset my world, the people who uselessly murdered my daughter, will pay dearly for this deed. I declare war on whoever was involved." With that she bowed her head for a few seconds in grave reverence and left the podium to a silent and stunned audience.

After Madame Chang and Hyacinth left the room it must have taken a few seconds for people to regain their composure and start the hubbub that was normal at a gathering like this. I shook the hands of Nagaoka, Miyahara and right in back of him Iishida. "It's good to see you looking well" I said. Iishida said, "From what I have heard we have the same thing in common. It is good to see you looking well." "I guess we do have similar wounds in common." And we started to leave the room.

As I was walking out of the room Shigatada Ari, President of Tamron Optical Company tapped me on my shoulder. "How do you feel" he asked. "Fine" I said, "I am looking forward to our meeting next week." He said, "Good, so am I." He added, "I have organized a geisha party with our board of directors so I hope you will stay the afternoon for business and evening for pleasure." "I will be there" I said and we shook hands and walked to the elevator together.

CHAPTER Thirty-one
Lunch With The Changs

Alex and I sat in the lobby of the hotel for a while reviewing our position with Nikon and the events of the past evening. We talked about Madame Chang's threat, which Alex thought to be serious enough to all who were involved in Juniper's death.

Alex said, "That is one lady you do not want to mess with. Robert, because Japan is considered a 'safe' country for a tourist or businessman to travel in - with all the violence that has happened in the last couple of days it is most unusual. I am not sure how the authorities will deal with it. For this reason, you should stay near the hotel and be with people who you know whenever possible. I just think we should at least take simple precautions."

I nodded and said, "Mr. Ari has invited me to a geisha party on Monday. That would take me out of the hotel for most of the day and evening." "I received an invitation to the same party" Alex said, "I will attend the business meeting and stay with you throughout the day and night - if that is all right with you?" "That is fine" I replied.

"Luke Albert will be expecting to talk to you sometime tomorrow - Sunday. Why don't you join Miyako and me for breakfast at the Jewish Community Center? Afterwards we will go to the office so you can talk to Albert." "The Jewish Community Center?" I quizzically asked. "Yes, I helped start the center after the war and on Sundays they offer a breakfast of traditional Jewish cuisine to its members and guests."

"My wife is a stalwart of the Jewish community, the temple and the kitchen. She has learned to cook many of the traditional dishes. I usually invite a few people from the industry for a taste of the 'old' country. Come along I am sure you will like it." I nodded yes. Alex then said, "I will pick you up at 10:00 tomorrow morning." – As he was leaving … he remarked, "take care today."

I found the room off the mezzanine where I was invited to have lunch with the Changs. Upon entering I noticed there must have been thirty people in the room. Obviously close friends of the Changs, company associates and some guests. I saw Nagaoka and Iishida sitting together and walked over to their table. I was immediately invited to join them.

The room was decorated similar to the room we were in for the service. Juniper's urn was in front of her picture with a selection of the rosette floral stands around the table. On the other wall was a buffet display of shellfish – lobsters, oysters and clams - that was very elaborately set up. A carving station was set up for those who wanted beef. Other stations were serving caviar, fish of different varieties and sushi. They all were elaborately displayed. I loaded my plate up with the

173

caviar and oysters.

While I was eating and bantering with my two noble company leaders Al Bernard came over to the table and said "Madame Chang would like to talk with you for a few minutes. Would you mind going over to visit with her?" I said, "Not at all." I excused myself and followed Bernard across the room to the Changs table. I was directed to sit beside Madame Chang. Hyacinth was across the table and was as breathtaking to look at as her sister was. Mama Cherry was also at the table; the other seats were empty. As soon as I was seated Bernard walked away.

Madame started off by saying, "Juniper mentioned your name a couple of times during her reports to me. She seemed to enjoy your company. I heard you danced with her."

"Only once," I said. "Yes" Chang sadly said, "And it was her last dance." I nodded. I looked across the table and I couldn't believe how much Hyacinth looked like Juniper. Hyacinth seemed a bit more reserved or shy but she was listening to every word. She kept on looking down at the papers before her. Our eyes didn't meet.

The Dragon Lady was no sentimentalist so I expected her to ask me questions about the negotiations. She asked, "Who attended the negotiations with you at the Copa?" I said Bob Claypool, a Director of TAG Photographic. "Who else?" "From our side, that was it. Across the table representing your side were Mama Cherry, Commissioner Cao and Juniper." I thought what Chang was doing was confirming Cherry's or Cao's story. She continued, "Did you notice anyone else who might be interested in your discussion." "Possibly Fritz Scheonheimer," I said. "Other then that – no."

I then said, "I should mention that at one point during the

discussion we were interrupted when Claypool received a note from our office." "What about this note," she asked. "What did it say?" I tried not to change the tone of my voice or look in anyway defensive. If fact, I made it a point to look directly into Madame Chang's eyes and said, "It was a confirmation that the number we were going to propose was satisfactory with our home office."

"Fine," Chang said, "What happened when you left the Copa?" "I ordered up the car from the doorman and your daughter got her wrap from the hostesses and we walked out onto the street. A number of people were leaving at that time and there were three or four cars lined up ready to pick up their passengers. We just thought it would be faster and easier to walk the three or so cars.

"I heard a car driving very fast with screeching brakes. I saw the window was down and I made out a gun - I think I shouted 'down' – heard shots - and the next thing I remember was my leg burning and bleeding and Juniper's lifeless face on the ground; then I blacked out.

Were you badly injured?" she asked, "Not really. A flesh wound that nicked and artery. Fortunately the doorman of the Copa knew his first-aid and probably saved my life." Everyone at the table was silent for a moment letting everything I said sink in.

Madame Chang then said, "Thank you for recounting everything that happened while you were with Juniper. – Oh – where were you headed?" she asked. "The hotel," I said. "It was getting late and I had a heavy schedule the next day." Madame Chang smiled and turned to look away.

Madame Chang turned back and asked – "What was your final offer for the disc?" Now she was playing the game with me - I thought. "US 75 million" I answered. "Are you still interested in completing the deal?" "Of course – under the same conditions we had agreed to." I said. "We must have a few moments to examine the disc to determine if copies have been made and if the disc is genuine. Then money can be transferred to the appropriate Swiss bank account."

"Good" she said. "We will meet Wednesday and complete everything by Friday – agreed?" "Agreed," I said. To myself I admired how smooth she was. She doesn't have the disc yet she is negotiating as if she had it. I wonder if she was planning to recapture it - or maybe the disc we have was a fake.

Just then a bellman brought a small box to Madame Chang. It was carefully wrapped in a small kerchief. She opened the box and inside was a roll of paper. She unrolled the paper and before her was a part of a finger. The paper note was written in Kanji Chinese characters. She read the note out loud in Chinese and English, "We apologize for our mistake and pain we have caused you. We ask your forgiveness."

Chang's face flushed red and tense. Her whole demeanor changed. She spat out through clinched teeth; "I don't want the blasted finger - I want the whole hand and then the head!" The severed finger was Yakuza's way to apologize. When something went wrong and incurred disfavor of the oyab-un (leader) the offender cut off one of his fingers as an apology and peace offering.

There was a hush in the room. People at the other tables were silent. Everyone was watching Madame Chang. Hyacinth said something sharply in Chinese to her mother and her mother took a deep breath and relaxed. Madame Chang then apologized for her bad manners and implored everyone to please eat and ignore her. She apologized in Chinese, Japanese and English. Domo suimimasen – I am so sorry.

While I was at the table Mama Cherry did not say a word. Her one expression was held throughout the entire conversation. It was inscrutable – I was not sure what she was thinking. All I know is that I had to tell the truth as best as I could or I would be one of the culprits whom Madame Chang would be looking for. The mere fact that we are still talking about closing the deal probably means that I have passed the test.

I didn't want to overstay my welcome so I thanked everyone for lunch and Hyacinth walked me to the door. She was very kind and gentle and didn't seem to have that bite or driving force that her sister had. All she said was, "Thank you for being with my sister during her last moments of life." I kissed her hand and said, "You are very welcome."

CHAPTER Thirty-two
A Meeting With Hiro And A Call To The Office

I was on my way to phone Hiro when Tanaka stopped me in the lobby of the hotel. He said, "Hiro Sacho-San would like to meet with you in his office." "I was just going to call him" I said. "Please lead on." We walked out of the hotel and Tanaka waved for his car.

Hiro met me halfway from his desk to the office door and we shook hands warmly. He said that he was happy to see that my wound was not critical and I was moving about so well. He directed me over to the comfortable leather chairs and we sat down. A young lady in a white kimono came in and put a few cookies and tea in mugs on the table for us.

Hiro started – "I want to confirm to you that we have the original disc and no copies have been made from it. It looks as though we have accomplished rescuing the disc with your help and we will respect the arrangement we made." "I am grateful to hear that" I said. Hiro continued, "The Seal team worked well with our field control team and we were obviously lucky that Mr. Roth was recovered unharmed."

"Madame Chang has caused a lot of problems with what she said this morning at the memorial service for her daughter." "Were you there?" I asked. "I didn't see you." "I was there" Hiro replied. "I was not happy with what I heard. Did anything happen that was unusual when you attended the luncheon?" I told him about the Yakuza's delivery of someone's finger. Hiro sat a moment or two thinking about that.

He started, "I think we are going to see the Yakuza make another stab at stealing the disc or stealing something else that would represent the value of your negotiations with the Yakuza's brokers. It is not the Yakuza alone – the Communist Chinese are in back of this and they will finance it to the hilt. They love to have the Russians and Americans bumping heads. There is no way the Chinese would miss this opportunity.

"Mr. Roth has gone home. We have to assume that Scheonheimer and Bernard are still in the game. The old expression of 'keeping your options open'. You most likely have the top bid but that doesn't mean the other bidders will not get approval to match your bid. – We have to make sure the negotiations do not open again. We have to put an end to their hope of getting any part of the project.

"The vulnerable people are the ones who immediately are working on the project –Koana, Wakimoto, Koana's assistants. These people could be brought into an uncomfortable situation and we have to somehow avoid that. The easiest thing to do might be to call a conference and bring these people together under our immediate supervision and protection for a couple of weeks.

When we feel we can expose the Communist Chinese plot and their involvement with the Yakuza, only then do I think they will back down. If we can embarrass them for their involvement with the Yakuza they will drop the whole thing like a hot potato. We need a little more time and more proof before we can turn this over to the press."

This was getting too political for me I thought. I understood the Communist threat. If we put that down and maybe do a little harm to the Yakuza then everyone backs off to look for some other project. However, while the Yakuza were on the rampage it might be difficult to control the situation. I am not sure if anyone can hold them down – money or no money.

One thing for sure was that the Yakuza couldn't care less if China, Russia and America were at each other's throats. The only thing they seem to care about was how they appear to their people – loss of face and loss of their strength is what matters to them.

Hiro thought he knew how he wanted to proceed and now there appeared to be some plan in effect he was a bit more relaxed. I asked him if I might use one of his secure telephones to talk to my office. I was shown into a small office by one of Hiro's secretary. I wrote the number down and she came back into the room and said, "Party is waiting" and walked out.

"Hello - Robert?" Doreen's voice came over loud and clear. She moved on very quickly "I am happy you called - I have left a message for you to contact me at your hotel." "Is there a problem?" I asked. "To some degree." she said. "As we speak, Luke Albert is on his way to Japan." "Confidentially," she continued, "He is going against his orders to stay behind his desk until released by the chief deputy of the division."

I could tell Doreen was very serious and concerned by the caution she was using in choosing her words. I said, "How can I help?" "There is only one man who can fill you in on the details of his last problem - the 'incident' we all refer to when we talk of Luke Albert. That person is Alex Triguboff. Alex can be depended upon. I have asked him to fill you in and then to take very good care of Mr. Albert." Out loud I said – "I have to take care of Albert?" Doreen responded with one word - "Yes." Finally she said, "He may add a complication that you will have to deal with - Alex will explain." I didn't know what to think.

I asked - "When will he arrive? "Pan-Am #001, the same flight you were on, at 5:30 PM your time." "Do I go to meet him at the airport?" "Miyahara will know what has to be done. I have already informed him of Mr. Albert's trip - leave the arrival in Miyahara's hands. He will get the factory people to meet him. Let's keep it a Japanese thing. You should meet him in the lobby of your hotel."

Doreen then said "Do not change any plans on his account. He is planning to tag along with you – no pun intended. I am sure you will work it out." She then hung up and I stood there for a while staring at the phone. I hung up and walked out of the office and found Hiro. I told him of Albert's imminent arrival. Hiro smiled and said, "Don't be concerned - you are running a good show and Albert is no dummy. He will let you continue." I was surprised he said that. I thanked him for his hospitality, showed him I was again wearing his special Omega watch and I went on my way to our Far East Office.

CHAPTER Thirty-three
The 'Incident'

When I arrived in his office Alex was smoking. He had a concerned look and the jovial attitude he has shown me seemed to be pushed away. Alex got to business very quickly. He said, "After the war there was chaos in Japan. Miyako and I were scrounging for food and trying to sell some possessions for water. We were surviving when one day in the thick woods we found an American soldier in the brush. He was an Army Ranger who somehow managed to keep himself alive hiding not far from where we built our home"

"We secretly got him into the house and tended to his wounds and brought him back to health. He was terribly dehydrated and had a broken arm. He said, he was working undercover for about three years. I asked if anyone else was with him and he said, 'No - they all are dead.' The war was over but Luke Albert was too weak for us to bring him to the authorities."

"After a couple of weeks I made contact with the Russian Embassy and because I spoke Russian and Japanese fluently I got a job as a translator. There were weekly dinners at the embassy and Miyako and I were invited. We would see these enormous displays of huge amounts of food in the embassy. We figured they wouldn't miss a couple of kerchiefs of food and they didn't. That food was what the doctor ordered and we were able to bring Luke back to his full health.

"As his extraordinary physical abilities came back he started to feel like a whole man again. He thanked us over and over again for saving his life. He thought it was time for him to reappear. He was tired of being a shadow with no support. He asked me to bring him to Tokyo so he could meet with his people. He said, he also wanted to see if he could get us a US passport. In my thinking – all I thought he was doing was expressing his good feelings for us – I thought an American passport was just a dream.

"I drove Luke to General MacArthur's office opposite the Imperial Place. He got out wearing his uniform cleaned and patched by Miyako. It didn't look too bad – from a distance. Albert showed the rank of lieutenant. I waited an hour and no Albert. I was getting nervous. Especially, when an armed group of four men came to me and asked me to get out of the car. I was searched, then with two guards in front and two in back, I was marched and surely thought I was going to jail for some sort of infraction.

"We got to the steps of the building and there was Albert with a heavyset major. He said, "The major is going to employ you. Major Gordon has been in charge of redoing the bathrooms to make them into western style. No one in his staff speaks Japanese. His best example of what has happened is that he wanted to raise the urinals in the men's room. They were just too low for us to use.

183

"He asked the Japanese workers to raise them. They did - they made them chest high - impossible to use. The Americans who beat the emperor obviously had to be very tall - just not quite that tall. You straighten that out and you've got yourself a job. Stay with us for at least six months and we will get you and your wife a US passport as a bonus and a thank you from the general himself." Alex then said, "I signed on without even asking what I would be paid.

"After the occupation I lost track of Albert. I did hear he was still involved in covert work. A couple of friends from the time of the occupation had a chance meeting with him on a street in Hamburg, Germany - he totally ignored them. That was very unlike Luke Albert.

"After a few years, he returned to the Orient. He was a mess. He had just lost a partner in a shooting in Munich that he blamed himself for. He felt he didn't respond to the signs of what was going down quickly enough. She was more then his working partner – she was his lover.

"Miyako and I tried to console him and nurse him back to health – a second time. He seem to be coming along when the Company offered him the opportunity to slow down and establish TAG Photographic and tie up the best lines possible in Japan for distribution in the United States. He accepted the job."

"He devoted himself to his work twenty-four hours a day seven-days per week. He made contacts and arrangements with the old Nikon network. He and I didn't realize it but the shooting in Germany was constantly eating away at him. He went on a trip to Hong Kong. Somehow he got involved with a prostitute and started on opium. He fell into an opium-induced trance that lasted several days. Photographs were taken of him and they were shown to him when he came to and appeared sober.

"He was threatened that the pictures would appear in Washington if he didn't cooperate. Albert said, 'Send the photographs to Washington' and walked out of the meeting. They ultimately did send the photographs – Albert went to Washington. He was slapped on the wrists and told not to travel until he could pass the Company's physical and mental tests. They didn't want him to travel until he had a clean bill of health.

"In actuality, the powers who oversaw Albert had no choice. Albert became very important to the TAG operation. All of the contacts with the factories had become very close personal friends of Albert's. It was Albert's territory and the people on the other end of the agreements respected that. Robert, you are really one of the first people to visit Japan on behalf of TAG. Albert greased the way for you with extensive telephone calls and telexes. I was instructed to assist you in anyway I could. – That is the story except for one key point – the person who arranged for the prostitute to meet Albert was Madame Chang."

CHAPTER Thirty-four
The Jewish Community Center Of Tokyo

Alex drove me back to the hotel. I didn't say a word – I was thinking about what he told me. It was a heck of a story and I guess I should feel that I was being groomed for the continuation of TAG.

Albert never consulted with his overseers to go on this trip. He obviously hasn't finished his medical work. He must have decided that this was retirement for him and he was taking care of business by joining me and giving me as much assistance as possible. He must have been going stir crazy and decided to face whatever music he will have to face when he gets back. He either gets another slap on his wrists or he will be asked to leave.

I got out of the car and Alex said, "I will pick you up at 10:00 AM tomorrow." I said, "I was looking forward to it and I will be downstairs by 10:00 – Bye." I walked in and checked my messages and there was the one promised by Doreen. I also had a telex with Luke Albert's itinerary and that a suite has been ordered in the Imperial Palace Hotel.

I was beat. The throbbing in my leg was getting fierce and it was sapping all of my energy. Fortunately I had not made any plans this evening. I decided to stay in my room, order room service and get to bed early. I showered, changed my dressing which seemed a little better – not as oozy - got dressed in a hotel yukata – (robe). Then I ordered and American favorite for dinner – a rare hamburger with French fries and a bottle of Kirin beer. At the last moment I also ordered a bowl of onion soup because I decided I was very hungry.

In no time it seemed there was a knock on my door and the waiter wheeled in my repast. It was beautifully set-up with a rose, white tablecloth and napkin and a sterling silver place setting. I was told to roll the cart out of my room when I was finished.

The onion soup had a thick layer of cheese on it with a hard piece of toast floating in the center. The soup was delicious. The hamburger didn't quite taste American – it seemed sweeter but it was very good. I drank my beer and tried to relax.

I gave Debbie a call and she asked how my wound was and I told her I was coming along - not to worry. She was very busy with her work and enjoying it. That made me feel good - she wasn't sitting at home pining away for me. She asked if I was on schedule and coming home on Friday of next week and I said, "I think I can clear everything up by then." "What would you like to do when you get home?" she asked. I said, "first I want a home cooked meal – something simple like meatloaf – that would be great! Then I would want another meal which was all of you." She sighed and said, "I love you and I said the same and we hung up.

It was only 8:30 PM but I was ready for bed. I turned off the light, placed my pistol under one of the four pillows on the bed and covered myself with the huge soft blanket and fell into a very deep sleep.

The buzz – buzz of the telephone went off and it was my morning wakeup call. A live person on the other end said, "Mr. Schein, it is 6:30 in the morning on Sunday" and gave the weather as I hung up before she finished. I rolled out of bed and struggled to my feet. It was dark in the room and I made my way into the bathroom banging against the walls trying to find the door to the bathroom.

I found my way in and splashed water in my face saying, "I must have slept ten hours straight through." I was reminded that I had to pee and then took a shower and did my morning ministrations. I re-taped my dressing and felt much better looking at my wound. It was healing and I didn't notice any more oozing. In fact, unless I was imagining it, I felt as though I was no longer walking with a limp.

I decided I should get dressed in my slacks and blue blazer, go down and get some juice and coffee and catch up on the world by reading the Japan Times or the Mianuchi English newspapers. I had a couple of hours to kill and it would be good to vegetate for a bit.

I went into the Orchid Room, which was empty and was seated at a table in the middle of the room – all by myself. Juice, coffee and croissant were what I ordered. I figured if the food at the Jewish Community Center didn't appeal to me - I was at least covered. There was nothing remarkable about the front page of the paper. The Korean War was in negotiations at Panmunjon the Dodgers lost to the Yankees and from what I could see the world wasn't coming to end.

That was until I turned to read the third page. This was the traditional local news page. There was a picture of the bodies of Fukuchi and Kobi with the headline "Yakuza Mixed Up in International Theft and Domestic Security Plot." The person who was doing the reporting was Chief of Police Icihiro Hiro of the Domestic Crime Agency.

Hiro was quoted, "The Yakuza tried to steal an important piece of computer equipment and was stopped only after the unnecessary killing of two members who worked for Mitsubishi Heavy Industries and Nippon Kogaku. The names are being withheld for the sake of privacy for the families. More details will be made available as the information is released from the prosecutor's office.

I guess what Hiro is indirectly saying, "Mess with me and I will turn the press onto you and the people will turn away from you." The Yakuza is Japan's Mafia but to a good portion of people they are looked at as the modern day Robin Hood. It's an interesting strategy I thought, if anything it will stop all of the whispering and backbiting going on in the police department and the government offices. I signed my bill and went out to sit in the lobby.

I sat down in a comfortable cloth chair and sank into the pillows. I had a full view of the lobby and the front door of the hotel. There must have been five or six guys walking back and forth in the lobby, each holding a small gift box and anxiously looking at his watch. I ended up calling this the Sunday escort parade or the Sunday prostitute walk. Each one of the guys was waiting for a prearranged 'escort'. When she came through the front doors the hugging and kissing going on was something you would expect to see in the movies. This was good fun to watch. The gifts, when opened, were broaches or pins or something in gold. They all quickly left the building to grab a taxi or a waiting car.

I recognized one of the guys from the industry. Joe Abbot was the distributor of Bronica in the States. Joe was a real cocksman – he tried to get into the pants of any skirt he could in Japan. I never saw him involved with anyone in the States but I think he did the same there as well. He bragged that he "never paid for it. Everything was always free". Joe was noted for being very cheap – the Jack Benny of our industry. I'm sure he didn't pay a lot, but he paid. If he didn't pay for the girl then he paid by giving her an expensive gift. I guarantee he then brought a gift home to his wife that was equal or better.

I looked around the lobby and I noticed something that caught me by surprise. I saw two of Hiro's men. They were not in their traditional dark suits but were wearing sport clothing like everyone else in the lobby. I guess they were 'undercover'. I recognized them because I remembered their faces from either following me or from Hiro's office. That is good, I thought. I was happy to see this.

Alex and his wife were on time at 10:00 and as planned I was standing outside. I noticed I still had my escort of Hiro's men. The ride to the Jewish Community Center was about fifteen minutes. We came to a gated house and were let in by a security guard at the entrance. The building was pure English style and was majestic. I asked the history and Alex said that a Japanese general and his family owned it for many years.

As we went inside I was given a tour of the Synagogue, the classrooms and the rabbi's quarters. The rabbi was named Tokia and he was originally from New York City. He was fluent in Japanese and had even written a couple of books in Japanese. We went downstairs to the Community Room.

Tables were set up – round and long tables – throughout the room. There was a separate one step higher level where members without guests dined.

When we sat down and made ourselves comfortable a number of the people came over to say good morning. As I was introduced I noticed a number of them had accents that later I was told was Israeli. Alex said, "Some of them spend months here and eat us out of house and home" he chuckled.

The first item that appeared on our table was vodka. It was in a small clear glass decanter and was ice cold. Alex said, "If you eat with me here you first must have vodka." I said to myself, "On an empty stomach I don't know if I can handle this." I sipped from the small glass and Alex said "Down the hatch - none of this sipping business." I complied and felt the warmth of the vodka as it went down. Alex immediately filled my glass. I said, "First some food then more vodka." He laughed and said "fine."

The food varied from pierogies to kugel to gefulte fish to chicken soup with kreplach, potato pancakes and fricassee. The usual fare was also available: bagels, cream cheese lox, egg salad, tuna fish salad and a few different types of herrings. All the various Jewish holidays were covered. It was a feast.

The problem with the meal was Alex pushing me to keep up with him drinking vodka. Finally, I gather that Miyako had had enough of his bad manners, pulled on his shirt sleeve and whispered in his ear. I guess it was something like "Enough already with the vodka - you have to drive later. Stop embarrassing your guest." I held up my hands in surrender and said, "I can't eat another thing."

Over coffee we planned out our week and how we would handle any situation that might come about with Luke Albert.

Alex didn't know that much about my negotiations with the Chang family and for the time being I thought it best to keep it that way. I did say the Changs are involved with why Albert is coming to Japan. All Alex replied was "I am aware of that. That is why Doreen called me." Hey, maybe he is already filled in but it is not my place to bring him into this. If Albert wants to do that OK - that is his prerogative.

Alex and Miyako drove me back to the hotel in the early afternoon. Believe it our not – Alex drove with no problems that I could see from drinking all that vodka. However, he did drive very slowly. As I was exiting the car Alex said he would come back about 5:30 to help welcome Luke Albert. Before walking into the hotel I noticed that Hiro's men were still with me.

I checked my messages and found one from Bob who indicated that he would come by in the evening so that we could catch up. Madame Chang was in the lobby talking to a couple of unsavory-looking characters. As I walked by I nodded and she nodded back. I guess I am not on her hit list. I took the elevator, got off on my floor and made it into the room when I realized that I'd had too much vodka. I needed a couple of hours to sleep it off. I placed a wakeup call, took a couple of Alka-Seltzers and crashed on top of the bed coverings, out cold.

CHAPTER Thirty-five
The Arrival Of Luke Albert

The telephone buzzed and it was Alex who said he was a little early and would be waiting in the lobby. I pulled myself together and found it was a heck of a job to freshen up and clear my head.

I went downstairs to the lobby and noticed that Madame Chang was still there and had a different group with her and Hyacinth had joined her. There was Alex in his relaxing clothing – golf shirt and slacks – all fresh and raring to go. He stood up as I came over and said, "These were the only chairs I could find together. Luke should be along anytime or if his plane was delayed we could be here for hours." "That's the breaks" I said, trying to be philosophical.

Soon thereafter I started to notice a few of the morning suited managers lining up by the front door and opposite them was a line-up of bellhops. They had gotten advance notice that the Imperial Palace Hotel limousine was arriving with a special guest. A car pulled up to the front door and out stepped Luke Albert to a hearty greeting from two of the doormen.

You would think it was old home week the way Albert was greeted by the managers. I guess it was. Albert hadn't been in Japan for at least two years and before that he was a frequent visitor – at the very least one week a month. The managers all knew him and he seemed to know them. There was much bowing and finally he was led inside where Alex and I greeted him.

Luke wore a dark suit and a formal looking tie. He looked rested – the flight evidentially went smoothly. I then noticed a rotund man in a colored shirt with and open neck button and loose tie wearing a tweedy sports jacket. He had sandals on and his entire presentation looked rumpled. Albert introduced George Michaels who was a computer guru from Washington.

I later learned that Michaels was one of the best-known computer wizards in the States. He worked with the largest computers available of the time. He was best known to have written a treatise on underground nuclear explosions and their atmospheric effects at Lawrence Radiation Laboratories. Michaels was not just a guru of computers but an honest to goodness genius. He obviously was the right person to evaluate the 5" floppy disc that had caused all of the commotion.

Albert had a smile when he shook my hand. He seemed to be happy to see me and that gave me a kick. He then hugged Alex and whispered a few things in his ear. They both laughed. Albert said he would like to get unpacked and wondered if we could meet in the Starlight Lounge and get caught up. Alex and I nodded and Albert's procession of managers and bellhops continued to the elevator. George

Michaels had to go to the front desk to sign in and then a manager and bellhop took him to his room.

As Albert's party was walking away I noticed Madame Chang looked in his direction and then quickly turn away. This might be very interesting, I thought. I tapped Alex on the shoulder and said, "Did you notice Chang's reaction when she recognized Albert?" He said, "Yes and that is what Luke whispered in my ear. He spotted her as soon as he stepped into the lobby."

We found our usual place in the Starlight Lounge. Soon, thereafter Luke Albert and, trailing just behind him, George Michaels joined us. When I saw Michaels I said to myself, "This guy looks more like a linebacker on the NY Giants than a computer guy. God, he's massive."

I said, "Bob Claypool and I think Lt. Cmdr. Andrew Hardwick will be joining us in about half an hour or so. They should also be involved in briefing you." Albert said, "Whatever you have planned is fine. Robert, I do not want to interfere with what you are doing. You have accomplished what I would expect a seasoned field operative to have accomplished. You have done a good job – especially for your first time out. Now, how is your leg wound?" "I am doing fine with it - no problem," I said. God, he he's massive."

Albert and Alex made small talk catching up on old friends while I had a conversation with George. George seemed like a gentle giant who couldn't care less about what he looked like. I learned he had a family with thirteen children. I couldn't get over it – 13 children! It also didn't appear that he had any intention to stop bringing children into the world - "The more then merrier," he said.

George then explained he needed about one hour to

properly identify the disc as being the correct or original disc then about another hour to establish if it was used to make copies. He had brought all the necessary tools including a device to run the floppy disc. That was one of the reasons they needed so many bellhops. The stuff he brought was heavy and he must have traveled with eight or ten boxes. He seemed very confident he could do what was being asked of him.

We then talked a bit about some sightseeing and I lamely explained that I hadn't much time to even get to the Ginza much less visit a tourist attraction. The closest I got to sightseeing was with the president of Mamiya, and he got shot during our walk.

Bob finally arrived with Andrew Hardwick. I started the briefing and made it as complete as I possibly could recall. I covered all of the bases from the submarine periscope cameras – the Nikon 'F' - the Digital Fiber Optics Scope, my abduction, the recapture of the disc, the recovery of Roth and the killing of Juniper Chang. Bob and Andrew filled in details as I went along.

It took us about an hour to go over the full review. Throughout the whole time Albert, Michaels and Triguboff listened intently. Albert interrupted only three times to better understand a point that wasn't clear to him. The hour seemed to pass in a flash. I started recounting everything that happen and it was over.

We ordered another round of drinks; martinis for Albert, vodka straight up for Triguboff, Kirin beers for Michaels, Hardwick and Claypool and Chivas for me. We also added a couple of orders of a variety of dim sum to hold us until we decided what we were going to do for dinner. If I hadn't done that I am not sure we could have kept Michael's stomach from growling.

Luke Albert then started methodically to lay out what he thought was important just as any good general would – he was issuing orders. He said, "The Yakuza are not done yet. They will try to do something to recapture the disc. They might look for a trade but, then they have to have something of value to trade – a person or a group of people for instance. They might decide to do something that will scare the living daylights out of the general public and thus the government. I am not sure what their devious minds are working on but I assure you - something is percolating as we sit here having our drinks.

"This is what I think we should be doing tomorrow. I will call upon Ichiro Hiro in the morning. It is a courtesy call giving him a chance to say hello and update me. I will tell him what our plans are to get through the week. I will also ask him to let George look at the disc.

"There is a definite time schedule here. We meet with the brokers Wednesday and we are supposed to complete the deal by Friday. If Friday comes and goes and they have nothing to sell to us they then will disappear and we go about our lives again. Robert, George and I will return to New York on Saturday the latest and put all this behind us.

"After my meeting with Hiro I will visit Dr. Nagaoka and pay my respects. I will also take the opportunity to finalize the details of the program we offered to get the new camera into production.

"Robert will go on with his planned meeting with Mr. Ari. You have to be very careful here Robert. Ari is known to have close contacts with the Yakuza. It has been stated that they were the original moneylenders for Tamron to get started and Ari arranged that. I recommend that Alex accompany you.

"I will join you both with George for the evening's geisha

party that Ari has organized. That should prove to be interesting. It wouldn't surprise me if a couple of the Yakuza were members of his board of directors.

"On Tuesday I would like to see what Robert has reported on at the Ohi-Machi factory in the Mitsubishi/Nikon clean rooms. I want to be able to fully support his information when we talk to the Navy Department in Washington. Unless you have other plans I would assume you will accompany me to the factory." "I'm good with that," I said.

Albert continued, "If all goes well I would like to gather our forces together Tuesday afternoon to plan our moves for Wednesday and the rest of the week." Albert's comments were short and to the point. It actually felt good to have him around. I was perfectly happy being a cast member instead of having to give the orders.

Bob said, "Where do you want us stationed – if at all - in this?" "Oh yes" Albert said. "I imagine Hiro will have his people all over us during the day. I would like Andrew's team to be available and on location in the evening wherever this geisha party is to take place. It would be nice if you could do it just the way you executed the protection of Robert when he was abducted.

"However, this time I do not want to inform Hiro or the local authorities of what we are doing. This will be an independent plan. In case the Yakuza have infiltrated any of our protectors I want to have a reliable backup plan. That is where Andrew's Seal team comes in. Please remember this has great legal, international and territorial problems. We must be very careful and very positive, if and when, we might have to get actively in the game."

"Bob, you will be the coordinator of everything. If we get

into any trouble you have to be able to reach Andrew's team, Hiro and the local authorities." I interrupted and said, "I do have this Omega watch that is a transmitter direct to Hiro." Albert said, "I am aware of that. I think I prefer that you wear it. It also has a homing chip in it that will help them to locate you, should you get separated and any problem arises."

Alex chimed in, "Luke, I think I am too old for this. Bob has been introduced as a director of TAG and maybe he should sit alongside of Robert. I'll assist with everything but at arm's length. I am more comfortable with that then being on the front line. It also is more my place as TAG's agent. I still have to live here after you guys leave. After all, I am not an official member of the Company."

Albert said, "I understand and agree with your suggestion. Bob, you accompany Robert for the day and Alex will help coordinate the background activities. Actually that might work out better for all of us." Bob and I nodded that we were in.

In the back of my mind I thought this is exciting but what am I getting excited about – I could be killed. This is more frightening than exciting – dummy, wake up. Albert made this all sound as though it was a maneuver of troops. I am glad he is doing the planning and not me.

After his briefing I said to myself – "I realize I have been very lucky these last few days. I hope my luck holds out the rest of the week. I'm not sure this is what I bargained for when I took this job – it seems I just fell into it – but as bad as this may sound - I love it. Maybe I am more comfortable with this danger stuff then I think I am. I must be out of my head."

The meeting had come to an end. George was the first one to speak, "When do we eat?" he asked and we all laughed.

Alex, Bob and Andrew begged off and left. Luke, George and I went to the mezzanine floor and chose an Italian restaurant. The saucy veal and pasta dinner was way too much for me to finish. George looked at my plate and I didn't have to worry about leaving anything over. In fact George cleaned Luke's plate as well.

CHAPTER Thirty-six
A Morning Of Surprises

I was awaken by my usual call and decided that I would try to do my Canadian Air Force exercise routine. I barely got through it but I did it and that made me feel good. My thigh wound was healing and I was walking better. After showering and re-taping I got dressed and went to breakfast where George and Luke Albert were already ordering and drinking coffee. Every few minutes people would stop by the table to welcome Albert to Japan and say hello.

When Scheonheimer stopped by he grabbed a chair and spoke with Albert as though I wasn't in the room. The conversation was about the Minolta distributorship. Luke, without a second thought, referred him to me which made my buttons pop. Scheonheimer looked at me and I repeated the line I had said to him earlier. "Our manufacturers would not be happy with us if TAG took on another camera line." Albert said, "There you have it Fritz. I certainly wouldn't recommend it to my board if there is such resistance from our current suppliers."

Fritz Scheonheimer knew who TAG really was. He thought our power could overcome any objections we might get from our vendors. Before Albert could say anything further I said, "First, we do not want do something that our competition could not do. That would be unfair competition. Second, our marketing setup is now organized for the lines we currently represent and adding Minolta would put us in a very difficult position with manpower.

"Third, to add another line, especially when we will be introducing a revolutionary new camera to the market, will spread us too thin. In fact, it might weaken our other manufacturers efforts. To jeopardize all that just doesn't make any sense." Fritz grunted, got up, nodded, and left the table.

I held my breath for taking such direct participation in the discussion and expected Albert to admonish me or kick me under the table. All he said was, "What's next." That simple comment made me feel super. He was acknowledging that I handled the situation correctly. Just then, the Changs with a large group of people entered the room. Madame Chang and Hyacinth came directly over to our table. We all stood up and said "Good morning."

Albert said, "Please accept my regrets for not being able to attend the memorial service for Juniper – I arrived in the late afternoon. I am very sorry for your loss." Madame Chang said, "It was an unnecessary loss. I am most saddened that this happened to my daughter. However", she continued – "life goes on."

"I imagine Robert has filled you in about our meeting on Wednesday to plan the exchange?" Albert said "Yes – I have brought one of our computer experts with me" and he introduced George Michaels. Chang gave George a once over and with a disapproving look said, "We won't need your expert until Friday."

"We would like to meet for lunch at Chin Zan-So with you, Robert, Mama Cherry and Mr. Cao, - shall we say about noon?" I interrupted, "We might like to add director Bob Claypool to the meeting." Madame Chang said, "That will not be necessary – we do not need so many witnesses to our meeting. Now that Mr. Albert is present, I am sure he will be able to fill in his board of directors with all of the information that is necessary."

Throughout the conversation Hyacinth stood by her mother's side not saying a word. As the two ladies, who were still dressed in black, walked away you could not help but notice Hyacinth with the grace of her walk and the way she carried herself. Everyone in the room – male and female – was watching her until she sat down.

Albert spoke first – "I wonder what she is thinking? She has dictated the meeting; she is dictating who is to attend and she has selected a pretty secluded location. The location works better for us but I think we might have to rethink some of our plan. That will wait until tomorrow.

"OK," he went on, "George you get all of your gear ready to come over to Hiro's office at about mid-day. I will have them send a car for you after I get Hiro's approval to test the disc. Spend as much time as you need to evaluate the disc as long as we have definite confirmation the disc is real before our meeting Wednesday. If Madame Chang has something up her sleeve about that disc I want to know what it is.

"Robert – what do you have in store for you this morning?"

"Not very much," I said, "I will prepare for the Tamron meeting but before that I think I will take a few minutes and go to the American Arcade and buy my wife a gift." Again, to my surprise Albert said, "Good idea. In fact I want to give you two of my business cards to visit two old friends who will properly take care of you.

"First go to the Arcade and visit the Hiyashi 'Used' Kimono Shop – it's the first shop on the left as you enter the arcade. Pick out the most appealing wedding kimono for your wife." "That is a very good idea but a wedding kimono, I think is a little too rich for my budget." "Robert" Albert said, "This is my gift to your wife. All you do is pick out the one you like and give the shop owner my card. You are not to pay for it."

I started to say, "That is very generous but unnecessary …" Albert interrupted saying, "When one of my people does a good job and gets hurt on top of that don't tell me what is necessary or unnecessary. It is my pleasure. George, go with Robert to make sure he does what I am asking him to do." George smiled and nodded his head.

Albert, who I thought was being very generous – left me speechless. He continued, "Buy a piece of jewelry for your wife like a broach or pearls or whatever appeals to you. Show the manager – Mr Takai - of Nakai Jewelers my card and you will get the best pricing possible. You will not have to do any bargaining and you will be getting the finest quality merchandise available in the store. Have a good time with your shopping and enjoy your morning." Albert got up and said, "Let's get on our way" and the meeting ended.

George and I went through the lobby, made a right turn and we were only yards from the American Arcade. We walked in and on the left - just as Albert described was Hiyashi Kimono. There were hundreds of wedding kimonos in neat piles. I showed the manager Albert's card and her face immediately light up. "Albert-San is well?" she asked. "Very well," I replied, "He will probably visit you during this trip." This seemed to make her happy.

I said, "I had no idea how to buy a kimono." "Honto?" (True) "Hai - honto" (Yes it is true). She went into an explanation as if she were a grade school teacher. She explained the difference in pricing - grade of silk, gold weaving, design, and so on. She then said many families could spend between US $20,000 to $50,000 for a new wedding kimono. If the family is in a financially tight spot, they will then sell the kimono after the wedding to a place like mine. Unfortunately, once it is used for a wedding the value of the kimono is only a pittance. The kimono will most likely only be sold to a giajin (foreigner).

The kimonos were something to behold. They were beautiful. I finally selected a white silk one with a magnificent woven picture of a large bird in flight filling the entire back. The bird was woven in gold and red threads. The manager had one of her girls model it for me and both George and I were impressed with it. I said "I will take this one and thank you for the lesson." It seemed that the manager already knew that it was going to be charged. She didn't even ask me my name and said it will be delivered to my room in the Imperial Palace Hotel. I gave her my maichi for future visits and she bowed - George and I nodded back and continued our walk.

"That was easy" George said. I replied, "If you live on an expense account all the time then you could afford to live this way. That was an incredible experience." George said, "That was fine - now I am hungry." "Come on George - you just ate breakfast." "Hey," he replied, "That was an hour ago." We stopped at a confectionery and we picked up some yokan, which is a sweet bean cake dessert. Then George purchased a

Coke from a stand and that seemed to keep him happy for a while.

I was looking around and I noticed that Hiro's men were not far behind keeping a watchful eye on us. Heck, walking with George - you couldn't miss us if you were trying to.

We then found Nakai Jewelers and talked to the manager Takai. He also was happy to hear that Albert was visiting Japan and asked that we send his yiroshku (regards). We said we would and George and I started to look at the jewelry. Takai was very patient. He took out bags of unstrung pearls and explained the differences among the pearls he was showing us. We got a whole lecture on pearls.

After he spoke I felt very confident and ordered an opera length, pink tinted, 8mm size pearl necklace with a sterling silver clasp. I also asked for a pair of drop earrings to match. He then showed me the presentation box it would be put in and will have it delivered to my room this evening. The cost for the whole thing was $400.00. That's a lot of money I said to myself. I really want to bring something back to Debbie to mark my first trip to Japan. Takai then stated they would probably be appraised for more then $1,500 in the States. That did it. I bought the set.

It was more then I had hoped to spend but that's from learning too much about buying something you knew nothing about before you arrived. A little knowledge is dangerous and expensive for the pocket book. George spent about $600 on small gifts, mostly pins for his wife and children.

All this spending of money made me hungry. I said, "George, let me treat you to a yakatory lunch." He asked, "What is that?" "Grilled chicken on a stick. I am sure you will like it." I had asked the concierge about a yakatory counter nearby because I had heard so much about them. Around the corner from the arcade was a small shop – maybe the size of a single desk office that had six bar stools. They were all occupied. The food was cooked on charcoal grills right in front of you. I guess this is the equivalent of Japanese fast food. We waited in back of the diner and as the patrons finished they cleared out.

When George and I sat the chef excitedly shouted "Tahoe!" - pointing at George. "Tahoe, nani desu ka" (What is Tahoe?) I asked. "Sumo Yokazuna" (Sumo Wrestling Grand Champion) he answered. All I said was, "Hai – wakarimas" (Yes I understand) In Japanese we played with the idea that George was considering sumo wrestling and was all had a good laugh. All this was going on while we were ordering the special of the day – which is the same thing every day - and enjoying the freshly grilled chicken. It came as quickly as you ordered it. I think George had three orders to my one. We finished lunch and went back to the hotel. George went to his room to gather his gear and wait for Hiro's car. I wanted to study the Tamron situation and I had about an hour or so to kill before I was going to be picked up.

Chapter Thirty-seven
The Tamron Visit Proved To Be A Little More Then Optics

I decided that I wanted to stretch my legs and see what the action was in the hotel lobby. I went down about a half an hour before my pickup was expected. I found a nice soft chair and started to look around to see if any of my escort parade people were marching around. Just as I thought I could pick one out one, Hyacinth Chang came over and sat down in the chair on my right.

She was still wearing black but this time it was a tailored suit with boots that had tall black heels. Her accessories were all in pearl – large pearls. This was no $20 suit you would find in S. Klein on the Square in New York City. Her mother was sitting across the lobby talking to Al Bernard.

Hyacinth started, "I am sorry we had to meet under the conditions of my sister's death. Juniper told me that she had her eye on you and that she offered to show you some interesting products in the New Territories of Hong Kong and maybe even China." "Yes" I replied, "She did make such an offer." "Are you still interested" she asked. "I could never turn down an offer from such a beautiful woman as you." She ignored the compliment and asked. "Then we can try to arrange a visit?" She asked. "I am sure we can but not on this trip. I think it would be best for me to get home by or on the weekend. I am bushed and need some time for my leg to heal."

"May I correspond with you" she asked. "Of course – please do," I said. I again gave her my business card but this time I put my home phone on it saying, "If you needed me and wanted reach me please feel free to call me at home." "Mr. Schein ..." I interrupted her and said, "Please call me Robert." "All right Robert - I hope we will be able to continue business after tomorrow's meeting. Thank you," she said, got up and walked away.

As I was watching her walk - and she had a walk - I said, "I wonder what she meant by her last comment." Just then Bob Claypool sat down where Hyacinth was sitting and commented You got one killed, you are going to try for two." Sarcastically I said - "And good day to you too."

A bellboy came up to us and said "Schein-San your car is waiting." A new black Mitsubishi sedan was waiting and the driver was holding the rear door open. The car even smelled new. It was very comfortable and I said to Bob - "We haven't seen any of these in the States yet." Bob replied, "If I had any money I would invest in Mitsubishi stock." About an hour later through heavy traffic on the outskirts of Tokyo we came to a small factory complex made up of very old buildings.

Mr. Ari and his staff were in the small courtyard to greet us. Just as we were shaking hands Hiro's men pulled into the courtyard and everyone seemed surprised. Mr. Ari said to his staff, "Diajobo des" (It's all right). Obviously he hadn't filled in his staff that I traveled with an escort.

We went into the building and after a short walk in a narrow corridor came to a small conference room fitted out with gray steel chairs and conference table. It was very clean but very spartan. We all had tea in large mugs and were introduced to Ari's chief lens designer Kawakami and his chief of staff and director Toki. As each one was introduced he bowed his head and we bowed back.

A translator who sat in back of Ari - a young lady whose name was never given to us, assisted the conversation. Ari struggled with English but spoke it. The young lady was there for him as a security blanket. He would lean back from time to time or she would lean forward and whisper something in his ear.

Tamron was a subcontractor to just about all of the camera and lens manufacturers in Japan. They manufactured many different sized lens elements and sold them to the primary camera makers. Ari also developed a line of Tamron lenses that used an adapter system to allow a lens to fit many cameras. Ari called it the Tamron Adaptall Lens System.

It was a good idea for the smaller camera stores. The store could purchase fewer lenses thus using less money for inventory and many adapters that were cheap. If you didn't want to spend a lot of money on accessory lenses you would purchase 'off-brand' lenses. This was generally a good lens and the adapter mounting system fit a variety of cameras. The popular camera makers like Leica, Exacta, Canon, Nikon, etc. hated this sales approach because they would be closed out of selling their brand label lenses. It was tough competition.

For Tamron to stay ahead of its competition its lenses had to be innovative and ahead of the camera manufacturer's lenses. For example, a camera manufacturer sells a 135mm f4 lens - that would mean Tamron would try to make a 135mm f3.5 lens and sell it at a lower price then the camera manufacturers. The objective for Tamron was to beat the specifications and prices of the camera manufacturer. It was a good approach and TAG was making money with the lens line in the States.

Ari personally showed us around the factory. He would stop at a work station and talk to the worker, ask about his family or how he was feeling and would show us what part was being made. Ari never introduced us to anyone in particular; all we would do is look at the part that was handed to us, make eye contact with the employee, bow our heads and he or she would bow back. It was all very civilized, I thought.

The machine, lens shop and lens grinding facility were in old buildings but the machinery appeared to be new. In fact, I would say some of it was state-of-the-art. The thing that fascinated me was the lack of space between workers and machines. The lighting wasn't particularly good and the workers were literally on top on one another. Every inch of space was being used. You could never get away with this in the States, I thought.

I didn't know if Bob was interested or bored but this was my thing and I loved it. The place was jumping. It was very busy and all you heard was the machinery. No shouting, fighting or people goofing off. Incredible! We were making our way back to the conference room and Bob leaned over and said, "You have got to give it to these guys; I can see why they are so tough to compete with." I looked at Bob and said, "I am happy to see you are paying attention." He smiled and we arrived back in the quiet of the conference room.

211

On the table were samples of what Ari wanted to produce for the coming year. The lenses were all interesting. One in particular caught my eye. It was large in the mount area for a 200mm f4. "What camera does this fit on?" I asked. I guess I asked the right question because the Tamron people started to chatter with each other and Ari was beaming. Ari explained that will fit the new Nikon 'F' camera that is expected to come on the market shortly.

"Holy shit!" I said to myself. The camera is not even on the market and here was a lens ready to fit it made by a competitor. "How can you do this?" I asked. Ari explained that he was a supplier to Nippon Kogaku and was shown the plans for the 'F' many months ago." Tamron is a subcontractor to NK. We were asked to make some of the mounting parts and lens elements for them. When I saw the camera I asked for and was granted a license to manufacture, under Tamron's brand, an adapter to fit the 'F' camera and here it is." "Brilliant," I said.

I then handed over my folders of orders and projections. Toki immediately took them to the office area to review what I brought. We talked about marketing and what was currently happening - day to day - in the States. Toki returned about 30 minutes later and told Ari in Japanese that he would be very happy to see what Mr. Schein brought him. They were pleased with our order levels for the Tamron lens line. I gather we were their largest distributor.

Ari said, "I wish to go over the orders and projections tomorrow with my staff. According to Mr. Toki he feels that I will be happy with what you have brought. I wish to thank you very much." "You are quite welcome," I said. We were then were asked if there was anything else we wanted to discuss. I replied, "Thank you – we will do that over dinner with Mr. Albert present." Ari seemed satisfied with that and the meeting came to an end.

There was a commotion outside the conference room and there appeared in the doorway George Michaels and right behind him Luke Albert. With Michaels in the room the room suddenly felt very small. Albert and Ari were old friends and they welcomed each other like old friends - hugs and pats on the back.

Albert started out by saying "thank you for allowing us to visit you today and we are looking forward to this evening's party. This large person is our computer expert George Michaels and I hope Mr. Schein and Mr. Claypool were able to assist the factory with our projections and orders." Ari bowed his head and said "Hai". "So" Albert said, "Let's go to dinner so this large man won't eat the table we are sitting at." Everyone laughed and we started filing out of the room.

Michaels, Claypool and I got into one of the waiting cars. Albert and Ari went to another and the rest of the party went to a third car. In back of this procession was one of Hiro's cars. I thought, "This must be the 20th car I am in - in only a week's time. Visiting Japan as a businessman seems to be an exercise of getting in and out of cars." We drove out into the countryside, which was beautiful. Rolling farms that I assumed were rice fields and small homes were speckled throughout the scenery. We were only a few miles out of Tokyo and I was amazed at the open space.

During the trip George delivered the message that he had examined the 'real' thing today. The disc was the original and no copies had been made. I said, "Then they must know we have the disc - what the hell could be their game plan?" We all speculated what it might be for a while and then just stared outside the window as the scenery flashed by.

The ride was long but I guess after being cooped up in the concrete city of Tokyo the open space was a welcome change. We all seemed to mellow and that may have been the plan to set us up for the relaxing fun of a geisha party. We arrived at a quaint and probably very old building called the Geisha House. Actually there must have been four or five small old buildings in the area. It seemed to be set in the middle of nowhere.

We drove into the courtyard and started to get out of the cars when a horde of young girls dressed as geishas laughing and squealing came running out to grab our arms and walk us to the entrance of the building. There they took off our shoes and gave us slippers. We went inside and were directed - with a girl on each side holding onto our arms - down a narrow corridor to a very large tatami room. They then took off our slippers and we walked into the room wearing our socks.

The room was bright and had shoji screens around the perimeter and shoji screens that could be drawn closed in the middle to make two separate rooms. Half of the room was set up with a low black lacquered table, flowers beautifully set in small vases at each setting and cushions on the floor. Additionally, there were black lacquered armrests with a cushion on top to make you more comfortable. A few simple wall hangings were on the perimeter. Everywhere you looked you felt that wonderful austere, clean Japanese look. The room felt warm and welcome even with its spartan appearance.

There were eight place settings on the table. As we started to assemble around it a new member of the party arrived - a director by the name of Yoshio. Ari as well as the other two Tamron members reverently bowed to Yoshio. We were introduced and we traded our maichi. Yoshio's card just said Director, with no department.

Ari then seated us. Our side was Claypool, Albert, Schein

and Michaels. The other side was Kawakami, Ari, Yoshio and Toki. The seating setup is very important to the Japanese and was an indicator of power. If there were five people on each side of the table Albert and Ari would be in the center and the next in command on his right. In this case Ari and Albert were facing each other and Yoshio was facing me. We were recognized as the second in command. Again, the Japanese are very orderly people.

We had no idea who Yoshio was but he looked like a serious person who moved like a cat. He was very well coordinated and powerful looking for his small 5' tall frame. Ari must have felt our question because he said, "Yoshio-San is a very important person to Tamron because he is involved in the finances of the company. He has closely assisted us with our banking associations for many years." We all bowed our heads and on the surface accepted Ari's description.

All I could think of was Albert's warning that an interesting member or two might join us this evening. So this is what the Yakuza looks like up close. We made eye contact and sipped the tea that appeared before us. Now that everyone knew who everyone else was the party was to begin.

Ari clapped his hands twice and a shoji slid to the side and eight geishas entered holding sake decanters and small dishes of nuts, seaweed and other dried specialties. A geisha sat on the right of each of us. There was a pecking order here as well. The most trained or oldest geisha sat beside Albert and Ari and the next beside me and Yoshio and so on.

My geisha for the evening was stunning. Her features were just like the pictures of the painted Japanese dolls. I could see she was fairly young and was wearing a beautiful red decorated kimono with a gold obi (belt). The kimono had long sleeves down to the floor that indicated she was unmarried. A married woman normally wears sleeves halfway down to the floor. Geishas are usually unmarried.

Her hair was a traditionally black wig made up high and full with combs and trinkets stuck in it. The nape of her neck was exposed by the way her kimono was worn and her hair prepared. To Japanese this is very sensual. It wasn't too bad for me to appreciate either.

With the girls at the table there was a lot of chatter to Ari to translate and ask questions of us. Simple questions like how tall we were; or how heavy was George and did he ever see sumo? This was supposed to lighten everyone up and get an interaction between everyone. We were all drinking sake, holding up our cups saying compai (bottoms-up). We would empty them in one swallow. As soon as the cup was emptied the girls would fill them up. It was a no – no for you to fill your own. Decanters were shuttled into the room by other young ladies dressed in more subdued and traditional kimonos.

One by one each man was asked to take his jacket off and put on a short silk 'happy' coat. I took off my jacket and my pistol and slipped the shoulder holster and pistol in the fold of the jacket and placed it against the wall. The shoji screen in the middle of the room was pulled together to make the room smaller and more intimate. If a jacket was on this side of the screen it was moved by one of the ladies into the other room. I noticed that Albert did exactly what I did with his pistol. I believe Albert and I were the only people armed in the room.

Different courses of food arrived. This was the cold portion of the meal - sushi, sashimi plates with small side dishes of cuttle fish and salad. The one thing that continued without stop was the pouring of sake and your geisha reminding you to drink it up. The group was getting a little more demonstrative and louder. Yoshio had his arm around his geisha and was whispering in her ear. Ari kept touching his girl's shoulder. Our group was a little more reserved and kept our hands to ourselves.

We were all trying to talk to each other though no one understood what the other was saying. I pretended that I didn't understand Japanese but would somehow understand by my geisha's words and hand motions what she was saying. In fact, I was translating every word and found it hard to keep it hidden.

The geisha by Ari's side clapped her hands to get our attention then showed us an orange. She then put the orange in the crook of her neck and leaned over to Ari and passed it to him. Everyone started to giggle. The next geisha took the orange from Ari and passed to Yoshio. Everyone eagerly participated but the funniest one was probably poor George. Because of his size the geisha had difficulty trying to lean over to him to give him the orange. He was just too big for her to get in any position to pass it. George, being a good sport, finally lay down on his back and she dropped it to him. I think everyone really warmed up after that. The laughter sounded good.

After that game a couple of geishas went behind the shojis that parted the room. I could hear a sámi shan being tuned. The doors parted about halfway and we had a makeshift stage. In place was a sámi shan player, a reader or in this case a singer and in the center was Mr. Ari's geisha, who was the dancer. The sámi shan started up and the singer started to sing. The geisha started her dance using her fan as a key part of the dance. One side of the fan had a picture of snow to signify winter and the other side was a picture of cherry blossoms to signify spring. Her dance and song - which only had a few notes in its range - were beautiful to watch and listen to. At the end the dance we all loudly applauded. The screens were closed and instruments and accessories put away. They girls re-entered the room again and found their seats alongside their assigned guests.

My geisha got up and wanted to teach us a song and dance called the Coal Miner's Dance. She started to sing in a musical scale and show me the steps – la la la da – la la la da etc. While she was singing she seemed to be taking a step and imitating a digging motion – the song continued and the motion turned to throwing the dirt over her shoulder. Still singing she imitated pushing the dirt - and then a clap of her hands three times – and she would start over from the beginning.

Immediately, Ari and Albert got into the action showing everyone how to do it. Albert knew the steps well and stayed right alongside Ari and the geisha in perfect timing and rhythm. I got into it and Bob tried it. George shouted, "If I did that the floor would fall in." Everyone seemed to be having a lot of fun. When everyone stopped we all went to our seats and were treated to cold towels to help cool us down. The sake continued to be served. At this point it seemed like no one was feeling any pain. The geisha party was doing what it does best, relax everyone and have a good belly laugh or two.

The next course served was a hot pot of soybean cake and vegetables, a plate of teriyaki salmon and a plate of cooked unagi (eel). I don't think we knew the difference if it was good or bad but everyone was taught to say oshi-des (it is good). The food was fine. Geisha houses are not necessarily known for their food.

My geisha was kind of a party animal. She seemed to have a twinkle in her eye and was looking to try to get your attention. I looked at her and she held a fist and went into the motion of once, twice, three, shoot. I knew that – then she held out her hand in a fist. She wanted to play paper, rock and scissors. Ari explained she want to play 'strip' paper, rock and scissors. I said, I don't know about that. Everyone booed and chided me for not doing it. I had no choice.

They parted the screens and we became the attraction or performers. I won the first couple of rounds and all she took off was a comb and a string around her obi. I knew I was in trouble. Bob ran over to me and gave me a quick "sake fix!" he yelled. I then lost about six times in a row and was down to my underwear. What do I do now I shouted? Albert walked over to the screens and closed them and we were in the room all alone. There was great laughter on the other side of the shoji screen. "Whew" was all I could say. My geisha smiled and went over to pick up my trousers and helped me put them on. "Thank God," I said aloud.

As I was putting on my socks I heard a crash and hysterical screaming. I paused for a second - then dove for my jacket against the wall. There was more yelling and a shot – then another shot. I pulled my pistol out. Just then the shoji was slowly being slipped open and a gun preceded a man who was obviously looking for me. As he turned toward me I cocked my .45-caliber revolver with my right hand and fired off two rounds with my left hand and hit him squarely in the head. He was thrown back by the bullets' impact and went down. That started a machine gun spray right across the center of the shoji screens above my head. Both the geisha and I were lying as flat as we could on the floor.

Suddenly there was more shooting and more screaming but not in our direction. I peered through the holes in the shoji screen and saw a gunman in black shooting in the outside corridor direction. One of the machine gunners had his back to me and I fired and he went down. That caused everyone to scurry. The gunmen were on the run and being picked off by the cavalry, I thought. - Good old Lt. Cmdr. Hardwick.

I cautiously started to enter the other room on my hands and knees. I had picked up Albert's pistol, which was against the wall in his jacket. When I saw him I slid it over to him. He immediately cocked the .9mm Beretta and was in a ready position when we heard "This is Hardwick coming in – don't shoot." We lowered our pistols and took a deep breath.

Claypool rolled over to his geisha and she was dead, shot between the eyes – there was a gaping hole in the back of her head. Bob said, "She was hysterical when they entered and started screaming loudly - the bastard killed her in cold blood." "How badly are you hit?" I asked. "Not too bad – A leg wound – it's not bleeding much." Bob replied. I asked George if he was all right and he replied, "Yeh – the next time you have one of these parties - don't call me."

Andrew was in full gear and stomped in. "We are checking out the rest of the house" he said. "Everyone OK?" "No – we need an ambulance" said Albert. "On the way" – Andrew reported. "Let's get a head count and see where everyone is" continued Albert. Saying that, he walked over to help up a much shaken man – Mr. Ari. He was in tears and couldn't speak. Toki and Kawakami were all right but where was Yoshio? We called his name a few times and there was no reply.

A couple of police officers and a few men in dark suits came into the room and were asking questions when Albert said "Let's do this outside and get some fresh air." George and I helped Bob and Albert helped a still shaking Ari out of the room. A cadre of young girls took all of the geishas out. Before we left I laid my jacket over Bob's dead geisha. We left the two gunmen that I shot and killed on the floor uncovered.

The air was fresh and crisp and it felt awfully good to be

alive. Albert called Andrew over, "Hardwick, get your guys the hell out of here. I don't want any international incident or any political shit cleaning this up." "Yes sir," replied Hardwick. He did some hand signals and his nine men got into formation and jogged out of the area. They literally disappeared.

If a small formation of trained men could disappear in a strange area then I am sure Yoshio will not be found tonight. Albert walked over to us after examining a couple of the bodies. "This was a planned Yakuza event. The dead guys have tattoos all over them."

"I suggest they were thinking of trading Robert and me for the disc. That is why they shot Bob in the leg. They weren't sure if he was to be one of the hostages they were to take. That would have been Yoshio's job. He was to identify who was to be taken. Yoshio was the one to tell them by hand signal that you were in the other room. George would have been a plus because of his computer knowledge. They were not sure of Bob but he would have made the hostage package more appealing. Having the four of us might have been good business on their part."

Chief of Police Hiro arrived with Tanaka. He came over to our group. He said, "Two of his men were careless and paid with their lives. The attackers garroted them. I am a little disappointed that you didn't bring us in on this, Luke. We might have had a better outcome. We have three people dead one wounded and five dead Yakuza. I am not too happy about this." He paused, then continued, "Fortunately this is a fairly remote location. I think we will be able to keep it out of the newspapers and then use it when we think we need it."

"Ichiro", Luke Albert said, "let's take a walk." The two of them walked off. Ari seemed to be coming to himself. He came over to us and humbly apologized for what happened this evening. I said, "not at all – we are sorry for being the cause of the disturbance. Until the shooting we had a wonderful time and will look to repeating it on my next trip – hopefully without all the shooting." Ari smiled and said – "Thank you" one more time and bowed very low. I responded in kind.

We had a police escort back to the hotel. On the way, Albert said, "Hiro explained that Yoshio was an Oyab-un who makes decisions on which deals the Yakuza will go into or not go into. This deal is obviously Yoshio's and he has screwed it up. He has a lot to answer for and a lot of deaths to explain. Hiro thinks we will be safe until that is finally resolved. That doesn't mean he won't continue his surveillance – he will.

"I then apologized for not including him but we wanted to make sure no one had infiltrated his organization." Hiro asked, "Are you satisfied now?" I answered, "I really don't know." Hiro then said, "We know and we know who it is and will take care of it in our own time. It was a good assumption, Luke."

Luke Albert said, "Bob, the medics patched you up pretty good and your wound does not appear to be serious; however I would feel better if you went and had it checked out in the hospital." Albert, without approval from Bob, directed the driver to take Bob to the hospital after dropping us off. As Bob said, "He is the boss and it is his prerogative to do what he believes is correct."

Albert went on, "If we can, I would like to have breakfast together tomorrow and get a review from Andrew, Alex and you guys. Let's try to make it at 9:30; figuring most everyone doing business leaves the hotel about that time. Let's have the breakfast in my suite. Agreed?" We all nodded and Albert said "Good."

CHAPTER Thirty-eight
Breakfast With Luke Albert

I got into my room took off my pistol and put it under a pillow on the bed, tore off my clothes and dropped them on the floor, climbed into bed and shut the light. I fell right asleep. I was up an hour later perspired and not very rested. I decided to take a hot shower. I stood under the shower for maybe a half an hour. I dried myself off put on the hotel yukata and tried to go to sleep again. I fell asleep and had dreams of shooting and shooting again and again. I would dream about the first kill then the second and it would repeat and repeat. I again woke up in a cold sweat and I was irritable. "What the hell is the matter with me" I shouted.

I sat up in bed, put my head in my hands and leaned over in the position of Rodin's Thinker. I must have sat there for twenty minutes trying to figure out what was happening to m. I had never shot anyone before - my conscience was working overtime – it was frightening. "Here I am playing macho-man and I can't sleep because I shot and killed – not one – but two people today.

"The terrible thing is, I took two lives and I didn't feel badly about it. I rationalized that they were trying to kill me and all I did was react the way I was taught. It was me or them. I was sure I made the right decision. Had I not been able to have this conversation with myself it would only mean that I would have been the one who was dead. OK we got that out of the way. Now maybe I can sleep."

I got under the covers and fell into a fitful sleep until my wake-up call started buzzing. I woke up like I had been in a fight. Thinking about it - I guess I had. I was fighting my my conscience. I decided to shower and go downstairs and get some coffee. Then maybe I will go for a walk, get some air before reporting to Albert's suite.

I dressed quickly in slacks, golf shirt and sport jacket. I rode the elevator to the lobby, grabbed a cup of coffee from a continuous brewing stand in the lobby - then standing alone by one of the leather chairs drank it down and went out of the side door for a fast walk.

I caught Hiro's men off guard and they started scurrying about getting into their car trying to follow me. I was giving them no mercy. I picked wrong-way streets and small side streets to walk to the Ginza. I came out in front of Matsuya Department Store. From there I walked around the store window-shopping. Matsuya Department Store is the size of a city block.

I then started back to the hotel. I was walking so fast I felt I was I was in a slow jog. I was trying to get rid of the excess energy I was feeling. I arrived at the hotel and found that I wasn't breathing heavily. In fact, for the first time since last night I felt like my old self again. I decided to go back into the lobby grab another cup of black coffee, sit in a comfortable chair and read the newspapers.

At 9:15 AM I rang the doorbell to Luke Albert's suite. Luke answered it and let me in. The suite was spacious. It was a two-bedroom suite with a huge room in between. The room was larger then my living room at home. In addition, there was a working fireplace and the decorations and furniture were French - maybe Louis XIV. In one corner of the room was a circular conference table and this was decked out with rolls, muffins and different breads. There was a hotel trolley that had sterno-cans warming eggs and various meats. It was a do-it-yourself breakfast and that was just fine with me.

Before I went to the table Luke asked, "How are you feeling this morning?" "I'm a little juiced up," I reported, "I didn't get much sleep last night." "That's what I figured" he said. "It is not easy accepting that you killed a person. It was also your first time around doing something like that. I was very impressed with the way you handled yourself yesterday. Do you want me to arrange someone for you to talk to when we get back to New York?" "You mean a psychiatrist?" I asked. "Well, someone who works for the Company who specializes in this area." Albert stated. "I don't think so. I pretty much rationalized everything that happened in my mind and I think I am OK." I said. "Fine, but, if any problems linger I want you to give me your word that you will come and talk to me..." I nodded and said, "Yes – I will."

The doorbell rang as if on cue; Hardwick, Claypool, Michaels and Triguboff entered the room. We all gathered around the hotel trolley and the round table filled our plates and sat down to eat, catch up and wait to start the meeting. Albert asked Bob how he was and Bob reported that he had a very slight flesh wound just above the knee that didn't require any stitches. He was a little sore and had a slight limp but was expected to make a complete recovery.

"OK" Albert said – "let's get started. First the casualties - the young geisha was shot between the eyes and killed instantly. Two of Hiro's men must have been garroted as the attackers were organizing to get into the building. Andrew, did you see them enter?"

"No, we were put down by chopper, after dark, about three miles away so no one would notice us. We were on as dead run to get there. If we landed earlier in the daylight we would have probably brought too much attention to our group. We arrived just as the shooting started. I put a few rounds into the dirt to let the attackers know we were there.

Once they starting shooting back, a large group of young girls and what I gather were their chaperons came running out of three different exits. My people surrounded the complex of small buildings according to our plan and actively returned fire. The enemy fired with AK-47 machine pistols in short bursts. One side of the building ceased firing – I imagine that was when Robert took that gunman out. My men made it inside and killed the other gunman.

"By this time two other bad guys were outside firing volleys of covering fire. We believe that is when Yoshio made it out of the rear of the building and escaped. From what we now understand there were seven gunmen. Two are unaccounted for and five are dead. Robert took out two – one with two bullets in the head and the other a clean shot through the heart. My guys took out three – one with a clean neck and throat hit and the other two were chest and abdomen kills.

"You then told us to clear out and we made it back to our pickup point – about a mile north of the building – with no injuries, everyone accounted for."

Albert said, "Alex, how did coordination work out?" "As soon as the firing started Andrew or his radioman gave me the signal over my transmitter/receiver which Andrew loaned me earlier in the day. I was parked outside of the area police station. I went inside and reported that the geisha house needed assistance. I also asked to use their telephone to call Chief of Police Hiro. Hiro confirmed to the sergeant that they should look into the matter. I then asked them to call for an ambulance as well. That was it."

"Oh, one more point" Alex said, "I learned the location of the party from Ari's secretary. I called on the pretense of getting instructions to the geisha house because I might be able to break away from my business and join the party. I recognized the location and was able to give Andrew a view of what to expect from the terrain and housing in the targeted area."

George then reported, "The disc Hiro has is genuine and is the original disc. No copies were made from it – it is as pristine as it was the day it was made."

"OK, that was good work, people," Albert said, "It is a problem that Yoshio got away with two of his clan's members. I don't know what they still have in mind for us. Hiro thinks that we will be left alone until the Yakuza deals with Yoshio or lets him make his case. The people pushing the Yakuza have a lot of influence over them. We will need some strong intervention to make this go away.

"I think we all agree that it is Red China who is the puppeteer. This information has been confirmed from our face-to-face negotiations at the Copa. Now that the whole deal is falling apart I don't know if the attack from them will get worse or if they will walk away from it. Knowing them from my past experiences, they won't walk away too easily if they have made an expensive investment.

"That brings us to Madame Chang's luncheon tomorrow. I have no idea what Madame Chang or Mama Cherry will bring to the table tomorrow. We are sitting pretty with the disc and they are sitting with nothing. It will be a very curious meeting to say the least."

I asked, "Are we going to set up with some security or do we go into this deal naked." "Robert, you know me better than that. Hiro's people will be in and around the facility. If anyone comes in or tries to get out it will not be easy if any mischief is to take place. I don't expect any problems but we will be prepared for it.

"Andrew, you and your people will stand down for now. I think we strained our international relationships enough last night. If we interfere again, I am certain we will be faced with some international outrage. We don't need that at this time. Since my conversation with Hiro cleared up the point that his organization might have been infiltrated, I feel comfortable with Hiro's people protecting us. Robert and I will go to lunch with the ladies tomorrow – it should prove to be a very interesting lunch."

We all hung around like a family and kibitzed after the meeting. We just seemed to want to be surrounded by people we knew and trusted. It was a warm feeling and for me it was important. It is amazing how close you get to people in a near-death experience. Except for Luke Albert I had known this group for almost two weeks and I felt as though I have known them for much longer.

Around noon we all - including Albert - piled into the

elevator and went to the Orchid Room and ordered rare hamburgers, French fries and beer as if we were in a pub in the States. We all seemed to want a taste of home after the night before. It was just what the doctor ordered for me. I think Albert went along with it just for me. That made me feel really good.

CHAPTER Thirty-nine
Tying Up Ends At The Nikon Factory

Albert and I were on the way to the Ohi-Machi factory when the conversation took an exciting turn. Luke Albert said, "Robert, I am very happy with the way you have handled yourself and performed these last few weeks. You have shown the steadiness and coolness of an agent who has been in the field for many years. Your business acumen has been outstanding. It has shown the TAG board of directors a development of maturity that they respect and are willing to invest in."

"When we get back to the States your office and title will have been changed. I am putting you into the office next to mine and you will be recognized in the industry as my protégé. Your title will be Vice President of Marketing and Product Development. Your income and perk level with go along accordingly with the standard package. You will be required to sign a five-year contract. That contract will keep you in the field doing the Company's work as well as TAG's work for at least that period." Albert said nothing else and looked straight ahead.

I wanted to jump out of my skin. I didn't know how to reply to this more than generous offer. I fought with myself to keep calm and said, "I am overwhelmed that we are even discussing this and you have shown such trust in me. I imagine there are field and sales people who will feel they are being passed over. I don't know what to say." Albert said, "Do I take that to mean you do not accept?" I looked him directly in the face making eye contact and strongly said, "Absolutely not! I accept and I hope I can continue to do you proud." "That's better," said Albert and smiled - "Then it's done" and we warmly shook hands.

My mind was racing. I said to myself, "I need a few minutes to collect my thoughts. This is unbelievable. I am afraid someone will pinch me and I will wake up. I couldn't ask for more. I knew Albert had his eye on me - I guess he saw something that kept his interest in me throughout these past couple of years. I am very grateful - I just don't know how I am going to tell Debbie. I guess making a good down payment on a house will go a long way."

We pulled into the courtyard of the Ohi-Machi factory. We stopped at the gate and as soon as we were let in the guard at the gate got on the telephone. We came to a stop in the front of the entrance of the Administration Building and coming out of the door were Miyahara, Wakimoto, Nakano, Segawa and Takeuchi. Just as we exited the car another vehicle came in and it was Hiro's men. They parked near the entrance and kept their distance.

We climbed to the second floor conference room. A young girl immediately served us the obligatory mugs of green tea.

She was dressed in a gray factory jacket wearing a black bobby-soxers style skirt, white socks and penny loafers. I thought she looked cute. She was very shy and slipped out of the room almost before we sat down.

This was Luke Albert's forum. Before we got to the business at hand he announced my promotion, to my surprise. It was applauded by all present and I shook hands with everyone in the room. Albert anticipated that there might be questions about the previous night and headed them off by saying, "There was a little excitement that Robert and I were involved with last night and fortunately no one from our group was injured. Other than that, I can't imagine that there is anything further to add." Everyone nodded and what could have been a sticky bit of questioning was put aside and the meeting started.

Albert said that his meeting with Nagaoka was a fruitful one. "The directors have accepted our offer to help get the new camera system into production." "Nagaoka Sansei said, it is a generous offer …"The directors have accepted our offer to help get the new camera system into production." "Nagaoka Sansei said, it is a generous offer and everyone of Nippon Kogaku thanks the U.S. government and TAG for their assistance."

Nakano added, "I was at that meeting and it ultimately was a unanimous decision by the board of directors." By this confirmation everyone was assured that the company accepted the decision and it was all right to proceed. Albert asked, "What do you need from us so that we can get started?" Nakano smiled, "Your line of credit and the signed agreement regarding what everyone is responsible for." "That will be written and completed as soon as I return to my office in New York," Albert replied.

Everyone in the room stood up and shook hands as if to finalize this partnership. "Good" Albert said - "Now let me take a look at what we are getting into." Mr. Wakimoto asked Albert and me to follow him to the basement facility so he could show him the two clean rooms. After that he indicated we would return to the conference room and be shown all of the Nikon 'F' camera system prototypes and the plans for the mounting of the 'F' camera to the Kollmorgan periscope.

After about two hours in the Mitsubishi Heavy Industries Laboratory with Koana we returned to the conference room. Our tea was refreshed and on the table was the Nikon 'F' and the same three lenses I first saw the week before. I made no mention of the lens I saw at Tamron but did ask, "Is NK considering offering any license agreements to the off-brand lens manufacturers?"

The answer was simple, "Yes - because we feel that we wouldn't be able to police their activity nor stop them from making a lens mounting system to fit the Nikon F body." They were probably right. It also, indirectly, was good business. The more lenses sold, that many more camera bodies would be sold.

As a final piece of business we were handed back our orders and projections that were signed with the factory's chop with minor changes. The changes reflected the production of products rather than placing orders that would remain on the back-order list under the category of open indefinitely.

Albert complimented all of the factory's efforts regarding the new products he had just seen. "The Nikon 'F' will be a fantastic breakthrough in the marketplace for NK and we look forward to many years of active business together," he said.

Albert had one last arrow to shoot. "In about a week," he

233

said, "I would like you to receive two Korean War correspondents from Life Magazine. I have been in contact with their picture editor and have been touting the quality of Nikon's lenses.

"I told them that they can get outfitted with Nikkor lenses that will perfectly fit their Leica camera bodies. This way they will not have to take their expensive German Zeiss lenses into the war zone. They can use our lenses, trash them if need be, and it will be our gift to them just for the honor of having them use our lenses. They have agreed.

"David Douglas Duncan and Karl Mydens will visit and ask to be outfitted with a bunch of lenses. Please give them whatever they want. If we can get an honest to goodness mention in Life Magazine with a couple of pictures under their names it will immeasurably help our marketing efforts." Everyone present agreed to be as helpful as possible.

We said our good-byes and climbed into our waiting car. Everyone lined up and bowed as we left the courtyard. Hiro's people waited until we were out of the courtyard so they would not obstruct our view. Once we cleared the line of sight they sped up to catch us and stick to us like glue.

The day seemed to just fly by. I was still in the glow of my promotion and couldn't wait to tell Debbie. I must have thought about it constantly since I was told. In my mind I decided I would surprise her when I got home. It will be hard to hold it as a surprise but it will be the best way.

Albert said, "He thought the meeting went very well this afternoon and complimented me for strongly recommending the submarine periscope camera and the new digital camera and periscope system. The Nikon 'F' will be renamed the KS-80 for Navy use and will be a big help in improving our periscope reconnaissance. As soon as we get back to the States we will visit the Navy Department in Washington and bring them up to date."

Albert continued, "The car will drop me off at our office and I will visit with Alex for a few minutes. Then I will use the secure telephone to talk to our board members and bring them and Washington up to speed. Robert, you go back to the hotel and please don't go wandering around. If you wait about an hour and a half or so it will be my pleasure to buy you a good French dinner to celebrate your promotion. We will stay in the hotel to reduce the security risk and not drive Hiro's people crazy. Deal?" he asked, and I said, "Deal."

Dinner was great. We had escargot for an appetizer, the maitre d' put on a big show when serving duck flambé for the main course and finally a soufflé for dessert. We tried not to talk shop and just get to know each other in an environment different from our offices in New York. It was an informative, fun evening for me. Three or four people from the industry came over to say hello to Luke Albert during our meal.

Al Bernard was one of the people who visited. Uninvited, he sat down and asked, "What is your meeting about with Madame Chang tomorrow?" Albert said, "Ask Madame Chang. I don't think it is proper for me to talk about it." "Wait a minute," Bernard said, "Does it have anything to do with my regular export photo business from Hong Kong?"

Albert was very cool, staring down Bernard - "Don't put me in the middle with you and Madame Chang. If she hasn't informed you about any kind of a meeting, then I must respect her wishes. As I said before, ask her not me. We did not instigate anything nor are we looking to increase our product book in TAG. So back off and go to your source before we get into any further uncomfortable conversation - thank you very much." Albert looked away and started to talk to me totally ignoring Bernard and he quietly got up and left our table.

Albert said, "He lost one major deal and I guess he is now paranoid about his association with the Chang organization. I can't say that I blame him but I think he has a safe bet that all will be well for his regular business." The evening ended about 10:30 and we left the restaurant, walked around the mezzanine for a few minutes and said we would meet at our usual time for breakfast tomorrow. Albert then said, "Goodnight and I hope you have a better sleep tonight then you did last night." I smiled and walked toward the elevator. "Wow" I thought "What a hell of a day!"

CHAPTER Forty
A 'Special' Lunch With The Changs

Over breakfast Albert mentioned that his conversation had gone very well with the board of directors and with Washington. I asked, "Are you going to get any grief disobeying orders by going to Japan?" He replied, "Maybe, but this has been a successful mission. There usually isn't too much of anything negative said when we can report a success. On the other hand, I am sure there will be a note or two (people covering their asses) in my historical jacket. I'm not too worried about it." "I am relieved about that," I said.

"Robert, I intend to visit with Ishida this morning just to say hello to an old friend. You are certainly welcome to come along." "No, thank you," I said, "I have a meeting with Bob to discuss the area of the property of Chin Zan-So. He has some overhead photographs I would like to look at. I want to be prepared in case there is any funny business and we have to be able to get out of there." "Good thinking; being thorough is what keeps people like us alive. I knew I picked the right guy. I will be back at 11:30 AM to pick you up." We broke off and went to our respective meetings.

At 10:00 AM I met Bob in our usual lspot in the Starlight Lounge. This was the perfect place to sit and talk this time in the morning. It was quiet and there might have been three or four people on the floor besides staff. Bob had an aerial view of Chin Zan-So. The property covered about seventeen acres with a series of buildings. There was the hotel, a restaurant area and a maintenance area. The gardens and ponds, even in the pictures looked magnificent.

One building between the restaurant and the hotel complex was recently named the Syngman Rhee Building. Rhee, the South Korean president, stayed there for a year or two while he was in exile. Many of the high level meetings or famous guests usually gather there or have coffee in the Rhee building during their stay in the hotel. The entire 17 acres were set off set off by a 15' to 18' stone wall. It was an imitation of the walls around the Imperial Palace.

"Other than the buildings to hide in there is not much of an opportunity to get out of there" I said. "It is what it is" Bob said. "Remember, there will be at least ten undercover people from Hiro's office. He will also have an army of police officers on call. I can't imagine anybody is going to get away with anything. If you feel very uncomfortable I can still call up Andrew's group." "Not a chance" I said. "Especially with what Albert said to Hardwick about an international incident. No way."

We ordered a pot of coffee and croissants and passed the breeze until I had to go to meet Albert.

Albert's car was right on time and I jumped in and we were

off to the meeting. Knowing what I now know, I think I was nervous about the meeting – well if not nervous, maybe jumpy. I couldn't sit still. Albert must have noticed and said, "Calm down Robert – I am sure everything is covered." "Just reviewing the layout in my mind," I said.

Albert changed the subject. "I have nothing but the highest regard for old man Iishida. He takes a bullet and it doesn't stop him, even slow him down. Quite a guy. He is very impressed the way you handled yourself after you were shot and wanted me to send his regards to you."

After about a forty-minute trip to the other side of Tokyo we arrived at Chin Zan-So. We were met at the door by a couple of women in dark kimonos. The inn and restaurant were beautiful. The overhead pictures did not do them justice. We were led into a garden area where Madame and Hyacinth Chang, Mama Cherry and Commissioner Cao met us. We were welcomed and asked to sit around a table that was placed on a little peninsula set in a pond. The flowers, lilies and trees portrayed a feeling of restfulness and quiet. On top of all that it was a beautiful day.

Madame Chang and her daughter were still dressed in black. The mother was in a stylish black dress with a string of huge pearls and Hyacinth in a black business suit very understated. Mama Cherry, I guess out of respect for the Changs, was dressed in a large black muu--muu with very expensive jewelry on her wrist and around her neck. Cao was in his usual Mao tan suit buttoned to the top, tight around his neck.

We were offered drinks and Albert ordered a martini, Madame Chang and Mama Cherry asked for tea, Hyacinth ordered an aperitif - Compari and soda, Cao ordered scotch neat and I had scotch over ice. We made small talk except for

Cao who sat in his chair observing and not changing his expression. Most of the conversation was started and directed by Madame Chang. It dealt with questions about the US market - stocks and bonds - and never touching on the subject of why we were there.

The main dish was what Chin Zan-So was famous for - shabu-shabu. Raw thinly sliced Kobi beef was placed in front of each diner. In the center of the table was boiling water over an open fire. Spaced around the fire for everyone to reach were different dressings or dippings. You boiled the beef to your desired taste, dipped it into one of the small dishes and then placed it on top of the rice and ate it as leisurely as you wished. While we were doing this, we were making trivial conversation - that is all except Cao.

The lunch was moving along and I was wondering when we would get down to business. Albert saw me moving around in my seat being jumpy again and gave me a swift kick under the table. He was right. This was Madame's negotiation - she had the right to organize it any way she wished.

By this time we'd each had a couple of drinks and were slowly warming up to each other. Albert handled himself beautifully. He appeared to have the ladies in the palm of his hand. He was telling jokes and giving financial advice from stocks to banking. He was a pro with the patience of a saint, I thought. It was time for dessert and we were asked to stroll over to the Syngman Rhee house where we might be more comfortable and secluded.

As we got closer to the Rhee house Hyacinth was walking alongside me and said that she hoped I would keep my promise and visit with her in Hong Kong and the New Territories. I assured her that I would arrange it after the first of the New Year. She smiled and walked a little bit ahead of me.

As we were entering the house Madame Chang was in the doorway and beside her appeared a man dressed as a waiter holding a tray. She said, "When you both take off your shoes to come into the Rhee house - I personally request that you give me your revolvers, which I will return to you when you leave Chin Zan-So."

Albert asked, "If we don't?" Madame Chang said, "I would consider that a lack of good faith and would end our negotiations. Please trust me with my request - you will not be disappointed." Albert looked at me and we both reached into our jackets and placed our pistols on the waiter's tray. Madame Chang then bowed and said, "Thank you."

The Rhee house furnishings were a combination of western and Japanese styles. One room off to the right was only a tatami room similar to the one in the geisha house the other night. The room to the left was made up of wicker furniture with a long glass table. The room was set up like an informal dining room. We chose the dining room over the tatami room.

At each place setting there was a small dish of Ichi-go (strawberries) and yokan (sweet soy-bean cake). In the center of the table was a display of a variety of sliced fruit. We picked at the fruit and continued our conversations from the garden.

Madame Chang finally said, "We are here to end our negotiations. It is my desire we do that expeditiously." "This is going to be interesting," I thought. "I wonder what she is going to negotiate with." Madame Chang clapped her hands and a tall Chinese man carried into the room a silver tray with a large napkin over it. He came to the end of the table and stood waiting for directions. I noticed that Hyacinth got up to leave the room. I imagined when nature calls, no matter the time, you answer it.

241

Madame Chang directed the man to put the tray in front of Cao. She then said, "Mr. Cao is my honored guest this afternoon." "Gentlemen," - looking in our direction - she then said, "I will ask Cao to uncover the tray in a moment." Cao was very curious. He started looking at the covered tray from all angles. The Chinese man who brought in the tray did not leave. He just backed up a few steps against the wall. Just then I noticed Hyacinth return to the room with her right hand behind her.

"Mr. Albert and Mr. Schein" she continued, "I promised I would get my justice at my daughter's memorial service. I now can go back to Hong Kong because as we leave here today I will have had my justice."

She then ordered Cao to uncover the tray. Cao did it with a quick grab and pulled the napkin towards him. There before us was Yoshio's head on the silver tray. I moved my chair back looking around the room to make sure no one else had joined us or looked suspicious. There was no question we were all tense. The scene was gruesome.

Madame Chang continued, "Yoshio was responsible for Juniper's death. His men have been killed and he – as you can see - has been dealt with. Before he died he told us who ordered Juniper killed. Madame Chang then screamed a paragraph or two in Chinese directly in Cao's face. Cao looked stunned and as he tried to get up out of his chair – just at that moment Hyacinth Chang applied the coup de grace. She pulled a sword from behind her back and using her right hand made a strong thrust at Cao, catching him directly in the center of his back. The sword had a strong force behind it and went through his body and pierced his chest. It was a shocking, bloody mess. It caught us all by surprise.

While Cao was still alive, with no sound coming from him,

Madame Chang said, "He organized this project from the beginning. If someone disagreed with him he had that person eliminated." Looking directly at me, Madame Chang said, "Juniper knew you had recaptured the disc. Her position was to admit our failure and go on to something else. That was a good business decision. It was not a good political decision for Cao. He disagreed with Juniper and ordered her killed. Then he tried to abduct the two of you Monday night, hoping to ransom you for the disc." With that statement Hyacinth withdrew the sword and Cao fell back into his chair – dead.

All of a sudden, one of the tatami floor sections lifted and two Chinese men appeared. The two men quietly carried Cao's body down the stairs of a passageway beneath the building. Hyacinth, the weapon and Yoshio's head all disappeared down the same stairs with the Chinese man who was standing in back of Cao. As Hyacinth descended the stairs she made eye contact with me and I could see this was a hard task for her and she appeared to be very sad.

Everyone else in the room was standing and backing away from Madame Chang who was sitting, ignoring us, and drinking her tea. What we had seen was a well-planned assassination of Commissioner Cao. Then, right before our eyes the scene disappeared. Quietly a clean-up crew, in a matter of seconds, changed a tatami that had blood on it and wiped up and cleaned up any evidence of Cao's presence.

Mama Cherry implored us to go into the tatami room and they closed the shoji screens to separate us from the other room. Mama Cherry made a very simple statement about the Yakuza. She said, "Because of their failure to keep the disc in their hands there was a loss of face for the Yakuza. The Yakuza wanted to make amends with Madame Chang and me when they found they were in an impossible position with their employer - Mr. Cao. They first gave us Yoshio and his crew

243

of four men and then they gave us Cao." "That said it all," I thought.

Madame Chang continued, "The Yakuza will no longer bother you regarding this project. However, I am sure other governments will be following your progress with great interest." Throughout the whole bloody mess neither Albert nor I said a word. We just watched and kept our mouths shut. I kept looking around expecting Hiro's men to jump in, but that never happened. I couldn't imagine why not. Maybe Hiro will explain later.

Then very formally Mama Cherry and Madame Chang reverently bowed and Chang stated, "The 'negotiations' are ended." As we left the restaurant our pistols were in large envelopes waiting for us on the seats of our car. We were walked out of the building by the ladies – they both bowed as we drove away.

On our way back to the hotel neither Albert nor I spoke. I think we were absorbing what we had just experienced. With the hotel in sight I said, "Funny, I don't see any of Hiro's men following us." Albert said, "I am sure Hiro was listening to every word. He knew we were not in any danger nor did we need any more surveillance. The cars that were following us – I'll bet - have all been called off."

CHAPTER Forty-one
Odds And Ends

Andrew, Alex, George and Bob met us for breakfast Thursday morning. We were all much more relaxed and didn't seem to have that weird feeling of being watched. Everyone was in a light mood. Albert invited our group to join us for our last night's dinner in Japan.

He chose the Italian Restaurant on the mezzanine floor at 6:30 PM. He said he had extended and invitation to a number of people from NK by telephone to join us for a sayonara (goodbye) gathering. He wasn't sure if they would or could make it. "They said they are working feverishly on the agreement and on the new camera system, Albert said. "I hope they do come because I reserved a private room."

I explained that my day was pretty much accounted for because I was receiving Fuji in the morning at about 11:00 and then Tamron at 3:00. I reserved a room in the small business center in the hotel. This was to collect all of the approved projections and purchase orders. It was a chance for the factory and us to point out any anticipated problems. It seems that all of the final decisions that a factory makes in Japan happens at the very last moment of the trip before you get on the plane.

Luke Albert said, "Out of courtesy, considering what happened at the geisha house, I might join you for the Tamron meeting. I want to assure Ari that we recognize he had nothing to do with the Yakuza." I said, "Great – I look forward to your participation."

The day moved like wildfire. Both meetings happened before I was able to catch my breath. Everything went to schedule with very few changes in our requests or projections. Before I knew it, it was time for the sayonara party.

I found my way to the mezzanine a little late – about 6:45 PM. I walked in and all of a sudden I heard Banzi! – Banzi! (Good luck! – Good Luck!) being shouted in my direction. I was being cheered for a successful first trip to Japan. Everyone was holding a drink and holding it high.

The room was mobbed with every one of the NK directors, Nagaoka and all of the people who worked with me in the factory. Much to my surprise I even had the opportunity to say goodbye to Koana. The drinks were flowing and everyone was walking about or saying hello or shaking a hand and generally having a good time. It was a very successful party - with no surprises.

When I returned to my room to pack and get ready for the trip back home I must have had ten other gifts for my wife that arrived from our various factories while I was at the party.

"I'm going to have to purchase another suitcase to get all this stuff home" I said out loud to no one in particular. This was overwhelming. I then went about my business trying to engineer everything into some order and method of carrying for the trip home.

Epilogue

On the way home Friday aboard Pan Am #002 Luke Albert said he had lunch with Hiro Thursday. Hiro explained, through hidden movie cameras and tape recordings, he had recorded the entire lunch with the Changs. He also photographed their escape through the secret passageway in Rhee House. He felt that Japan was better off with Yoshio dead than alive.

Cao was a Chinese citizen and he thought the Changs would handle covering up his death better then he could. Cao was secretly transported on a Chang airplane to Hong Kong. Hiro said, "It was a much better position to have them handle it instead of Japan having to explain why a Chinese commissioner was killed in Japan."

Hiro chose to be jury and judge because he now had hard evidence that could be used in the future should the Changs threaten Japan in any way again. I imagined Hyacinth and her mother have worn out their welcome in Japan for quite some time.

When I got home I couldn't wait to get my hands on my beautiful wife. As soon as we walked into the apartment we didn't say a word. We hugged and felt each other like we had been apart for a millennium. We scrambled to the bedroom and made love until we were finally exhausted. I thought, "If this is my welcome home – traveling and being apart from one another for short spells is not so bad."

I had a smile on my face when I looked to my left and Debbie wanted to know what I found so funny. "Oh," I said, "I have great news." "So do I" she said. "You go first" I implored her. "OK, I think I found this great house for us on Long Island in the City of Glen Cove." "Whoa," I said, "That was fast, but my news is still better." Debbie looked at me quizzically – "I got a field promotion and we now make three times what we made before I went on the trip – you can buy any house you want."

A big smile came on her face and then she began to laugh. "What is so funny," I asked. "I still have bigger news then you" she said and paused – I couldn't think of anything bigger then what I told her. Now I looked at her quizzically and then it hit me – "We are pregnant?" I asked and she shouted – "Yes!"

After a wonderfully relaxing weekend it was time to go to the office. As I walked in Doreen came to the door to greet me. Wow, I said – "This never happened before." She even planted a kiss on my cheek. I was amazed – then she took me by the arm and we walked past my old cubicle, down the corridor to Albert's office and just before going into his office made a left turn into what was now my new office. I knew it was my office because it had my name and new title on the door.

I didn't know what to say – Doreen patted me on the back

– said "good luck" and closed the door. I was flabbergasted. I just stood there taking it all in. Windows, mahogany desk, a couch with side chairs and my own high back executive desk chair. My pictures of Debbie were already on my desk. Doreen took care of everything.

Luke Albert was slapped on the wrists – again – for not following the deputy director's orders. The success of our trip made it hard to seriously discipline Albert. Albert was put on probation until he cleared the medical office and was allowed to continue as TAG's president.

In subsequent months I corresponded with Hyacinth Chang and we were arranging a meeting to visit in Hong Kong some time the following year in February or March.

By December, only three months later, we successfully delivered the first 125 kits of the KS-80 submarine periscope camera to the Navy. The camera was so successful the Navy also developed the KS-81 Anti Submarine Warfare kit for PBY's to fly with. When a pilot saw something suspicious in the water he triggered off a few shots and had the pictures later developed in the Navy's laboratories.

When photographers David Douglas Duncan and Karl Mydans returned from Korea their Life Magazine picture editor was very impressed with their results. He could not imagine the sharpness and the quality of the pictures they took. This prompted an eight page article in Life Magazine that gave quality creditability to the Nippon Kogaku Factory and to Japanese products.

The Nikon 'F' became one of the most successful Single Lens Reflex quality cameras in the world. The name Nikon is now a household word.

The digital camera system and fiber optics periscope is still under development and evaluation and will take a number of years before it is properly tested and made operational for military usage.

After the war, many industries prospered in Japan and developed quality based products. If you visited a camera store in the late forties or early fifties with a Japanese product you were looked at with suspicion that you were selling 'junk'. In fact, some stores would even throw you out. That happened to me more than once.

Nikon and other Japanese manufacturers changed the world's perception from junk products to quality products. A great deal of thanks has to go to the occupation and General MacArthur. Zenji Wakimoto always used this example of the quality and the unique product revolution in Japan:

"During the occupation equipment was stripped from many factories and sent to the United States. The shipbuilding factory of Mitsubishi had a projection device that sped up production for building ships. It would project an image on to a large piece of steel and a team of people with hammers and punches would follow the projected outline and that would show you where to cut the steel."

"When this equipment was stripped from the Mitsubishi shipyard they needed a replacement. Wakimoto, NK and Mitsubishi developed a production device that coated large pieces of steel with a photo-sensitive material, projected an image on the steel, electro-statically developed the image and finally an automatic cutting tool follows the cut line by referencing the difference in the gray scale.

"The Japanese today are the leaders in the world in shipbuilding"

Because manufacturing equipment was shipped out of the

country during the occupation, Japan's industry was forced to develop new equipment to do the work. The new equipment, in many cases, was more modern and automated than anything available in the United States. Whenever a Japanese product was declared successful in the States Wakimoto would say, "Thank you General MacArthur."

I referenced in the story a small meeting where the Japanese Defense Agency would not release the Nikon Periscope drawings to Kollmorgan Corporation. This is one of the reasons why I repeatedly ask myself ...

"Who Really Won The War?"

- End -

Printed in the United States
45509LVS00002B/376-399